DEFENDING THE FUTURE

NO MAN'S LAND

SERIES EDITOR

MIKE McPHAIL

eBooks
Pennsville, NJ

Special thanks to "DAN • E"
…Fix it!

PUBLISHED BY
eSpec Books LLC
Danielle McPhail, Publisher
PO Box 242,
Pennsville, New Jersey 08070
www.especbooks.com

ISBN: 978-1-956463-87-3
ISBN (ebook): 978-1-956463-86-6

Design: Mike and Danielle McPhail
Cover Art: Mike McPhail, McP Digital Graphics
Copyeditor: Greg Schauer, John L. French

AUTOGRAPH DUTY ROSTER

Mike McPhail	Brenda Cooper
Nancy Jane Moore	Maria V. Snyder
Danielle Ackley-McPhail	Ann Wilkes
Laurie Gailunas	S. A. Bolich
Lee C. Hillman	Deborah Teramis Christian
Lisanne Norman	Judi Fleming
Jennifer Brozek	

eSpec Books Titles in the Defending The Future Series

Breach the Hull - Reissued
So It Begins - Reissued
By Other Means - Reissued
No Man's Land - Reissued
Best Laid Plans - Reissued
Dogs of War - Reissued
The Best of Defending the Future
Man and Machine
In Harm's Way
Answer the Call (2025)

eSpec Books Titles Related to the Defending the Future Series

A Legacy of Stars by Danielle Ackley-McPhail
Dawns a New Day by Danielle Ackley-McPhail
Daire's Devils by Danielle Ackley-McPhail
From the Archives: The Die is Cast edited by Greg Schauer
Radiation Angels: The Mission Files by James Daniel Ross
Shattered Dreams: The Shardies War by Bud Sparhawk
Devil Dancers by Robert E. Waters
Issue in Doubt by David Sherman
In all Directions by David Sherman
To Hell and Regroup by David Sherman
(with Keith R.A. DeCandido)
Written in Light by Jeff Young
Vox Astra: The Black Box by James Chambers
Vox Astra: When Clouds Die by James Chambers

This book is dedicated to:

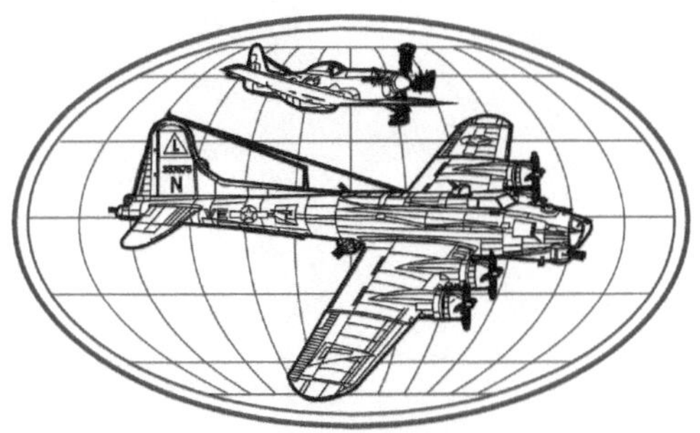

The Women Airforce Service Pilots (WASP) of World War II

1943 - 1944

And to all those who followed their example to "Answer The Call."

Contents

CRACKING THE SKY
Brenda Cooper

THE MEMORY OF SMOKE CLUNG TO MY HAIR AND INHABITED THE BACK OF MY THROAT. My boots cracked through a heat-dried veneer of ash that coated low hills. I walked where fire had been three days ago, before it was storm-killed by soaked clouds sent over the Cascades by NorAM command. It would be sweet if NorAM decided to follow the deluge up with some mist or a bit of drizzle, #but they'd probably burned their whole weekly weathering credit with the one act. Not that I wasn't grateful. NorAM'd probably saved our sorry lives. Almost surely. But I was still so sticky with sweat it was hard to watch our thin column wind up the ravine in front of us, much less watch for enemies.

Nothing moved but us, at least as far as I could see. Not even the air. There had been wind the day the fire had raced toward us (I thought it was set against us, and a few others did, too, but no one in command agreed). The wind screamed through us again the day NorAM created the storm and set it loose on the fire. Everything felt hot, barren, and still.

It had been pretty here. The ground had been dotted with scrub and yellow flowers. Now it lay grey and hot and still. At least the heat must have scoured it free of nano-mines. I still half expected a pile of dangers to be headed our way, some scary franken-science thrown out from the illicit labs we were advancing on.

Alongside all of us, the dogs marched in lock-step, their metal feet occasionally sliding on bits of rock.

In front of me, Mario and Joe marched side by side, looking way too unbothered by the sun.

Kris looked as melted as I felt. Bitch was a bit more cheerful than me, though. "Still no sign of life. We're going to make it."

"They could have sent UAV's."

She had the bad grace to laugh at me. "And ruined your fun?"

"UAV's don't die."

"They cost as much as we do."

"More." But people were still good for a lot of things that unmanned aircraft just weren't so good at. Opening doors, assessing, reading the fear in an enemy combatant's eyes.

The first few of our line had all reached a shadowed cleft between two low hills. I trudged up a scant incline near the end, next to Kris, exposed as hell.

As if they knew we'd been talking about them, the steady echoing thrum of copter blades came up from behind us.

I tensed.

"Safe!" Louis called from five people ahead of us. He meant it had told him it was ours, sharing the right codes in the right sequence. The dogs trusted it, too, clanking along without missing a beat. So maybe NorAM had decided to give us more help. Maybe they'd learned something. The UAV's body was the size of my head, the rotors a stack, the whole thing flying canted a bit forward so the tail seemed to reach for the sky. The sound of its flight made my shoulder blades itch. I squinted, the sun making the silver blades into diamonds too bright to stare at. Why now, instead of after we were closer to the lab?

Why so close to us? Why one?

Instinct finally kicked in, in spite of Louis's words. I dove sideways into Kris, tumbling her. Her eyes went wide but she said nothing, catching enough balance to scramble on all fours. Simon and Jillie reflexed after us.

Mario turned, mouth open, his eyes so dark I was sure he was about to bark at us for being scared little girls.

He never got any words out. Mario's hand flew up to his skull and came away slick and red and I could feel the heat of little machines racing through his body, the fear of them turning me soft and small inside.

He writhed and fell.

The four of us, me, and Kris and Rob and Jill, raced away like one. My dog, Hunter, slowed to stay beside me. I ran with a hand on Hunter's broad, full back, wishing there was power and time to mount and race away. The big dog's metal skin felt hot to the touch. But then everything was hot, the sand, the dog, the air, my anger.

I didn't want to glance back toward Mario's body, but I did. Most of the line was down, the dogs on their sides, faces scarred with soot. Someone had managed to knock the silver copter out of the sky. My quick glance didn't say how many people from the front of the line had made it. If any.

The fear of things too small to see drove us a long way in spite of the sapping heat and the surreal burned and wetted and baked ground.

We re-grouped behind a stand of rocks. Small cover, the rocks hot enough to burn hands where we touched them, tinged with silicates so they shimmered, big enough to throw shade if the sun weren't directly above us.

Jillie looked over at me, her face shocked. I checked the rest of the group. Eight had made it to the rocks. Eight people and eight bots, so sixteen. I checked what I'd been left with. Two new recruits, the speed of death thrumming through them so deeply fear seemed to leak from their sweaty, dirty pores. Jillie and a thin boy from Seattle who leaned over, puking. The scientist. The two trainers, busy already, checking the metal dogs for damage, probably glad as hell to have something to do. Kris, the ever optimistic and bitchy. Simon, who was only happy when he was actually fighting, who got an orgasmic look on his face in hand-to-hand, and yet wouldn't kill a spider if it landed on his mouth in the middle of the night. Thank god for Kris and Simon and the trainers. Maybe between us we could protect the two newbies.

Simon had already managed to climb up the rock pile in spite of the heat, peel his binoculars out of his pack, and look toward the carnage. I caught the shift in his uniform from ash gray to the tan of the rocks. He grunted softly from about five feet above me.

"What do you see?" I asked him.

He shook his head. "Stupidity."

"No shit. See any more copters?"

"Damn things are fast."

I pulled the handheld out of my pocket and swiped up the tracking chip info. Close-together green dots for us, dark for humans and light for robot dogs. Three more humans on the far side, two with fading vital signs. I whispered an apology to them since we couldn't even try and get there yet. Red death dots made a ragged line across the open spaces. I called for overhead pictures. I got back two-inch pixels, which was enough to see that everyone had died in place, and even the dogs had made no more than a few steps. They'd been targeted. The poison that killed people didn't kill robots. So whoever sent the UAV knew who and what was coming for them.

Illegal nano for sure, scattered by an illegal UAV. NorAM would tell—I breathed in deep, re-thinking who was left —NorAM would tell *me* more once they analyzed the info.

Shit.

I did want command. But not now, and not here.

NorAM would have the same information I had, except maybe our condition. We'd lost two of the scientist embeds, but we still had one left. Alissa Frietag, a small woman with twice the strength she appeared to have, and a fierce determination to get into the labs. I stared at her for a moment, assessing. Small, so thin I would be able to wrap my hands around her waist with only a little effort. She looked pissed-off instead of scared.

Good. So all we had to do was protect Alissa, get into the well-defended lab, and give her some time to assess it before we destroyed it. Yep, that should be easy.

I typed my message to NorAM. *We're okay. Sci1 looks fierce. We need cover.*

Or to withdraw, but I didn't have to tell them that. They knew. If we withdrew, GenGreen would simply destroy everything and smile and invite us and a bunch of media in the front door just in time to see a lab devoted to feeding the starving. We didn't want to leave them time for that. Other NorAM forces had blocked the roads out. Of course, we could just get them from the air. But people up the chain wanted the lab intact. Apparently there was some experiment or knowledge so valuable that we weren't willing to just blow it up and move on.

I half expected to be recalled within a day of starting out. The goal had been to come in unnoticed, but the UAV screamed that GenGreen and its private armies had noticed us. The fact that our code was compromised suggested they'd also paid off someone. With luck, that would be a dead rat from our group, but more likely it would be NorAM.

I scanned the horizon again. Listened. No wind. No rotor blades. Puking boy had stopped hacking and spitting.

Damnit. Time to lead.

"Everybody gather up."

Simon started to clamber down the rock, but I gestured for him to stay. He'd be able to hear me from up there. The dog handlers got the big bots to stand and look at me, too, cocking their not doglike heads sideways at me in a dog-like motion. Good. At least someone had a sense of humor.

I glanced down at my handheld. The screen was still blank.

"You all okay?"

I looked them each in the eye. At least they all looked back at me. Five women including me, three guys. The men were Simon, Scott of the weak stomach, and one of the two dog trainers, John. Then me, Kris the steady and bright, Jillie, Alissa Frietag the scientist, and the other dog trainer, a woman named Paulette.

The communit buzzed in my hand. I glanced down and saw what I expected. I looked back at the group. "Orders are to keep going, move more evasively, get to the lab. They'll send in some cover and some help after we get it secure."

"Ma'am."

"Scott?"

"Just us. To take the whole place?"

I nodded. "What supplies do we have?"

John spoke a litany he'd pretty clearly memorized. "Water. Food. Handhelds. First Aid. Light. Blankets."

Crap. I glanced at Paulette, who stood with one hand on her robot's head as if it were flesh and blood. She swallowed. "The same."

So we were eight for eight on supplies and zero for zero on big weapons? We wouldn't starve while we were destroying an enemy lab with our bare hands. Good thing.

John must have seen the look on my face. "We do have some rockets and launchers, and a few mines."

"Our handguns," I added. "And the knives on our belts. Any useful solar?"

Paulette shifted on her feet, swaying. "Not enough for the dogs." Her face had gone white. "Enough for us."

Jillie's eyes widened and she looked like she was about ten and desperate for a friend. I knew what she was thinking. That we'd need to raid the supplies on the other dogs. I didn't look directly at her, but I made sure I could see her relax when I said, "We're not going out there." Stray microbots could kill us as easily as they'd killed everyone else. It might be slower without a direct hit, but three of the damned things in your soft tissue guaranteed death. There would be no recovery of the other dogs or their packs, or anything else. Not until NorAM could send containment suits out. Not today.

I updated NorAM with our status, and requested a storm.

They suggested quite formally that we do without.

I counter-suggested quite formally that without power we would die before we got the job done instead of while we were doing the job.

I stood still, staring at the screen, waiting for them to discuss amongst themselves and then get back to me. I was half-hoping they'd say no and decide we could go back or wait for more people and stuff or something.

Instead, they answered way too fast. They promised lightning.

Whatever was in that lab mattered to them. I swallowed. I'd been trained. I'd even succeeded in a live exercise. And out of our group, I was the only one still alive and rated for it. I glanced at the dog handlers. "We do have the laser?"

John nodded, his eyes gleaming a bit.

I surveyed the group. "We are going to crack the sky and bring home some power."

Allisa's tongue darted out between her full lips, and she looked like she was about to be seated at a banquet table. Jillie's eyes widened again, and the trainers glanced at the dogs. Kris and Simon, who knew the calculus, nodded.

We had orders to go forward, so no turning tail. Probably wouldn't work anyway, since GenGreen would follow us and keep whatever they were protecting at the level of rumor. We could go forward. Would. We carried the worst weapons on us—some as small as the ones GenGreen just killed most of us with. We would need power to eat and drink and scatter signal around, power to feed the tiny weapons, power to control the lab. Stored power, available on demand.

In addition to the power to get there.

That had been on the other dogs, along with the more power-hungry of the weapons. We'd run them a long way to get here. The robotic dogs were stronger than us by far, faster, fleeter if less graceful. But when we ran out of juice, we just reached into our will and found more. When robots ran dry, they stopped.

So be it.

Death or a miracle.

"Rest. Simon and I will take a watch."

They nodded, the old hands falling almost immediately to the ground, accepting rest. Jillie and Scott followed. Alissa Frietag leaned back against the stones, closing her eyes and whispering under her breath.

I clambered up beside Simon and sat looking out over our distant dead and toward the buried lab. The very idea of it made me feel small and fragile even if I was one-sixty with my boots on and no real fat. Bulky for a girl. We were all fragile when it came to nano and biologicals and whatever else GenGreen and its partners were dreaming up to protect their solution for the world from the combined North American Government, which had a different one. The NorAM populace had voted almost as one from the wet northern reaches of Canada to the sweltering, hurricane-slapped coasts of the Yucatan. They'd said to stop intervening, preferring to take their chances with nature than to trust the multinationals.

There was no money in letting nature balance itself. Hence the science wars, and this small battle.

The dead between us and the next hill attested to the seriousness of this small battle. Our own corporations, or at least multis born here, killing us. Assholes. I swore I'd do my best. Both to kill the big scary lab and to stay alive.

I was gonna miss Mario, even if he was a loudmouthed idiot.

Simon opened the conversation. "This sucks."

"Yep." And that closed the conversation.

We sat close to each other, taking comfort in the silence of long friendship. We'd been on three attacks like this before, and come back from all of them. I wasn't so sure this time, but no soldier says those things to another. Instead, we watched the empty blue sky and baked quietly on the rock, the sun glinting on the great field of ash that surrounded us.

NorAM interrupted to tell me the others had all died. No one left on the far ridge. I imagined it. One of the dots had been healthy. They'd watched the others die, gotten too close. Prayed to be safe. Maybe they'd even donned their protective suit, the crappy one that came in all our belts. But something too small to see and big enough to kill them had gotten in anyway. It made me feel cold even in the punishing heat.

The rocks started throwing longer shadows. Simon and I traded with Kris and Scott. I wiped the sweat from my face and felt sure the heat would keep me fitful and maybe even awake.

A fat warm glob of rain struck me on the cheek and I shook awake, swinging my head like an animal. Wind cooled the air. Dark, roiling cumulonimbus clouds towered overhead, the front edge of them splitting the sky like angry foam above my head, blue, then gray, white above, tinged gold by the setting sun.

Kris looked down at me. "Almost ready?"

"Are they?"

I had given her my comm. She shaded the screen with her hand and said "Forty minutes."

I took five minutes to perform routine body maintenance functions, and five more to verify that everyone else did the same. I gathered the humans all into formation, packs at their side and ready, each with a weapon in hand.

The dog handlers had already chosen John's dog for the first receptacle in line. I didn't ask how he'd drawn the risky straw. Just thanked him for being ready.

At least there was so much wind I didn't need a posted UAV spotter any more. Anything over about twenty miles an hour tended to slam them off course, into the ground, or both. I was willing to bet the occasional gust was past the twenty mile an hour mark. In fact, there was a serious whine in the part of the wind that passed up above us. Damn NorAM physics jocks.

John handed me the launcher.

"Did you name your dog?" I asked.

He swallowed. "Max, sir. Ma'am."

His confusion felt almost touching. John passed Max's hand controls to me, and me and the metal dog walked away from the group, as far out into the open as we could get. Wind tore at my shirt.

All the blue had been blown out of the sky.

Max came to my waist, with four legs that had two joints each, and a hollow tail. His belly was big, and right now all that it held was empty space and some magic built from Tesla's dreams and our materials. Too classified for me to get the details, and too new to be completely sure it would work.

Lightning slammed upward from the ridge we had been going to, would go to again. Rain sheeted down, sharpening the smell of the charred soil.

John and Paulette called out the other dogs, lining them up one after the other, tails in mouths, a long string of conductivity. Hunter was last. John said something to Max, and the big robot tilted its ugly black head back and opened its jaws. Someone had painted sharp teeth like a shark's onto the dull gripping surfaces.

John handed me dark goggles. I slid them on, the world almost black, John now a silhouette. He handed me a long slender rod with a firing pin on the outside. The laser gun felt heavier than I remembered, harder to manage. I pointed it up at the roiling clouds, ignoring the rain that nearly blinded me.

The two trainers raced to the rocks to join Simon and the others.

I pulled the trigger and nothing happened.

I checked. The gun worked. The laser beams shot fast as lightning itself into the clouds, but invisible. The clouds had simply ignored my call, my act, the light.

They had to be ready, to be almost pregnant with charge.

I giggled, absurdly, soaking wet and wondering if the storm were a lover I'd just tried to drive to premature ejaculation.

The laser had enough power for three charges. I'd wasted one. I took a deep breath and stared up into the rain and the dark clouds and smelled the damp, charred air.

Another lightning bolt flashed down near the rocks and thunder made me cringe and cover my head.

My timing was still off.

Practice for this had been controlled. The storms had been smaller.

I closed my eyes, let the water fall on the goggles. Braced. Waited.

Fired.

I opened my eyes.

Thunder smacked again.

White light surrounded me, the world turned to day in spite of the lenses between my eyes and the bolt. Max stood unmoved but full, and I had the briefest glimpse of the dog with light pouring out of every hole in its body, out through its tail into the other dogs, a line of lightning eaters.

Then I couldn't see, and all I felt was a deep thrumming in my body, and a sharp pain behind the eyes. I shook, relieved and scared and pissed off as well, mad at NorAM and GenGreen and the whole difficult, warring world. The thunder kept rolling away from me, hiding any other noises.

John's voice, a whoop. "We did it! You did it!"

Someone took the laser gun from my hands. Simon spoke. "I'm taking off the goggles. Keep your eyes closed."

I felt them slide away.

"Look at me."

His face existed. Thank God. I could see, and what I saw was Simon grinning, ear to ear. "Now what, chief?"

I swallowed and stood up, my legs shaky, the back of my head still mushy and pain-wracked. Nothing good was easy. Unless we called it again, the lightning would move on. We had what we needed from it, and all that was left was danger. We could wait it out. "Is everyone here?"

Simon nodded. I verified he was right. They looked shocked and bewildered. Some soldiers. But at least everyone had their packs. "You're a damn good second," I whispered to him, and then I stood up and addressed everyone else. "By the time I finish this briefing, the worst of the storm will have moved on, and we'll go take the lab. We're going to ride in there."

Scott's eyes widened. "On the dogs?"

"No. On each other." Dingbat. But then he was in as much danger as the rest of us. Maybe more for being wet behind the ears. Whatever was in the lab had better be good. "We're moving light and fast, following the storm, hoping to take them by surprise. We'll have enough power to get there on the bots. I don't know if we'll get back that way or if we'll walk." Which meant I didn't know how much power we'd have on the way back. Once we succeeded—if we succeeded—NorAM wasn't going to burn more climate credits on getting back the easy way, not unless we had something they wanted fast. That was an idea. I looked back at them. "The extra supplies are still here. We meet back here. Has everyone marked this on their maps?"

Jillie looked sheepish and fiddled with her wrist unit until she could nod and say, "Yes," just like everyone else had.

I tested communications, made sure we could all hear and speak to each other. "Use voice when you can," I reminded them. "Security."

Lightning fell again, far away now, a thin streak that forked in three places and was gone. I waited for the thunder to die down and then I said, "All right. Go."

We skirted the dead, going so wide we missed the ravine. Better to add ten minutes than pick up some windblown death. On the smooth ground, the dogs had pretty even gaits, about like a horse walking. Over hills or rocks, they rocked and lurched, irritating my still-sharp head and scraping my inner thighs. There were reasons we don't usually ride the damned things. Plenty of bots had been designed to carry soldiers, but the pack dogs like these had it as a second priority. Or maybe a third or fourth.

It hurt.

I had ridden the dogs in the wild, but Jillie and Scott had only mounted in training exercises. They managed, but only because I paired them each up with a trainer. Behind them, Kris and I rode together. Simon protected Alissa, the pair of them a bit in front of us and off to the side.

For the first hour, we followed the storm. Dusk yellowed the lagging edge of the clouds, and Alissa pointed out a fresh storm behind us, maybe five miles away. "Backup?" she screamed the question to me over the wind and the rain and the space between us.

I shrugged. Sometimes weathering made more weather, as if sun or wind or rain called to its own kind. If it was NorAM storm, they hadn't told me. But then maybe they wouldn't. Maybe we'd wake up in the morning to August snow. If we made it to morning.

As we neared the top of a long, low hill two huge figures rose up. Bipedal, metal, too thin to be manned. Legs like tree trunks and torsos like limbs, thin and wiry and fast. Six arms, or maybe more. They held rocks in each hand.

I ducked.

Hunter feinted right under me, then left.

Rocks landed on either side of us.

Voices screeched in my ear. Too many to make sense of.

Alissa gripped her dog's ears, which held its head down.

"Let go!" I screamed at her. "Hold its neck. Handholds."

Just as she let go, a rock the size of her head pounded into the ground at her dog's feet and the robot dog rose up on just its hind feet, striking the ground with its tail to help balance. Alissa threw her weight backward instead of forward and landed with a hard thump on her butt. Immediately twisting away from the dog.

A rock fell between the scientist and the robot dog.

It stepped back, avoiding the rock, programmed to stay with its handler.

I charged her attacker, drawing two of its rocks toward me. It was agile enough to pick another rock up as it threw two at me. So a brain for each hand? My immediate reaction was to go eye for an eye. Sometimes old-fashioned weapons are just fine, and since I'd never even seen a rumor of a six-armed rock-throwing robot, this couldn't be far out of beta. By the time I'd pulled the pin, the bot had hit Alissa's dog in the torso, leaving a dent. It stood over her small form, which lay curled under its broad belly in a fetal position.

Well, I'd probably have gone fetal, too.

I threw the grenade and watched it arc up toward the robot. I turned away, hoping Alissa was smart enough to cover her face.

Hunter shied, if that's what you call evasive actions in a robotic dog the size of the small horse.

After the initial explosion I heard metal screech and turned to look. A leg complete with a long string of cables that must have pulled loose from inside the robot lay behind us, evidence there had been something for Hunter to avoid.

A rock slammed into us, hitting a glancing blow to my thigh. Hunter took the blow, moving with it, taking three fast steps like those daisy steps from aerobics. I managed to hold on. My thigh hurt like hell. I tested and my leg bent normally if I forced it. No telling if I could put weight on it.

Wind had blown the wet ash clear enough for me to make out the robot, no longer standing, but with at least two working arms.

No time to look around and see what else was happening. I raced to Alissa's side and barked at her, "Stand up!"

She looked up at me with a face streaked with tears and ash, but she nodded and pushed herself to standing. She reached for the holds to mount.

"No. Use it as a shield and run."

Alissa stood blinking at me with shocky eyes for just a second before she understood what I meant and started heading away from the now-stationary rock-thrower, keeping the robot dog between her and the damaged enemy. She started off in retreat and I herded her forward and around, paying close attention until we appeared to be out of range.

I looked for the other robot. Simon or Kris had done a better job than I had, and it lay inert.

I called for everyone to come here, counting as they appeared. John and Jillie, John with one arm hanging and a bruised cheek. Jillie looking like hell but smiling. I hoped it was happiness at being alive and not something more manic.

Kris and Simon rode in from the left, Simon looking ecstatic. I knew where his happiness came from. He must have been the one to bring the bot down. If this had been the middle ages and the six-armed bot a dragon, Simon is the guy who would have raced toward it on a black charger, whirling his sword above his head. His voice blossomed in my ear. "If that's all they have, we're okay."

I suspected we wouldn't be that lucky. "Paulette? Scott?"

No answer. Everyone else had the discipline to keep silent while I called for them.

Finally, Scott's voice. "She's hurt. My dog died."

"Are you okay?" I asked, grateful he didn't seem as shaken as he had the day before.

"Yes."

"How badly hurt is Paulette?"

"I think her leg's broken."

Thank God. I'd been afraid of something worse. "Do you remember field medicine."

"I think so."

"Is Paulette conscious?"

"Yes."

"She can talk you through."

He sounded shaky as he said, "Okay."

Simon broke in. "Hurry up. There's another storm coming."

I'd almost forgotten that. The sky was darker, but it was also later in the day. The wind came up again, only this time at our backs. The lab was close.

"Scott," I said. "Good luck." And then to the others. "Group around me."

I still had no clear idea how six of us were going to get into a secret GenGreen lab. There had to be better defenses than what we'd seen so far. I took time to report in. NorAM was quick to respond. "Keep going. There are reinforcements on the ground."

I glanced up over my shoulder. "Is that our storm?"

"Get Alissa to the lab."

"I'll do my best." I closed my communit. Aye, aye, sir. Thanks for doing the impossible so far, and keep on going. Of course, I'd signed up for it. On purpose.

Lightning split the sky behind us, followed a few seconds later by thunder. Maybe they sent the storm just to drive us. Hopefully Paulette and Scott would be okay. "Let's go!"

The dogs had the GPS data, and this close, there wasn't much routing I had to do. The last bit of the journey was mostly a balancing act trying to stick to Hunter in spite of my head and my thigh. Rain made the broad backs of the dogs slippery as hell.

Kris did fall off once.

We got close enough I started watching for the fence.

NorAM messaged us all to turn around and look the other way. Them talking in our ears was a security risk of the first order and so I turned my head even before telling Hunter to turn. Looking up and down the small line of us left, I was pleased to note everyone had understood the order.

Light pinned us bright and blind. Then again. Flash. Wind, or maybe the electricity of what must be simultaneous lightning bolts, lifted and twisted the stray hairs around my face. Flash. Thunder boomed, a deep cracking sound as if the sky had been hit with the hammer of the gods. More noise poured through right above us, enveloping us, making it impossible to talk.

We stood, still looking away. I hadn't known they could do that. *We* could do that. Another ratchet up in the weather wars.

It scared me as much as the lab.

NorAM's voice again. "The fences are all fried. The building's main security is probably off, but there may be generator power. Go, now. Copters will be along. Ground troops are arriving now."

Another scary thing. "Did you catch the traitor?"

"Yes."

Hopefully there was only one. "Wait for orders," the NorAM dispatcher said, enough happiness in her voice that I guessed whatever the lightning and the new troops were supposed to do was getting done.

I glanced over at Alissa. "Are you okay?"

"I will be." She still looked fierce. Like the scientist in a television show I used to love that chased down Japanese whale boats. Something to be said for fierce scientists. Our back was still to the lab and the conflict, and we watched a sliver of black cloudless sky slowly grow as the storm above us blew further east. From time to time we heard thunder in the distance.

It had stopped raining by the time they called for us. I smiled at the look on some of the NorAM shock troop faces as I brought Alissa Freitag into the compound on top of a wet, banged-up robot that barely resembled a dog. I had no mirror, but I'm sure we looked like wild women, drenched in rain and sun and wind and thunder.

I kind of liked the picture that drew for me.

Two scientists had come in via the road, and been protected in the back until the lab defenses were neutralized. NorAM replacing what we'd lost, and probably unhappy about it. But then they'd wanted us to be entirely stealth. Which is probably why so many died. Not that I got to make high-level battle plans or even hear what data went into them. It felt good to have done my part, and that all of the soldiers who had escaped with me were alive. And I liked seeing Alissa run up to the others and start organizing immediately, no question, as if she were the field commander among the scientists.

Maybe she was.

John and Jillie and I attended to the robots and set them charging. After about twenty minutes, a small crew returned with Scott and Paulette. I complimented Scott on a decent job of field-bandaging, and he blushed.

Just as we were about to leave, Alissa came up to me, almost bouncy. No—more than that. Electric with excitement. Her eyes were shining as she said, "Thank you. You have no idea how important it was that you got me here."

"What did you find?"

"Bees."

I must have looked stupid. I had been expecting a breeding farm for human organs or something else scary. "Bees?"

"Genetically changed to kill the few remaining regular bees, and then they would have died out. Would have killed off the whole honeybee line of pollinators. At least that's what they were trying to do."

"Bees were worth all that?" I meant the people dying, the scientists dying, the robots with the rocks, all of it.

She was more direct than me. "The deaths? Yes. GenGreen wants to destroy enough life that we have to depend on their products."

I swallowed and watched her, hoping I'd see her again somewhere besides on television. I could get into helping scrappy scientists save bees. Even if I wasn't quite sure of our methods either. But thunder and lightning and bad weather were the slow way to kill the bees. If I understood what Alissa was saying, we had helped stop a fast way. And even I knew that had become the game. Fight the cancers day by day and hope the body finds remission.

"Are you supposed to tell me this?"

Her sharp brown eyes shone with mischief as she said, "I believe in the power of information."

"And I believe in the power of science."

She shook her head. "Don't. Science is on both sides of this."

I winced. "You're right. Maybe that's why I'm a soldier and you're a scientist."

"And maybe you just saved a lot of the heirloom food left."

We napped in a pile of soldiers and robots until dawn. Alissa said nothing else to me, and NorAM gave no more comment than, "Well done. Come home." As I led my severely reduced crew out of the lab and headed us home, I realized that I felt more sure of our side than I had before we got into the lab. I remembered the power of calling down the lightning and splitting open the sky just for us to continue a war, and I hoped I wouldn't have to do that again. I let us stay mounted until we were out of sight, and then I gave the order to stand down and walk. Our backsides would get home in better shape that way, and besides, the sun had already warmed the air and a light breeze plucked at my uniform.

GAMBIT

Nancy Jane Moore

THE COMM SQUAWKED IN CASSIE RAMIREZ'S EAR. IT STARTLED HER, THOUGH SHE had been lying awake for the last hour, worrying. "Yeah?"

"Transport moving out there, lieutenant. About a hundred klicks out."

Not again. They'd only been running this check point for three Earth-standard days, and already they'd been challenged by four bands of rebels. So far everybody'd backed down. Would this be the group that didn't? She shivered, and not just from the cold that never went away on Titan.

"Lieutenant?"

"Acknowledged. On my way. Got any coffee made?"

"Yes, ma'am. Good and strong."

At least Titan grew good, cheap coffee. The bioformers had installed genemodded coffee plants on every planet, asteroid, and moon they'd transformed. On Titan the plants had done particularly well.

Cassie pulled her exoskeleton on over her fatigues and set its heat at high. Both skel and fatigues were patterned in the dark green camo that marked the Combined Forces Peacekeeping Corps, and both had her name and rank displayed over her left breast. But it was the skel—made from silicon merged with one of the Ceresian metals—that allowed humans without Titan-specific gene tweaks to survive outdoors. She buckled on the weapons vest, locked its circuitry plug into the skel, and checked to see that the weapons were fully charged.

She ran her fingers through her short, bleached blonde hair, then pulled the skel's headpiece up. She'd need the light source outside. Saturn still shone orange in the sky, but Titan at its brightest resembled Earth at full moon. And the bright peak had passed.

Bobby Rowan had tried to convince her that the glow from Saturn was the same as sunlight. "It's caused by the sun, right?"

She had laughed. "You just want it to be sunlight, so you don't feel so far from home."

He'd laughed, too. "Maybe I do. It's summer now in Vancouver. The sun comes up before five, doesn't set 'til after ten."

Typical Earther. Tied to a particular city in a particular country. And homesick for it.

It hurt, to think of Bobby laughing. They'd fought four days ago, fought badly, maybe irrevocably. And over what? Politics. Fucking politics.

The bareness of the clearing where they'd set up the check point emphasized the density of the trees surrounding it. Their leaves gave off an acidic smell, overpowering other odors. Tall, wide-leafed, most of them a genemodded evergreen with foliage that tended to turn yellow, they'd been planted in the twenty-second century to give Titan a breathable atmosphere. The solar collectors orbiting the moon brought them just enough sunlight for photosynthesis.

The checkpoint consisted of a cluster of instabuild cabins, one set right at the road to block traffic, three others forming a mini compound. She stepped inside the one that housed scan and comm, and helped herself to the coffee. "Anything else show up?"

Gavin, the scan tech, shook his head. "No, ma'am. Transport still headed our way."

"Only one?"

"That's what's showing up, ma'am."

"Funny. They usually have several. Wake the rest of the crew when they get within fifty klicks or so. I want a full staffing out there."

He looked at her. "You got a bad feeling about this one, lieutenant?"

"Just want to be cautious. The political situation's gotten pretty tense." She tried to keep her voice off-hand, calm.

He nodded.

Cassie added more coffee to her cup, and went outside. Even with the skel on high she could feel the cold. Earthers had it worse; they'd never been genemodded at all. But even those like her who had grown up in the other settled parts of the solar system didn't have the heavy gene tweaks the Titanians had needed.

Still, the chill in her bones didn't come from the cold. Ten years experience—more than half of it in combat—was causing it.

She sat on the stoop of one of the buildings—she wanted to pace, but it would look bad—sipped more coffee, and realized she was scared. A very bad sign.

You're just being paranoid, she told herself. That's what Bobby would tell you.

That's what she'd fought with Bobby about the day before the platoon moved from guarding diplomats to running the point.

They'd started—and ended—the evening in one of the coffee houses that dotted the once-popular resort city of Revelations. The city had changed hands a dozen times during the war; now it was certified neutral territory, site of the peace negotiations, headquarters of the PK troops.

Cassie had gotten there first. She was sitting where she could watch the door, so she saw Bobby before he saw her. He stopped in the doorway and pushed back the headpiece of his skel. In the interior light—the café catered to the peacekeeping forces and kept both heat and light at higher levels than Titanians preferred—his red hair shone like a beacon.

Seeing Bobby always made Cassie feel ridiculously good. She tamped the feeling down.

He spotted her, and began navigating her way, stumbling as he tried to avoid bumping into the closely packed tables and chairs. Earthers struggled with Titan's light gravity—one of many reasons why the PK force was largely stocked with people like Cassie who'd been born off-Earth.

She stood up to give him a quick kiss. He pulled her close, and they stood there a little longer than she'd intended. She broke it off first—public displays of affection always embarrassed her.

He took off his gloves and rubbed his hands together as they both sat down. "Ah, nice and warm in here." He motioned to the waitress to bring him some coffee, and grinned widely at Cassie.

She tried to grin back, but she didn't feel as cheerful as he did. Lots of rumors had been flying through the troops about major problems at checkpoints. Her soldiers were jumpy, which didn't bode well for their assignment.

She said, "I see you're in a good mood. Peace talks went well?"

"Not bad. We made a little progress." Bobby served as aide de camp—chief assistant—to Gudrid Amudsen, chief peacemaker for the United System Governments' diplomatic corps.

"Really? How unusual. Did the True Harkers actually agree to something?" She hadn't intended sarcasm, but it came out anyway.

Bobby's grin faded. "I wish you'd have more faith in the negotiation process. Nothing's going to happen overnight—these people have been fighting for thirty years."

"And after six months of talks all we've got is a cease-fire best defined by its breaches. I heard the Harkers moved into Jehovah City again."

He sighed. "Yeah, we got a report on that."

"And the government negotiators didn't walk out? I would have."

"Obviously they've got more faith in the negotiations than you do."

"Or maybe they're just scared. They ought to be scared. The True Harkers are winning this war. And we're just sitting here on our hands, pretending both sides are the good guys."

Bobby said, in a disgusted tone, "So we should just intervene on the side of the government?"

"You already know I think so," Cassie said. They could practically have this fight by the numbers now. "Half the USG nations are scared they'll actually have to do something. And the others are more interested in continuing the war so they can sell weapons to both sides."

Bobby sighed, and reached over for her hand. "Cassie, nothing's ever going to be completely smooth when so many different governments are involved. I know USG has screwed up before. They'll screw up again. Humans aren't even close to perfect. We're still learning how to get to the root of conflicts, and we're going to make mistakes. Especially in religious wars. But Titan isn't Ceres."

Cassie yanked her hand back angrily. She hated feeling patronized. "I goddamned well know Titan isn't Ceres. But that's no excuse for screwing up here like they screwed up there."

Bobby stared down at the menu. He took a deep breath, and said, "Cassie, could we not have this fight tonight? We don't have much time to spend with each other."

Maybe if she hadn't felt so nervous about the checkpoint assignment, she'd have been able to let it go. "If you weren't so damned enamored of all the nice-sounding peacemaking theory, you'd agree with me. The True Harkers want to run Titan. They're not going to negotiate in good faith as long as they think they can win."

"Then why in hell are they at the negotiating table?"

"So they can hang out here in Revelations near the shuttle point, and buy weapons from some of those so-called diplomats."

He closed the menu with a slap. "Now you're being paranoid. Do you believe every rumor some scared private starts?"

"I heard it from an air captain who was trying to enforce the embargo. He told me all the ways light craft could get around his blockade."

"And you bought into his paranoia. Look, Amudsen says the weapons embargo is holding tight. A little stuff is getting through, sure. It always does. But nothing significant, nothing for you to worry about."

"And if the great Amudsen says so, it must be true."

Bobby stood up. He ran his chit through the table register to pay for the coffee. "I'd better get back. Long day tomorrow."

They'd planned to spend the evening—and the night—together, knowing it would be several Earth weeks before they saw each other again. Bobby stood there, shifting his feet awkwardly. Cassie didn't want him to leave, and she knew he didn't really want to go. All she had to do was say something conciliatory. It wouldn't even have to be a full apology. But she couldn't.

She said, "Yeah, it's hard work, dithering around."

"Fight's over, Cassie. Both sides lost." He turned on his heel and walked out.

Four days later she was still replaying it all in her mind. Maybe she was overreacting. Maybe the talks would work. She didn't have Bobby's education—the war on Ceres had prevented that. All she had were instincts honed by combat experience.

She didn't know anything about religion, and just knew the barest facts of Titanian history—settlement by the followers of a so-called messiah named Jesse Harker, followed all too shortly by a long period of abandonment as Earth and the closer settlements struggled with other conflicts. And now a war brought on by religious schism. It made no sense to her, but she'd been raised by people who considered religion outdated mythology. Maybe Bobby was right; maybe she was just jaundiced by her own experiences.

And even if she were right, what difference did it make? She and Bobby didn't make policy. If she had just shut up, they could have spent a pleasant night together.

Comm clicked in. "They're about 25 klicks, ma'am."

"Acknowledged."

She stepped into the scan cabin, grabbed a little more coffee, and drank it down. "You're sure there's nothing else moving out there?"

Gavin looked offended. "Yes, ma'am, I'm sure," he said stiffly.

Cassie put a hand on his shoulder to let him know she wasn't questioning his competence. She knew her people, knew which ones she could count on, which ones had to be watched. Making sure the headpiece of her skel was set firmly in place, its sensors locking on, she walked over to the point. "What've we got, sergeant?"

"They're showing up on short range now, ma'am." All the skels had short-range scan built in, along with weaponry and comm.

Cassie pulled her own scan up. "Looks like a mag-lev transport."

"Yes, ma'am. Scan shows about ten passengers, plus a couple up front. Think they might be refugees?"

"I doubt it. We probably got another round of True Harkers. Refugees don't travel by mag-lev. They walk."

He nodded.

She double checked his assignments. Everything in order, as she'd expected. She buzzed Gavin. "Everybody else up?"

"They're moving, ma'am. Whining and bitching, but moving."

"Tell 'em to move faster. And spread out into the forest. Back up formation. I don't want our whole force on the point."

"Yes, ma'am."

The feeling of wrongness got stronger. Nothing you can do about it, she reminded herself, and shook it off. The transport was pulling up to the point.

It stopped at the barricade. A large truck, steering compartment in front, a back area suitable for hauling either troopers or supplies.

A couple of her soldiers stood in front of it with the sergeant; several others had moved behind it.

A man wearing a skel in the dark blue of the rebels stepped out. Her sergeant said, "I want all your people out of there."

The rebel looked back inside the transport, apparently got confirmation from someone in there, and muttered an order into his comm. As the soldiers came climbing out the back, another man alit from the front compartment.

Officer, thought Cassie, watching him move. He looked at the various soldiers, clearly sizing up who was who, and walked over to her.

He had his headpiece up, just as she did. She wished she could see his face. The insignia on his skel showed him to be a captain.

He said, "Lieutenant, I've got orders to relieve the security detail in Revelations."

"I haven't been told anything about a replacement detail, captain." Clearance from Combined Forces headquarters was required to allow replacements past checkpoints.

"We just got word ourselves a few hours ago. Maybe your people are slow letting you know. If you check, you'll find we've been cleared."

A plausible story. They were the right size troop for security. And communications did screw up from time to time. But she didn't like it.

"Nice bluff, captain, but I don't buy it. You turn that transport around, load up, and go on back to your base. Our orders say no one crosses this zone."

"Lieutenant."

"You have five minutes, captain. I suggest you start now."

"What happens in five minutes?" He sounded amused.

"We take the transport. You walk home."

"Come on, lieutenant. It won't take you those five minutes to check with your headquarters about our orders. You're neutrals, after all. Why make this nasty?"

Cassie hesitated. Maybe she was judging too quickly. Maybe that voice screaming 'don't trust this man' in her head was just her own paranoia, her dislike of the rebel position.

The captain moved closer to her.

She took a step back.

"Just check, lieutenant."

It sounded like an order.

And then Gavin was screaming in her ear. "Incoming. Almost on top of us. About ten small craft. They got smart missiles, lieutenant."

Shielded. They must have been shielded from scan. Neither side on Titan was supposed to have that capacity.

The whole troop had heard Gavin. Her people were moving and targeting weapons. As she dove for cover she hit her long range comm button, calling for immediate air support. Not that it would do any good. Their fighters would take fifteen minutes to get there.

The rebel captain had moved behind the transport and was giving his own orders. Obviously he'd known when his other people showed on scan. One of the rebels fired, and she saw her sergeant go down. The fuckers had ammunition that pierced PK skels, more weapons they weren't supposed to have. Cassie fired a projectile at the shooter, and saw him fall. At least their weaponry pierced the rebel skels, too.

"Set your skels as moving targets," she said into comm. That setting made it harder for enemy weapons to lock on. It was new tech, not fully reliable, but it beat nothing at all.

A whistle in the air. Missiles. The barracks and scan cabin went up. Gavin. Another loss. But at least the other shift hadn't still been in bed.

A midair explosion. Some of their automatic intercepts were still working. But late, way too late. The scan block had slowed them down.

She'd been moving as she watched what was going on, and now she had the rebel captain in her scan. She looked at him to lock target, but before she could fire she felt something graze her head. Her mind registered that whatever it was had pierced her skull. And then she passed out.

✦

Cassie struggled to open her eyes. The ground was moving under her; no, she was riding in the back of a transport. She shivered; she wasn't wearing a skel.

Her head hurt like hell. She tried to bring a hand up to feel it, and realized that her hands were tied behind her. Some kind of steel cord. Shit.

Damn, her head hurt. Someone had shot her, she remembered. She wondered if she'd just moved at the lucky last moment, the point beyond which a smart weapon could no longer correct, or if whoever fired had only intended to wound her. That she was still alive argued for the latter. Hostage, maybe? Didn't make a lot of sense. But the way her head hurt, nothing made a lot of sense.

Cassie shivered again. Minimal heat on in the transport. Definitely Titanians in the front.

A knife would cut the cord, she thought. She had one, concealed in her uniform belt. Had they found it? She managed to sit up. Her head throbbed with the effort. Wriggling around, she managed to move her hands to her side, and slid her thumb inside the webbed belt. It touched plastic. She shifted enough to get a finger in, too, and managed to grab the knife. Idiots. They'd figured she was disarmed without the skel and weapons belt.

She was supposed to be. PK forces weren't supposed to carry extra weapons, but all ex-combat troopers did. Her people did, for sure.

Her people. Had any of them survived? The fight came back to her, far too vividly for her headache. If she'd only called in backup earlier. Though she'd had no reason, nothing but a bad feeling. Can't call in air strikes on bad feelings. Except she knew damn well you should pay attention when something felt wrong. Maybe later you'd figure out how you knew.

Cassie saw Sarge fall again, saw the buildings go up. Let some of them have made it. Please.

She felt the knife in her hand, pressed the button to extend the blade, and tried it on the cord. It cut easily. At least the rebels hadn't gotten hold of the latest tech in everything; the restraints the PK Corps used were proof against all available cutting tools.

She flexed her fingers, felt her head. Sticky. She didn't seem to still be bleeding, though.

She tried to look around. Titanians were tweaked for low-light vision, too, so they hadn't bothered to put lights in the back of the transport. The fading glow coming through the back window allowed her to pick out a pile of skels lying in the corner—green camo. PK skels then. It looked like less than twenty. Maybe some folks made it. Other stuff piled up seemed to be weapons belts and other supplies.

Cassie wondered how many were in the front. Probably just one—why use more than one guy for transporting an injured prisoner and stolen gear?

Cassie crawled to her feet. Standing up made her head hurt worse. Her balance felt off—no skel to compensate for light gravity. She moved over to the door to the front, pressed the open plate gently. Locked. She might have expected that. The back one was probably locked, too. Not that she felt much like rolling out of a moving vehicle. What she really wanted to do was curl up and go back to sleep. Except she was too cold.

A skel. That's what she needed. She crawled over to the pile, and started pawing through them, looking for hers. A sound behind her made her turn. The inside door was opening. Shit. Whoever was piloting had probably heard her trying the door. Or had been watching her on comm.

A man ducked through the door. A large man, with hair even blonder than her bleach job. He wore rebel blue, but no skel. In one hand he held a gun. "You're mine," he said.

Cassie climbed shakily to her feet. Standing up made her see double. She stumbled, backed against the pile of skels for support. He walked straight toward her, holding the gun casually, not even threatening her with it. He'd probably already locked it onto her as a target. If her eyes could be trusted, he held an energy weapon, not a projectile—it would stop her if it hit any part of her. But it still had to be pointed in her general direction. If he kept walking in like that, she'd be able to move straight into him and get out of range of the gun.

So what the fuck was he trying to do, walking straight in on another soldier? No one attacked like that. Unless he thought she was so injured she couldn't do much.

An image from the past, from Ceres twenty years ago: A half-drunk asteroid pirate, walking toward her that same way, holding his weapon the same way, the same half smile on his face. He'd been celebrating the initial invasion's success. She hadn't been a soldier then; she'd been twelve, terrified, not sure what he wanted. Though that had become obvious when he had gotten close enough to rip her shirt open.

Cassie'd had a knife then, too: a blade from a set of carving tools in her father's hobby workshop. A small, but very sharp blade, made of metal refined from the high-grade ore mined in the asteroids. The closest thing to a weapon she'd been able to find as she fled the house. She knew how to carve with it; she didn't know how to fight with it. She'd struggled with the pirate as he pushed her to the ground, pulled her pants down with one hand while holding both of her wrists with his other.

She could think of nothing to do but cut at his fingers with the tiny knife, and she did. He pulled his hand back with a scream of pain and then lunged for her throat with both hands. She'd stabbed upward with the blade, eyes shut, hoping something would happen. He'd screamed, pulled his hands back toward his left eye. It had given her time to run, and she had.

Now she looked at this True Harker, this Titanian rebel, and tried to call up the look of pure terror she must have given the pirate. Though all she felt for this stupid rebel was contempt. She wobbled a bit as the transport turned, and realized she could see three of him. Probably she didn't need to try to look vulnerable.

Come closer, she thought, almost begged, and he did, finally grabbing the front of her shirt to pull her toward him. She came with the pull. Now her body touched his, making his gun useless for the moment. He stumbled back, but didn't completely lose his balance. She stumbled with him, fumbling with the knife in her right hand, trying to find flesh to cut. The blade touched something and he screamed, tried to push her away.

But she grabbed hold of the shoulder of his gun arm, and pulled him with her as she fell heavily with his push. They bounced twice, then landed with one of his arms and the gun trapped under her body. Both of her hands stayed free. Now her knife found flesh again. He screamed, and grabbed her right wrist, trying to wrest the blade away. With her left hand she stuck her fingers in his eyes. He tried to bring his free hand up to protect his face while still holding onto her wrist. She cut at his wrist as his arm moved and pushed her fingers further into his eyes. His grip loosened. She pulled her knife hand loose and plunged the blade into his carotid artery. Blood spurted. Cassie rolled aside so that most of it missed her.

She pulled out the knife blade, shook it clean, closed it, and pushed herself up to a sitting position. And sat there, watching him die. A voice in her head said, 'You didn't have to kill him, Cassie.' It sounded like Bobby. She knew it—he—was right. She wasn't a twelve-year-old kid with no training. She had choices.

Cassie said aloud, "Yeah, but I wanted to."

She pushed her conscience to the back of her mind. For now, she had to concentrate on surviving. Her head hurt worse than ever.

The transport was still moving. Probably had a destination programmed in. She didn't think she wanted to go where it was headed. And she needed to get rid of the corpse. She pushed him up against the transport's back door, and then crawled into the front compartment.

It took her a couple of minutes of fumbling around to find the back door controls, put them on open, hit the override when it reminded her they were moving. A quick look back told her the corpse had fallen out. She managed to shut the door, and tried to call up her position. The mapping all ran together. She couldn't find any lights. Her vision was getting blurry.

Change the coordinates, her brain urged her. She put in new ones at random, felt the transport lurch to a stop, turn around, and start back in the other direction. Then she passed out again.

She wasn't cold. That was the first thing that registered. The second was that someone was washing her face with warm water. Cassie opened her eyes immediately and grabbed the wrist of whoever was washing her. A voice gave a little cry. "Please. I'm only trying to help you."

Her eyes focused, and she looked into the face of a young girl—maybe sixteen. The girl's face was contorted with pain. It took Cassie another couple of seconds to realize she was grabbing too hard. She released the wrist, said "Sorry" and then "Thank you."

The girl rubbed her wrist, then started washing Cassie's face again. Cassie lay there. She had no idea where she was or who this girl might be, but it felt so good to be taken care of. After a few minutes she realized that she was lying on a couple of blankets on the ground, and that a powered one had been put over her. That's why she was so blessedly warm.

Over to her right she could just make out the mag-lev transport. It had crashed into the trees that lined the road. 'Those must have been some coordinates,' Cassie thought.

The girl had finished washing her face. Now she was combing through Cassie's hair, looking for the source of the blood.

Cassie winced, involuntarily inhaled. The girl had found the wound. She picked up a tube, squeezed out something, began to rub it on the spot. Cassie winced again; some kind of disinfectant. She willed herself to hold still while the girl finished the job.

"Thanks," Cassie said. "You're good at that."

"We've had practice," she said. "What happened?"

"I got shot."

The girl said, "I can tell. But where are the rest of your people? You're one of the offworlders, aren't you? My mother said you must be from offworld, because you were so cold. Though that could have been shock, I guess."

"Yeah. I'm part of the peacekeeping force. Trying to keep you people from killing each other."

"You're not doing a very good job," the girl said.

A woman who had just walked up behind her said, sharply, "Myra."

"No, she's right," Cassie said. "We're not doing a good job at all."

The woman knelt down beside her. She held a steaming cup. "Soup."

Cassie took the cup in hands that surprised her by shaking, had a sip. "Thank you. Decent of you to take care of me."

The woman looked a little uncomfortable. "We found your truck. We ...we needed some supplies."

Cassie nodded. She looked at the woman, guessed that she might be forty or so. Dark-skinned. Graying hair. Probably Myra's mother. The girl was dark-complected too. She took another sip of the soup, and looked around. Several other people milled about. Mostly women,. The few males Cassie saw looked young. All of them looked tired.

Makeshift shelters had been set up. Over by the transport, someone was going through supply boxes, sorting items out into piles. *Refugees,* Cassie thought.

"We couldn't take your stuff and not help you," Myra said. Her mother gave her a look.

Cassie had the feeling there'd been an argument about helping her. "About the stuff, it's okay, you taking it." Though of course, it was nothing of the sort. They'd been given specific orders: no assistance to refugees. Official policy said people should be discouraged from leaving their homes. Camps had been set up for those who made it despite the lack of help.

Still, even if she'd liked the order, this was neither the time nor the place to follow it. She needed these people. Her head still ached badly. Her last memory was setting coordinates on the transport; she didn't recall the crash at all. "It's okay," she said again and drank the rest of the soup. She set the cup down, snuggled back down under the blankets. More sleep would be nice.

"Don't do that," said Myra sharply.

Cassie opened her eyes wide, stared at the girl.

"Head injury. You need to stay awake."

Cassie sat back up. "Any coffee in those supplies?"

Coffee helped. Cassie got up, and walked over to the transport. The refugees had left the skels and weapons in the back. She'd have gone for the weapons before the food, if she'd been in their shoes.

Her skel was in the pile, blood still on the headpiece. Suspecting that the circuitry was damaged, she scavenged a whole headpiece from one of the others, careful to avoid looking at the name plate. Sooner or later she'd have to see whose skels were in that pile, which of her people were dead. But not yet.

Blood remained on the back door of the transport, too. Killing the rebel was a fuzzy memory. She wasn't ready to remember that either. She wondered what the refugees had made of the blood.

Cassie pulled on the skel, cranked the heat up to high, and grabbed a weapons vest from the other pile. Pulling the headpiece into place, she brought up the light controls. Now she could actually see. Her hands ran through systems check automatically. She touched the control for long-range comm; time to call someone to get her out of here. But she hesitated.

She owed these people. If she called in medevac, they'd lift her out, and they'd take the supplies. And turn the refugees back. Policy. She didn't want to do that to them. They could have left her in the transport, just taken the supplies. Exposure would have killed her. Her hand dropped away. She'd think about it later.

The refugees gave her a wary eye as she walked back through the group in the skel. Myra and another young girl came up to her. The second girl seemed to be about the same age as Myra, but looked completely different: fair and blonde, and about a head shorter. She stared at the skel. "You really a soldier?"

"Yes, ma'am," Cassie said. The thought made her tired again.

"But you're a woman," she said, making it more of a question than a statement.

"Yes, I am."

"I want to be a soldier, but everybody tells me I can't because I'm a girl."

"Hush," Myra said.

Cassie said, "Well, everybody's wrong. Lots of women soldiers out there. Nothing unusual about it."

"But not here, not on Titan," Myra said. "Jobs have been opened up to women in the last twenty years or so, but not in the army."

"Well, Titan's kind of unusual that way. Someone told me it's because in the first few years of settlement your population was dropping, and you needed women to have as many children as possible." Though she'd never understood Bobby's explanation of why they hadn't just used *in vitro* methods—another one of those religious things she didn't get.

The thought of Bobby hurt. She wondered if he knew she was missing, wondered what he thought. Wondered if he even cared.

"But now it's different," Cassie said. "Now your population is stable; no need to protect women for childbearing."

"That's not what the rebels say," Myra said. She was scowling. "They say women shouldn't even be in the schools. That's why we're trying to get to government territory. My mother says we aren't going to go back to the dark ages with those people."

"I'm going to become a soldier like you, and go back and kill those bastards," the other girl said.

"Emilie!" Myra's voice was shocked. She put a firm hand on the girl's shoulder.

"I am." Emilie brushed the hand off, and turned and ran.

Myra said to Cassie. "The rebels killed her father and brother. She's been wild to get back at them ever since."

"I can understand that," Cassie said. Oh, too well could she understand. "But you. What do you want to be? A doctor maybe—you seem to have medical skills."

Myra shook her head. "A biologist. I want to work on the genemods, help open up the other continent."

It struck a chord, somewhere deep in Cassie's soul. She'd wanted to be a biologist once. Her mother had been a biologist who studied the interrelationship of native bacteria and genemodded plant life on Ceres. At twelve, Cassie'd wanted to grow up to be just like her mother.

Her mother had died giving her a chance to run away. And since then no one had asked Cassie what she wanted to be. The Combined Forces had plucked her and others like her out of the refugee camp on Luna. Ceresian survivors made good soldiers.

She wondered what she'd say now if anyone asked her what she wanted to be.

Cassie knew she wasn't going to call for a medevac. Oh, hell. The GPS locator. Automatic in her skel. She muttered instructions into the skel's comp. With luck no one had locked in on her yet.

People were packing things up, piling them in wheeled carts. Wheeled carts! She walked up to Myra's mother, who seemed to be one of the group leaders. "Pulling out?"

"Yes. Lots of ground to cover. You coming with us?"

"If you'll let me."

"We might need a soldier. If you'll fight for us."

"I'll fight for you." Now when had she made that decision? "The weapons and skels—in the transport. You should take them, too."

Now she'd crossed the line. Trading food and medicine for first aid might be excused as an emergency situation; giving refugees weapons would not. Stupid. It would destroy her career if she got caught.

"We don't know how to use them."

They didn't even want them. All she had to do was say okay, let it go.

But her mind wouldn't let her. It kept playing back images of her own escape off of Ceres, pictures of a makeshift group of people—mostly children —making their way among bombed-out ruins. Not all of them had made it.

"I'll teach you. The skel will work as body armor, protect you. And the scan will show what else is out there. Might get us past any rebel patrols." She could help them avoid the Combined Forces checkpoints, too. At least without a vehicle they could cut through the forest. Though if they got too close to a point, they'd show up on scan.

A moment of hesitation, then a nod.

There were eleven skels, but several had been badly damaged. A little scavenging produced eight working ones. Now Cassie couldn't avoid seeing the names. The pain of loss was quick, sharp, almost physical.

And just as quickly she turned it into anger. Her family had died on Ceres; her soldiers had died; but these people would survive. She clenched a fist; swore an oath to herself.

Perhaps thirty seconds passed as she did this. No one seemed to notice, except Myra. *That girl already knows too much,* Cassie thought.

Not counting the smaller kids there were fourteen refugees. She got eight of them to agree to wear the skels, Emilie and Myra foremost. Cassie disabled the locators as she helped the volunteers put the skels on and lock on the weapons belts.

As the refugees walked along, she moved up and down the group, giving basic lessons. She set weapons to sim mode, so everyone could practice looking at a target to lock it, and then fire. Sim told you when it hit. She also showed them how to switch to fully powered. If any trouble came up, it would happen quick.

She only showed them the energy weapons. Projectiles required more skill and the explosives were too damned dangerous in inexperienced hands. Emilie and Myra took to them eagerly, as did one other young women and a couple of teen-aged boys. The older women seemed uncomfortable with the idea of shooting anyone.

Cassie taught Myra and Emilie the rudiments of scan, and put them at the front. Skel scan would only read about five klicks ahead, but that was better than nothing. The first three times they called her over—excited about something they'd seen—turned out to be false alarms. It occurred to Cassie that she'd spent three months in basic, learning how to manage her skel and weapons. How could she expect these girls to get it in a few hours?

But the fourth time turned up something. A vehicle. Cassie read her own scan. Five people. Weapons. Judging by the maps pulled up on one of the refugees' comps, they hadn't crossed out of rebel-held territory yet. Cassie didn't completely trust the maps, but pulling up her own would require the GPS.

"Probably rebels," Cassie said. "That's the most logical assumption, anyway. Figure they're running scan. They know we're here, but they may think we're friends of theirs. Who else would be moving through here, armed."

Myra looked wary; Emilie eager. The others seemed very nervous.

Somehow, Cassie got everybody herded off into the trees. She and those in the skels took up positions near the road.

An open vehicle stopped about twenty meters off. Five men got out. Cassie stepped into the road. A couple of the refugees stood just in front of the trees.

The leader said, "You're in True Harker territory. No offworlders allowed."

"We're a special detail. Taking a couple of government agents back to Revelations." As she spoke, Cassie locked her weapon on the leader. She didn't think much of her bluff. The rebels would want whoever she claimed to be transporting.

"Turn 'em over to us."

"Now you know I can't do that. I have orders."

"So do I."

Scan registered movement in one of the men standing to the leader's right. Targeting. About to fire. Cassie fired her energy burst at the leader, who went down, dead or stunned. She retargeted toward the second man as she moved for cover. He suddenly collapsed from fire coming from behind her.

The other rebels were moving now, trying to target. Her own people were standing still. She screamed through the comm at them to move, move.

She heard the pop of a projectile weapon, saw one of her people freeze and another leap to knock her over. The second one—in the skels she couldn't tell them apart—took the shot in the upper back and fell forward. The first one returned fire even as Cassie fired her own projectile at the rebel shooter. Three down.

The remaining two rebels were sheltered behind their minitruck, firing from cover. *To hell with it,* Cassie thought, and targeted the truck with a smart bomb. The explosion disintegrated the truck and blew the two men back twenty meters into the trees. Fight over.

She checked the readout on the rebels on the ground. Two dead. Two heavily stunned. One seriously injured. None would be moving anytime soon.

Several people were huddled around whoever had gone down. Cassie ran over to see what she could do.

Emilie sat on the ground, crying, cradling the injured person in her arms. "Why didn't you blow them up before? Then Myra wouldn't have been shot."

Cassie dropped to her knees beside the two girls. The projectile had hit Myra's right shoulder. From the ragged way she was breathing, it must have hit her lungs as well. A serious injury. With quick medical attention, she'd do okay; without it....

Cassie sent out a priority call for medevac, set it to repeat indefinitely. Then she reset the GPS on her skel and Myra's. Might as well make them as easy as possible to find.

"Why didn't you blow them up before?" Emilie said again.

"Because I hoped I wouldn't have to," she answered quietly.

"Why not? Why not kill them all? They kill us all. Oh, please God don't let Myra die."

Cassie muttered the same prayer under her breath. She reached a hand over to Emilie. "I've called for a doctor. We'll save her."

She told a couple of the refugees to watch the stunned rebels, make sure they stayed down. Someone else brought her the first aid supplies. She cleaned the wound and injected Myra with a painkiller.

The injured rebel probably needed attention. She knew no one else here would help him. Another charge for the court martial, probably, if she didn't treat him. She sat there, mentally adding up the charges. Weapons to refugees. Taking sides. Not to mention killing people. One more seemed almost trivial.

But there wasn't anything else she could do for Myra, so she walked over to check on the injured enemy. He looked to have broken bones, a probable concussion, maybe internal injuries, but he hadn't died yet. Nothing she could do would help anything but his superficial injuries. She gave him some of the same painkiller she'd given Myra.

He looked at her with hate—his skel had disintegrated in the explosion. She felt too tired to hate him back. Her head had started to hurt again.

It took thirty minutes for medevac to arrive. Two other aircraft followed close behind, both sending out PK signals. She took the medic sergeant to Myra, pointed the others toward the injured rebels.

The medic knelt down, took inventory of the injury, called the robot stretcher over. He looked at Cassie. "She's not ours, is she? I mean, in spite of the skel."

"No. That keep you from treating her?"

"Not with an injury this bad. But I'm going to have to report it, lieutenant."

She nodded. The second ship had landed. Someone walked toward her. "Not going to be any secrets here, sergeant. Just save her life."

He was using a half headpiece, so she could see him grin. "That's our job, ma'am."

The person coming toward her wore captain's bars. Cassie stiffened to attention, saluted.

The captain returned her salute perfunctorily, and said, "What the hell is going on here, lieutenant?"

"We were attacked by that troop of True Harkers, ma'am. Had to defend ourselves." Cassie didn't know this captain personally, but insignia on the skel made her military police. Not a friend.

"Using explosives, I see. Who are all these people wearing our skels?"

"Refugees, ma'am." Way too late to come up with any lies or plans.

The captain looked around, took in the whole situation. "You have any idea how much trouble you're in, lieutenant?"

"More than I'd like to think about, ma'am." Behind the captain another aircraft was landing. Someone jumped out before it even came to a full stop. In the light from the aircraft she could see the red hair.

The captain said, "You'd better start thinking about it."

Cassie said, "Yes, ma'am," but her eyes strained to see the man running toward them.

Definitely Bobby. He caught his breath, gave the captain a perfunctory salute, and turned to Cassie. "Amudsen needs you right away. They're holding a big hearing on embargo breach, and want your testimony."

The captain cleared her throat. "I'm afraid you can't take Lt. Ramirez with you right now, lieutenant." She emphasized the last word. "She's under investigation for some very serious offenses: arming locals, unauthorized combat...."

She didn't say the word "murder," but Cassie knew it was implied. She waited for Bobby to give her a horrified look, to ask if the charges were true.

Instead, he said, "Apparently you didn't hear me, captain. I'm not acting on my own authority. Delegate Amudsen sent me to find Lt. Ramirez. We're dealing with a major problem: rebels ambushing peacekeeping troops, using high-tech weapons they shouldn't have access to. A little more important than some minor skirmish between rebels and refugees."

Cassie could almost see the captain take a mental step backward. The MP certainly knew about the checkpoint incident, and the embargo breach. But she also probably knew about Bobby and Cassie's relationship—it wasn't a secret. Bobby might be bluffing; on the other hand, crossing Amudsen would not further her career.

She needed an out, and Cassie gave her one. "I'll make myself available for your investigation, ma'am, as soon as Delegate Amudsen no longer needs me." She met the captain's eyes, let her body imply "my word as an officer."

The captain exhaled. "I expect no less." She turned to check with the soldiers that accompanied her, who were rounding up the refugees and checking on the rebels. Cassie heard her tell a soldier, "Load these people up. We'll take them to the camp at Revelations."

Not a perfect ending for the refugees, but at least they'd be out of danger, out of the war zone. And sooner or later Combined Forces would start recruiting soldiers out of those refugee camps, the way they'd recruited her so long ago. Emilie would get her wish, though she probably wouldn't get to fight on Titan.

Cassie turned to Bobby. "Now, what are you really doing here?"

"Just what I said. Amudsen sent me to get you. Though I'm not sure she expected me to rescue you from the MPs. Did you really do what that woman said you did?"

"Yeah." She waited for a lecture, some words of recrimination.

Bobby said nothing.

She said, "Look, like you said, Amudsen didn't expect me to be in all this trouble. She wants to see me, the MPs will make sure I get there. You don't have to put yourself on the line for me like this. Especially when you think what I did was wrong."

"I don't think what you did was wrong, Cassie."

She stared at him.

He kicked at an imaginary rock on the ground, then stumbled because he'd overestimated the gravity. Cassie caught his arm. "Our whole damned policy here, that's what's wrong," he said.

"But they really are investigating what happened at my checkpoint, the embargo breach?"

"Oh, yeah. Big hearings. Headlines on every news service in the system. That's why I've been looking for you. They've heard from a few members of your platoon, but you know how big-time tribunals prefer testimony from officers."

"How many members of my platoon?"

He knew the question meant how many died. "Five," he said quietly.

Fifteen lost. Her fists clenched. Even on Mars she'd never lost so many at once. She found herself wishing she'd killed the injured rebel instead of giving him the painkiller.

"It gets worse, Cassie. Our generals knew the latest tech had slipped past the embargo. Amudsen knew." The expression on his face said he felt betrayed. "They just needed a fucking incident to pull the plug. Bastards."

Somehow Cassie couldn't feel any outrage. She'd used all hers up. Generals worked like that. Diplomats did, too. All an individual soldier could do was go along. Or break the rules and take the consequences.

Bobby went on. "The True Harkers aren't ever going to negotiate in good faith. The core of their leadership believes in all that crap they put out—they're going to do everything they can to win, because they'd rather die than compromise. You can't negotiate with people like that." He kicked the imaginary rock again, this time with more success. "I'm sorry I acted like such a prig, the last time we saw each other."

"I acted pretty bad myself."

"You stood your ground. You always do. That's one of the reasons I like you." He grinned at her. "I'm going to put in for a transfer, get out of this bull-shit diplomatic stuff."

She was shocked. "What about your career?"

"Fuck my career." He said it loud enough that several people turned their heads to look at him. "Fuck it. I could never do what she does, could never send people out to die so I could use them as chits at the bargaining table."

Cassie put a hand on his shoulder, to give him comfort. But even as she did it she thought of the times she'd sent people out, knowing they would die. She hated having been the chit—the unknowing chit—but war worked that way. Probably Amudsen had started out as idealistic as Bobby. Maybe what she had to do gave her nightmares.

Bobby went on. "I've been so stupid. I really wanted to believe the problems were as simple as I expressed them in my thesis. I could see what was happening here, but it didn't fit my theories, so I didn't want it to be true."

He took both her hands. "Think I could run a checkpoint? No, probably not. I'd probably fuck that up, too. Maybe something dead end. Supply or something. Or just be enough of a pain in the ass that they ship me home the next transfer. How about it? Want to transfer with me? Just mark time until our terms run out, and we can find decent work?"

Cassie said, controlling her voice carefully to keep it from breaking, "I imagine the only place they'll transfer me is the stockade station off Luna."

He looked startled, as if he'd forgotten her situation. "You don't sound scared."

She laughed. It was better than crying. "I work at not sounding scared. I'm terrified. Even if they don't lock me up, just kick me out, I've got no place to go, no job skills except killing people." Suddenly she was shaking.

He put his arms around her, held her until she stopped.

"I'll use whatever clout I've still got with Amudsen to keep all that from happening," he said.

She let him hold her close. It felt so good. But she said, "That'll only work if it's in the bigger interest, Bobby. Just like everything else. I gave weapons to refugees, killed rebels. If they need to hang me out to dry to get the negotiations going again, they will."

"Then we'll put them on trial—the USG, the whole shebang."

She smiled. His words might be grandiose fantasy, but they helped. "Will you come visit me while I'm doing time?"

"Hell, if they lock you up, I'll steal a ship and come bust you out." He pulled her close to him again. "We'll fight it together, Cassie. I'll stand by you, whatever happens."

Something in her relaxed. Not alone. For the first time in countless years, not alone. Someone else would fight with her, would help her as she tried to find the next step. She might still lose. Probably would. But if she could just remember this feeling, this moment, she could bear anything.

GODZILLA WARFARE
Maria V. Snyder

VAL'S COMM LINK BUZZED IN HER EAR, WAKING HER. NOT ANOTHER PROBLEM WITH *the simulator*, she thought. *Damn thing breaks more than the mining trolls on Mars Seven.*

She toggled it on with a little more force than required, hurting herself, which just added to her annoyance. "Harris here, this better be important."

"Sergeant Harris, report to Captain Bachman's office immediately," a mechanical voice said.

Oh shit. Val rolled out of bed, sorted through the pile of uniforms, searching for one less wrinkled than the others. An impossible task. Finally, she found a pair of fatigues that didn't look like it had been on the losing side of a fight. She dressed, tied her long auburn hair into a regulation knot, and sprinted for the captain's office.

This is it. Time for the you've-outlived-your-usefulness-talk. Time for the let-the-younger-generation-take-over speech. Even though, at forty-two, she was still able to outsmart the newbs, the invention of the planet-wide shields had rendered her expert skills obsolete.

She paused outside the captain's door to compose her expression before peering into the retinal scanner for identification. The base on Mercury Three was far enough away from the action to be safe from a direct attack. Indirect was the new strategy. Thus the talk.

The door slid open, revealing a waiting area with a receptionist. Val fully expected to be gestured to a seat in the typical army hurry-up-and-wait manner, however the private working the desk admitted her into the captain's office without delay.

Double shit.

The captain sat behind her desk and watched Val approach and salute. Bachman's immaculate uniform lacked a crease. The knot of her blonde hair had been twisted into perfection. Val resisted the desire to yank at her semi-wrinkled shirt.

"Sergeant Harris, I have an assignment for you," the captain said.

Biting down on her surprise, Val waited.

Captain Bachman glanced at the collective's screen. "There's an unexploded MFG-66 on Jupiter Nine and since you're the expert in disarming those... what do you call them?"

"Godzilla bombs, sir."

"Why?"

"It's a reference to a mythical Earth creature that can destroy a city, sir. Since the MFG-66 has enough energy to flatten a city with a population of thirteen million or less, we've code named it the Godzilla, sir." And it managed this feat without using nuclear energy. No sense contaminating the planet you were fighting over.

"Interesting." The captain tapped on the screen. "There is a bullet waiting to take you to Jupiter Nine. Please report to deck twelve, barrel two right away."

Val hesitated.

"Sergeant?"

"We're at war with J-9, sir." And a whole list of other ungrateful colony planets.

"Not at present. We have signed a cease-fire agreement with them, and are currently involved in treaty negotiations. This mission is an act of good faith on our part, sergeant, so don't screw it up or UFoP will come down hard on us."

"Yes, sir."

The captain confirmed what Val had surmised on her own. The war with J-9 and the other colony planets hadn't been going well these last few years.

Val swung by her tiny office next to the beast, a.k.a. the simulator, to gather her equipment. She hadn't been assigned a field job in over seven years. A few of her instruments were out of date, but so was the Godzilla. Odd. This whole mission felt... off. Not much she could do about it. Val sent a message to her second, putting her in charge of the newbs' training and nursing the temperamental beastie. *Good luck.*

She reported to barrel two. The bullet to J-9 was piloted by a scruffy-looking lieutenant whose skin had the grayish tinge of someone who hadn't seen sunlight in years. *Another old soul. Wonderful.*

He flashed her a toothy smile when she saluted. "No need for formalities on my ship, sergeant. Call me Leo." He eyed her gear bag. "How much does that thing weigh?"

"About three kilos."

"And you?"

"Fifty-four. Why?"

"This baby's stripped down for extra speed, not comfort. Let me pitch about sixty kilos and we'll be all set."

Leo piled various gadgets on the deck. He held a stack of vomit bags, debating. "Do you get Kasner-speed sick?"

"No."

"Great." He tossed them onto the pile. "Let's go."

Val wedged herself into the back seat, strapping in even though, with this conveyance, you either arrived or you didn't, there was no in between. The ship's name came from the simple fact that it resembled the old projectiles that had been used on Earth. Cone full of navigational equipment and controls, a seat for the pilot, followed by a seat for a single passenger, a small cargo area, and ended with the Kasner-Phillips engine. Constructed for the sole purpose of getting from one place to another as fast as possible, the bullet was literally shot out of a barrel and into space.

They hit Kasner-speed as soon as they broke Merc-3's gravity. Val had forgotten how truly awful the experience of traveling at Kasner-speed was. The destroyers she'd been assigned to before baby-sitting newbs traveled at the more leisurely pace of Phillips-speed.

By the time they arrived near J-9 and her body coalesced, Val wished she'd kept a few vomit bags. *Getting too old for this shit.*

"How ya doing?" Leo asked.

"Fine. How much longer until landing?"

"As long as the Jups open their shield, we should be on terra firma in twenty."

"And if they don't open the shield?"

"We'll go skating, baby. Put on a nice fireworks show for the Jups as we burn!"

Val sighed. *Fly boys.* "I meant what's the plan if we're refused entry?"

"Oh. Turn around, go home. They're the ones with the pimple."

The dimple. Bombs that crashed but failed to explode left craters that the explosive experts called dimples. But she wasn't going to correct an officer even if he had spent too much time at Kasner-speed.

Despite Leo's personality quirks, they landed with nary a bump twenty minutes later. When they finished decontamination, Val and Leo entered the port and were surrounded by a dozen armed soldiers.

"Ah, the welcoming committee," Leo said. "Let me handle this, sergeant." He introduced himself to the squad's sergeant. "I believe you requested an ED expert? I'm just the pilot, but I've brought Sergeant Harris. If you have an ED to disarm, she's your girl."

Val kept her expression neutral despite the desire to cringe over the lieutenant's intro. The J-9 sergeant's hard gaze swept over her with frank appraisal. She reciprocated. About her age, he had the weathered look of someone who'd been in one too many skirmishes. Buzzed black hair and blue-colored eyes, he stared at her with open suspicion.

They confiscated her gear bag and "escorted" her to a conference room, while they led Lieutenant Leo... elsewhere. She sat on one side of a square metal table that had been bolted to the floor. No windows, no decorations—other than six chairs all secured to the floor—Val realized the purpose of the room probably wasn't to confer, but to interrogate.

If they think I'd make a good POW, they're in for a surprise. I haven't been relevant since those damn planet-wide shields. The civil war with J-9 and a number of other planets had gone on far too long. She understood that they desired their independence from Mother Earth. But they didn't want to pay Mother back the octillions of dollars she invested in equipment, supplies, and labor needed to colonize a raw planet. Nope. They wanted a free ride.

Mother didn't have a problem with the colony planets that signed the pay-their-way-to-freedom contracts. Although these semi-free planets had formed the United Federation of Planets (UFoP)—a laughable tiny group for such a big name. Too bad they didn't remain small and insignificant. The UFoP agreed to stay out of the civil fights as long as Mother Earth adhered to fair warfare tactics. They also now had enough member planets and firepower to enforce the rule.

The sergeant from the port entered the room with two of his men. The door closed with a distinctive click. The men stayed near the door as the sergeant approached. She stood.

"Sergeant Harris, I'm Sergeant Gideon. I'm to brief you on the situation." He didn't offer his hand.

They sat on opposites sides of the table. Gideon tapped on the surface of the table. It glowed as it accessed the J-9 collective. A live picture of a barren landscape showed a number of small dimples. As the view zoomed closer on one, it revealed the crater the bomb had created. The MFG-66 had made an impressive scar, digging deep. The view followed the impact path and then the bomb itself—a melted distorted mass, but still deadly. Val wondered how the Godzilla ended up in the middle of nowhere where it couldn't do any damage even if it had detonated on impact.

"I'm leading a team to the crater. You'll remain here and give me instructions to disarm it. I have experience with explosives," Gideon said.

Interesting brief. At least he wasn't planning on using a remote robot. Those things had a twenty percent success rate with the Godzilla. "No," she said.

"It isn't up for debate, sergeant."

"Sergeant Gideon do you want to die?" she asked in a reasonable tone. "Do you want that MFG-66 to detonate because your expert can't smell, touch or get a sense of the bomb through a screen? Now, I don't care if you blow your team to little tiny bits, but my boss ordered me not to screw it up. So unless you take me out there, I'm not going to cooperate."

Gideon stood. "I'll discuss it with my superiors."

"Good. And make sure you tell them that, when *we're* onsite, *I'm* in command. It's not negotiable."

His demeanor remained dispassionate, but anger burned in his gaze. She almost laughed. Working with unpredictable explosive devices in hostile environments over the years, Val couldn't be intimated by one man's ego.

The three soldiers left. Val tried to get a better view of the Godzilla, except the screen turned off at her touch. *Probably set off an alarm. Good, it will keep them on edge.*

An hour later, Gideon returned Val's gear bag and led her to a shuttle along with six armed guards.

"Tell your pilot to land two kilometers from the crater," she ordered Gideon.

After they reached cruising altitude, Gideon sat across from her with his STR-23 rifle in his lap. Val ignored him as she prepped and calibrated her instruments.

When they landed, Val had them wait thirty minutes before opening the hatch. Not that they could out fly an explosion, but the vibrations from the landing should have settled by then. Gideon's impatience grew, causing his men to tense up as he bore the wait with ill humor.

At the end of thirty minutes, Val said, "Your men will stay here, sergeant." She paused to let him refuse. He didn't disappoint.

"It's not up for debate," she said, keeping her tone even. "Normally, this is a one-person operation. Explosives are temperamental, and ones that have burned through an atmosphere and crashed are overly sensitive to the slightest vibrations. The more feet tromping around, the higher the risk of setting the damn thing off." Val rummaged in her bag. Pulling out two pairs of soft-feet, she handed one set to Gideon. "Put them on the bottom of your boots. They're hard on the ankles, but sore ankles are worth not dying."

They exited the shuttle and covered the two klicks in silence. Val noted the air was cool and dry. A breeze blew from the east, stirring the lifeless soil. Nothing except a few clumps of rocks and a couple smaller indentations marked the empty expanse.

When they reached the edge of the crater, Val surveyed the damage. "How long ago did this hit?"

"That's classified," Gideon said.

"You're going to make this as difficult as possible for me, aren't you, sergeant?"

"I have my orders, sergeant," he shot back.

And that would be a yes. She climbed down the steep side of the crater. Grabbing a handful of scorched dirt, she rolled it around her palm and smelled it. She moved to another area and repeated the test. Val wiped her hands and followed the path of impact until she neared the Godzilla. It was half buried.

Opening her pack, she removed her sniffer. She stood downwind from the MFG-66, testing the air for chemical leakage. Then she sampled the soil. The Godzilla's casing hadn't ruptured on impact, the good news. The impact had happened a few weeks ago, the bad news. An already old bomb—the Godzillas hadn't been manufactured in the last seven years—combined with chemicals degrading on the ground created one twitchy bomb.

Which raised the question, why didn't they just set it off with one of their own explosive devices? She asked Sergeant Gideon.

"Classified," he said.

Something stank. And it wasn't the burnt fuel.

Val mulled over the few facts and watched Gideon's expression as she theorized aloud. "You tried to trigger it, but the Godzilla's defensive scrambler sent your bombs wide, which explains the other two impact craters."

He kept his neutral demeanor, but a slight twitch in his jaw gave him away. She was on the right track. Val gestured to the bomb. "This is a recent hit. Which should be impossible due to your shield. Our ships no longer carry the Godzilla. It could have been launched from a Hermit ship. But, again your shield should have destroyed it."

His eyebrows rose, but he smoothed them just as quick. "Is that what the G stands for in MFG?"

"That's what we call it. There is a technical name the higher ups use."

"What does the MF stand for?"

"Official or ours?"

"Yours."

"We refer to that device as the Mother Fucking Godzilla."

Gideon laughed, and the tension between them slipped a few notches. Until Val realized he had been trying to distract her from putting all the clues together.

She picked up the thread of logic and gathered it. "Someone sliced into your collective and turned off your shield just long enough for the Godzilla's entry. Didn't they?"

"That's impossible. No one has sliced into our collective."

Yet he had stiffened as if she had hit a nerve.

With Gideon a step behind her, she approached the bomb. The vibrations in her chest increased ten-fold as sweat dampened her uniform. The number of times she'd defused a bomb didn't matter. Each had its own quirks and challenges. Each one could be her last. Each caused the adrenaline to rush through her body.

The bomb appeared to be far bigger than the standard Godzilla, but the outside markings matched. After confirming the absence of dangerous chemicals, she located the access panel.

Val handed Gideon the sniffer. "If this reads over ten parts per million, tell me."

He nodded.

Glad her hands remained steady, she opened the panel, revealing the bomb's innards. She stared at the complex twist of wires, circuit boards and switches. Except she didn't recognize the configuration. Not right away. When she understood just what sat in front of her, she cursed.

"What's wrong?" Gideon asked.

She replaced the panel and backed away, pulling the sergeant with her. Val didn't stop until they reached the crater's edge.

"What's—"

"I need to speak with my colleague," she said.

"The bullet pilot? Why?"

"It's classified."

Now it was Gideon's turn to curse. "This better not be some stunt or attempt to influence the treaty negotiations."

"It's not."

He stared at her. "I'll hold you to that."

"It's a Death Star," she whispered to Lieutenant Leo. They were in the conference room and she suspected it had been bugged, but she needed to talk to Leo.

"Holy shit with a halo and a white robe! Are you sure?"

"Unfortunately. Are the treaty negotiations going badly for us?"

"I don't know. You can ask the ambassador, he's at the J-9 capital. That is if he'd talk to you." Leo swept a hand through his non-regulation shaggy hair. "Damn girl! Can you disarm it?"

"No. Not alone. It's wired so you need two people, working in tandem."

"But you've done it before. Right?" A crazed hope shone in Leo's eyes as he clutched her sleeves.

"In the simulator, with my assistant. We had one successful session." And only one other team had managed to duplicate it. Not a real achievement since they stopped training on it when the planet-wide shields proved to be an effective defense against the Death Star. Which had been the point. Intell on the Death Star's incredible power had leaked before the device was ready to launch. The panic had been epic.

"Out of how many practice sessions?" Leo asked.

"You don't want to know."

"Time to vacate the premises." Leo stood.

"They won't let us go." Val went up on tip-toe and whispered in his ear. "The Death Star is in delay-action mode."

Leo's face paled to pure white. He swayed. "Why bother to send us?"

"Think about it," Val said. She had. During the trip back to the base, she did nothing but mull it over.

Her theory wasn't pretty. Mother Earth had signed a cease-fire with Jupiter Nine because the colony had been winning the war. The planet-wide shields had countered Mother's one effective offense. With J-9's new guerilla attacks on Mother Earth's bases, Val suspected Mother had to be desperate. So Mother played nice with J-9, sending an ambassador and his retinue to negotiate terms and conditions. Once inside the shield, one of the team had probably managed to shut the shields down long enough for a bomb to slip through.

Mother probably acted surprised. *How did that happen? Must be from a Hermit ship from the past since it was an old MFG-66. We'll send our best expert to take care of it for you.* Except the expert wasn't qualified to disarm a Death Star—no one was. And after the expert "triggered" the bomb, Mother would be all apologetic to the UFoP. *Oops, our mistake. Sorry. Someone must have stolen the schematics to the YFS-97, a.k.a. Death Star* or as the late Sergeant Val Harris liked to say, *You're Fucking Screwed in ninety-seven different ways.*

Val admitted it was an elaborate ruse to appease the UFoP, but she suspected Mother Earth would rather turn J-9 into an asteroid belt, than turn it over to the Jups without a pay-back contract. She was a spiteful bitch that way.

Val could almost hear the gears and switches humming inside Leo's head as he put the clues together.

"And here I'd been worried I'd be forced into retirement. Far better to retire than be a flipping martyr," Leo said.

"Actually, to be a martyr, you have to be the one to decide. In this case, we're being sacrificed."

"Thanks for taking away the only shred of dignity I had left. Did you torture animals when you were little, too, sergeant?"

"What do we do?" she asked.

"Kiss your ass good-bye and find someone willing to fuck your brains out before the big bang."

Val frowned at the lieutenant. He was not helping. Conflicting emotions churned inside her, Val had been glad the Death Star program had never been activated—the loss of life would have been astronomical. Plus it sickened her. But she was loyal to Mother Earth and felt she was right to expect to be compensated for all that hard work in colonizing a planet. Her warring thoughts connected and produced a blast of inspiration.

"Lieutenant, can you contact the ambassador and tell him I *need* to speak with him?"

"You have a plan?" Leo asked.

"I have an idea."

"Bless your wicked little heart." Leo pounded on the door and demanded they be taken to the ambassador.

Surprisingly, Sergeant Gideon agreed, escorting them to another interrogation room thinly disguised as a conference room.

The ambassador swept in a couple hours later with a scowl already deepening the lines on his wide forehead. "Report, lieutenant. And it better be important or you'll both be court marshaled for interfering."

Val studied him. A thick, but powerful build, receding hairline with enough gray to appear respectable. His agitation seemed genuine. Leo glanced at her to begin. Time to test the extent of his knowledge. Did he know he was on a suicide mission?

Keeping her voice pitched low, she explained the situation.

At first, the ambassador huffed in disbelief. "No one on my team could have taken down their shields." But soon his survival instincts kicked in. "There was mention of a Hermit when we flew in. Are you one hundred percent sure it's a YFS-97, sergeant?"

"Yes, sir. No doubt."

"I never should have pissed off General Reffan," the ambassador said. "The old bastard never forgot and here I am, thinking I'd been promoted."

And Val had thought she was useful for the first time in years. Leo's sad gaze matched hers. Another old soldier who had outlived his usefulness. She let the bout of self-pity run its course, then shook it off.

"Ambassador, you need to inform the Jups of the situation," she said.

"So they can tell the UFoP before we blow to smithereens? How much time do we have?"

"Not enough to argue with me, sir." She ignored his outrage. "They have the right to know, and I need the complete and unquestioning cooperation of Sergeant Gideon. The only way he'll give it to me is if he's ordered to by a superior officer. Plus he should know what he's dealing with."

"You're going to try to disarm the cursed thing?" Leo asked.

"Yes. There's not enough time for an evac, it's either try or do what you suggested earlier, lieutenant."

Leo leered at Val. "I knew you'd see it my way eventually."

The ambassador, though remained confused. "Why not have the lieutenant help you? That way we don't have to say a word to the Jups."

Val poured a glass of water. She handed it to Leo. "Please take a drink, lieutenant."

He lifted the glass and downed the contents in one gulp. When he handed it back, Val took it from his shaky hand. Too much time spent at Kasner speed affected the nervous system. He was okay to fly, but disarming the Death Star would take a steady hand.

"What are the odds of success, sergeant?" the ambassador asked.

"Does it matter?"

"That bad?"

"Yes, sir."

"A what? Sergeant Harris, you're not making sense," Gideon said. "What the hell is a Death Star?"

She suppressed a sigh. His superior officer ordered him to cooperate with her without hesitation or question, but failed to state a reason, leaving that bit of nasty news to Val. "The bomb buried in your planet is a YFS-97 not a MFG-66. It's carrying enough energy to destroy your entire plane, and it's set to go off in twelve hours." They had wasted six precious hours talking with the J-9 authorities.

He rocked back on his heels as if she had punched him. "You're wrong. They've been obsolete since the shields."

"According to *your* people, it managed to slip through when the shield opened to allow a supply ship to land. With the right timing, dead accurate maneuvering, and the bomb's special coating, which makes it invisible to your sensors, it is possible."

"But it was shot from a Hermit ship sent over a decade ago. It wouldn't have the latest tech."

She waited, letting him realize the Hermit either had been a decoy or another ship disguised as one. Unlike Val, Mother Earth hadn't given up on the YFS-97 program.

He blanched as fear widened his eyes and his lips parted. "Shit."

Val watched as Gideon swiped a hand over his face, wiping away the horror and transforming into a soldier. He straightened and met her gaze. Black stubble peppered with gray darkened his strong chin. She wondered if he had a wife and kids or a girlfriend waiting for him at home. Or if he was, like her, married to the job.

"What do you need from me, sergeant?" he asked.

"Hold out your hands."

He did. They were rock steady.

"I need you to make the impossible possible."

Gideon quirked a smile. "Is that all? And here I was worried."

They returned to the crater. This trip was completely different than their first. Gideon sat next to her and she explained everything she could remember about the Death Star. Since a delay-action device was a different beast than an unexploded one, the shuttle could land right at the crater's edge.

Val removed both access panels. They were located on opposite sides. Pointing out the important circuits and wires to him, she said, "At times, my instructions will seem counter-intuitive, but you need to do exactly what I say. Understand?"

"Yes."

When Gideon called that he was ready, a cold wave of terror washed through her. The only successful disarms had been with teams of two females. She should have requested a female sergeant.

"Harris?" Only Gideon's face could be seen above the bomb's body. "Let's do this."

Pulling in a deep breath, Val stared at her hands. Despite her out-of-control heart rate and her guts turning to liquid, they remained still.

"All right, Gideon. Located the red-and-black wire that has been twisted with a green-and-yellow one. On the count of three, cut the red-and-black wire." She positioned her wire cutters then glanced up. Gideon stared at her, waiting.

She said, "One. Two. Three." Snip. Val braced for the roar, the flash of light, but nothing happened.

This is going to be pure hell. Consider the alternative, Val. Right.

"Okay, now I want you to cut the green-and-yellow wire on three."

Once again he met her gaze while she counted, cutting the wire without looking at his wire cutters. Her assistant hadn't done that. Anxiety boiled in her stomach.

She continued with the initial sequence. If the steps weren't done in order and in tandem, the Death Star would detonate. The device's internal clock couldn't be stopped or disconnected without severing the contacts with the explosives. In other words, there were no shortcuts.

Val had lapsed into a rhythm, when Gideon broke her concentration.

"Harris that's insane. You're sending current *into* the pads. It should be diverted." Little streams of sweat ran down the sides of his face.

"Twist the wires together on my count."

"No. You're a Godzilla expert. They sent you to fail, remember?"

Ouch.

"You're going to kill us all," he said with a voice pinched tight with panic. "There are over five million people living on this planet. I won't do it."

She tried logic. "We're all going to die anyway."

"But I *won't*... can't be the reason." Gideon stepped away from the panel.

"Damn it, Gideon. We were working. Ninety-five percent of the simulated sessions had failed by this point." She made up the statistic; it sounded reassuring and was close enough to the truth.

He paused.

"Stop thinking. This baby is unlike anything you've dealt with before. But I have experience. Now twist those wires on three, sergeant."

Gideon nodded and returned to the bomb. Val allowed a second of cool relief to flow through her burning muscles before she counted.

As they worked, Val disconnected from what might happen to the task at hand. But statistics caught up to her. Two people cutting, splicing, and re-wiring circuit boards at the exact same time was near impossible.

The YFS-97 shuddered and activated with a series of clicks. She jumped back.

"What happened?" Gideon asked.

"We're done."

"But we were so close!" His voice rose in panic. "Why didn't it explode?"

Her thoughts jumbled, twisting until they resembled the pulled out guts of the Death Star. *Kaboom, kaboom—where's the kaboom? Leo had the right idea, I should be on the floor with Gideon, spending my last minutes—*

"Harris." He shook her shoulders. "It's not over. Finish the mission, soldier!"

She blinked at him. "They sent me to fail. I've achieved my mission."

"Yes, they did send you to fail. After years of loyal service, you were deemed disposable. How does that make you feel, soldier?"

"Mad as hell."

"What are you going to do about it?"

The clicking increased in volume and speed. Kaboom come soon. Val almost giggled, but a chunk of vital information formed in the middle of her spinning thoughts. *No kaboom. Why not?*

They had been near the end. Only a few connections were left, which meant the YFS-97 had to find another way to detonate.

"Go!" She pointed to his panel. Grabbing her pliers, she shouted instructions to Gideon over the noise.

It didn't matter if they worked in tandem as long as they both finished the last step before the Death Star re-routed its ignition. Sweat dripped and she panted with the effort.

"Last cut, Gideon," she yelled. "Blue wire, snip it off before it enters the boxes on either side and pull it—" A shower of sparks arched across her wire cutters. Then a huge fireball slammed into her, knocking her off her feet.

Kaboom. Mission accomplished. She crash-landed. All thought disappeared.

Pain and semi-consciousness returned at the same time. Every centimeter of her body hurt, and she had lost her vision and hearing. Val swore. Except it didn't help when she couldn't hear her own cursing. She also couldn't move, which would be alarming if she had the energy to care.

Real consciousness came with some serious pain, but the meds helped blur the sharp edges. And the return of both her hearing and vision aided in her recovery.

Gideon visited. "Welcome back, sergeant."

"But... the fire. What..."

"I've no idea. I yanked the blue wire just as the fireball hit you. It dissipated. The clicking stopped. I'm here and not blown to bits. So I'm not complaining."

"How long..."

"You've been out of it a couple days. Leo's beside himself. He wants to go home, and is driving us all crazy."

"Pilots have... a harder time... being a POW. There's been... studies." *And I probably won't do much better.* However, when she considered the alternative, being a POW didn't seem so bad.

Gideon smiled. "You're welcome to stay—you are a hero, after all—of course, only a few people will ever know about it. However, you don't *have* to stay. As soon as you're feeling better, Leo will fly you back to your base."

Confused, Val asked. "What did I miss?"

"Your ambassador made a deal. If you saved our planet, you would be allowed to leave. But there is one condition."

"Home, sweet home," Leo cried as he landed the bullet.

"Leo, it's a barren rock with a military base. Not what I'd call home," Val said as she tried not to get sick in his ship.

"Better than some foul swamp with huge creatures that consider us dessert."

"Ugh. You've been to the base on Venus Five?"

"Spent two years there." He shuddered. "I'll take a barren wasteland any day."

Her sore muscles protested as Val climbed from the bullet and entered the decontamination area. But she forgot all about her aches and pains when she spotted Captain Bachman and four MPs waiting for her on the platform.

"Sergeant Harris, come with me," the captain ordered. "Lieutenant Leo, please report to your commanding officer."

"Yes, sir." They both snapped a salute.

Leo shook her hand good-bye. Grinning, he headed in the opposite direction. *I'd grin, too if I could claim ignorance, telling everyone I'd hung out in the pilot's lounge drinking the entire time.*

The captain led her to a debriefing room and gestured to a chair. Val scanned the room. The place had been rigged with video and audio sensors.

"Report, sergeant," the captain ordered.

"I disarmed the bomb as requested, captain. I've nothing else to report."

"You disarmed a MFG-66?"

So she had known. "Yes, sir."

"Are you sure?"

Val feigned confusion. "Of course, sir. The explosive device was clearly labeled. There is even video footage—"

"Sergeant Harris, I don't care what the video showed. I want an honest report."

Then you shouldn't have lied to me, bitch. Swallowing the bitter taste in her mouth, Val detailed a textbook disarming of a Godzilla bomb for the captain.

Clearly impatient, the captain banged her hands on the table. "What took you so long to return?"

"After I disarmed the bomb, I supervised the proper dismantling and safe storage of the explosives, which required a few days."

"That wasn't part of your mission, sergeant."

"Sorry, sir. I misunderstood. Since you had informed me that my mission was an act of *good faith*, I felt it was my duty to ensure the safety of the Jups."

The captain kept trying to trip Val up. However, Bachman wouldn't directly ask about the Death Star. And with the ambassador's report, confirming Val's statement, Captain Bachman couldn't charge Val with treason.

The Jups had been smart to pretend all had gone as planned. They kept Mother Earth wondering and worried about what happened to that Death Star. *Good, it will keep them on the edge.*

Val tendered her resignation a few months later. Although upset, Captain Bachman couldn't stop her. She packed her few belongings and met Leo on deck twelve.

"Free at last?" he asked.

"Yep. What about you?"

"I'll never retire. I'm a speed junkie." He grabbed her bag and shoved it in the cargo area of his bullet. "Where to, my dear?"

"Jupiter Nine."

"Oh?"

"I hear they're looking to hire an explosives expert."

"Really? Are you sure it isn't because of a certain yummy Sergeant Gideon?"

"I wouldn't use the word yummy to describe the sergeant."

"What word would you use?"

But Val only smiled at her friend as she settled into the passenger seat. While she waited for the bullet to fire, she thought of the perfect word for Gideon.

Kaboom.

GHOSTS ON THE BATTLEFIELD
Danielle Ackley-McPhail

THEY WERE CALLED THE MORRIGANS. RAVEN. CROW. CORBY. JACKDAW. ROOK. AND their unit leader, Captain Jayne Corvidae, known as Scarlet Jay. They were AeroCom's battle-honed goddesses of war. They had more campaign ribbons across their collective chests than any other flight in the group, and more demerits on their records than their entire wing combined, mostly for fights started by greenies eager to prove themselves tougher than the dames. Still, fighting's fighting, no matter who starts it.

Or who *finishes* it.

They held that record too, though they didn't consider it something to brag about.

They were the Morrigans. They had more important things to do than crow.

Jay popped her head through the common room arch as she hurried by. "Briefing room, ten minutes." A machine-gun series of "Ayes" followed her down the corridor, cutting off sharply as she straight-armed her office door, letting it slam behind her.

"Damn it! I can't believe he's doing it to us again!" She took a swing at the old-fashioned training bag she'd had installed in the corner. If it weren't chain-anchored to the floor it would have slammed into the wall.

"Ten minutes isn't going to be enough, is it?"

Jay spun around and glared at Raven—First Lieutenant Chen Po—who had just slipped in the door. It was an effort to unclench her jaw—and her fists—to respond to her lieutenant. Breathing deep, she squared her shoulders, ran a hand over her spiked bristle of vibrant red hair, and put an arm out to steady the still-swaying bag. When she was as calm as she was likely to be, she spoke.

"We're shepherding another crop of green."

Raven grimaced and closed the door behind her as she moved fully into the room. "Nope... a *week* wouldn't be enough."

Raven was right. They were a combat flight, use to taking the fight to the enemy in atmo or space, but ever since General Calloway took over command of their group two months ago they'd been on baby-sitting duty, responsible for buffing off the rough edges on each batch of fresh pilots assigned to his command. There was only one thing worse than sitting on her thumb or banging heads with airmen that hadn't yet clued to the fact that they weren't winged gods, and that was guilt. Calloway made sure her duty periods were all three rolled into a great big miserable ball. The two of them had a history. Back in flight school she'd made a stupid mistake, cut the wrong corner. It had resulted in the death of the General's son, Justin. Calloway didn't much care for her, which she could understand and respect. What she didn't hold with was the fact that he was taking it out on her pilots as well.

"As of 0600 tomorrow we'll be patrolling the DMZ in two-hour shifts. One Morrigan, one newbie," Jay said as evenly as she could, with a hard-knuckled grip on her temper. Her deep brown eyes narrowed with annoyance as she handed Raven a stack of personnel jackets. "There's one clear problem child in the bunch. He's with me on first patrol. The rest I'll let you sort out."

Raven nodded, sending her short, straight black hair swaying around her face. Then, with a knowing glance, said, "Okay. Take one more swing."

The training bag was still rattling its chain as they left the office, expressions neutral, backs straight, and eyes hard-edged.

It was 0Dark00 on the planet Demeter. Jay was running the preflight on her bird, an AC-360PH—AeroCom-360 PlasmaHawk—straddling a single hybrid aerospike engine. The fighter wasn't the latest or—some would say—the best, but even the most skeptical admitted that Scarlet Jay could work magic behind the stick. She didn't know if it was magic precisely but she knew the old girl the way a cowboy knew his horse, every trick and habit and the fine nuances of each little shimmy. Up in the atmo they were one and they got along just fine, even if the Hawk did have a tendency to argue.

Her checklist done, Jay slid her digital pad in her flight suit pocket and reached up past her jumpseat into the dead space between the jet's skin and its frame. The tinkle of a small bell ringing reached her ears and she smiled faintly as the sound of the biker bell she'd tucked up there faded. It had been a gift from her Granddad when she'd gotten her wings; to keep the gremlins away, he said. Granddad had been both a pilot and a biker and understood such things. He was long gone, but that bell went on every bird she flew. It was like having him at her shoulder, looking out for her, reminding her she had a right to be there. In the tough spots, she'd even dare say she almost heard his voice in her ear.

"Man... whose bad side are you on to get saddled with that?" said a voice from behind her, way too informal, she might even say insubordinate. She turned, and her suspicion was confirmed. It was her greenie. And he was bad-mouthing her fighter. There was no reason to point out that if he were permanently assigned to the squadron, he'd be flying the same thing.

She looked at him over her shoulder as she slid down the rails she'd climbed to the cockpit. What she saw was a golden boy: from his burnished hair, to his light brown eyes, and straight on to his attitude. "Get your preflight done, Pilot Panski. We lift off in thirty."

"Already done," he answered.

He piloted an AC-010 NovaStream; the absolute newest craft in the division. It was a couple rows over up the line. Not exactly line-of-sight from her location, but Panski would have had to have walked by her PlasmaHawk to get to there.

"Really? Must have been awful early. I've been here an hour and I can't say I saw you come in." She spied the outline of a familiar hand-held device in his flight suit pocket.

Technically, the NovaStream was capable of remote preflight. She didn't know whose bright idea that was, but it resulted in enough deaths in the testing phase that the remotes had been banned, and yet every once in a while a newbie tried to get away with using one. But, as she herself had learned long ago, there were some things only eyes-on could tell you and there wasn't a seasoned pilot in the ranks that wouldn't stand hard on those skirting the rules.

As she hit the tarmac, Jay pivoted and took three long strides to where he stood.

"Hand over the preflight remote," she ordered.

With a sullen look buried deep in his eyes, he pulled it from his pocket.

She plucked the non-issue gadget from his hand, her eyes hooded as they locked with his. "Did you happen to notice the bars on my collar, Panski?"

His face went expressionless and he instantly snapped to attention, belatedly saluting.

She continued, "Regulations state on-site, manual preflight is required before going airborne, is that understood, *pilot*?" Her tone and demeanor would have made Granddad proud. She didn't usually stand on ceremony, but she could pull rank with the best of them when it was called for. This was a lesson he definitely needed to learn.

"Ma'am, yes, ma'am." She almost couldn't even see the way his jaw muscles tightened in protest as he responded.

"Now go do your walk-around. And be sure to double-check the navigational array. Maintenance warned that there's been a problem with drift on some of the flights."

While Panski strolled toward his jet, Jay turned and headed for flight control, the contraband remote in hand. Her mind was still on the pilot, though. Even if she hadn't read his jacket she would have known all about him. This guy came not just from a career military family, but from presidential stock. That combination went one of two ways; they either produced a next generation of soldiers that was squeaky clean and by-the-books, or ones that walked around with a sense of entitlement and felt their connections lifted them above military protocol and deportment. There was no having to guess which side Panski came down on. She only wished she couldn't see so much of her younger self in him.

And it's my job to readjust his perspective, she thought. *Joy.*

"Hey, Deeley." As she entered flight control she tossed the remote to the sergeant behind the desk. "Add that to the contraband lockbox, please." While he took care of that, she pulled out her digital pad and slid it into its port on the mainframe—a safeguard against wireless interception—logging in their flight plan and officially beginning their duty shift. "See you in two hours," she called as she again pocketed her pad and left control.

There were sounds of life rising around the flight line; jets being maintenanced and fueled, pilots coming off patrol, and Panski trying to chat up Raven, who was waiting with Jay's helmet in hand. He had so picked the wrong Morrigan. He was also done with his PF awful quick.

She ran her hand over her right arm, where the flight suit hid an old scar from her cadet days. For a moment she considered going over and running the check herself, but if they were on the ground much longer they would be late for patrol. And Calloway was just looking for reasons to add another black mark to her jacket. They just didn't have the time. She was going to have to give Panksi the benefit of the doubt.

Jay accepted her helmet with a nod and a, "Thanks," before turning on Panski. "Get it in gear, pilot." She nodded him toward his bird, then turned back to Raven.

"We're patrolling the east leg of the DMZ. Intelligence indicates some isolated Dominion activity along that stretch, but otherwise it's been quiet." As she briefed her second, she tugged her comm hood, with its integrated earpiece, into place and settled the helmet—emblazoned with a stylized diving scarlet jay—overtop. She tightened the chin strap as she continued, "Run some flight exercises, get the Morrigans and the new pilots use to operating together. Anything comes up, you know the drill."

In response, Raven reached out and knuckled her helmet, the Morrigans' private ritual for luck. "See you back in two, SJ. And don't worry... I'll keep them in line for you." She then stepped back behind the red safety lines and saluted as Scarlet Jay climbed into the cockpit.

One of the ground crew scampered up the rails to lock her harness into place. When he was done and slid back down to the flight line, Jay powered up.

"How you doing today, Hawk?"

"All systems optimal," the flight computer responded; the vocal tones not quite neutral, though by no means mistakable for human.

Jay affectionately rubbed her hand along the control panel then began warm-up procedures, activating her comm, starting the engines, and, as a back-up, running internal diagnostics before signaling flight control they were ready to taxi. As she waited for confirmation, she commed Panski, "Pilot, you have my wing. Once we are informed of our runway you will follow my lead, heading 03-niner, climbing to seven thousand feet, and maintaining patrol altitude. Acknowledge?"

"Acknowledged, captain," the pilot responded, his voice expressionless over the communications system. "Heading 03-niner, climb to seven thousand feet, and maintain patrol position."

Tension crept along her limbs as Jay powered up the rest of her systems in habitual sequence, flipping toggles and pressing buttons until the control panel was fully engaged. Her eyes trailed across the gauges and displays.

No warnings flashed, no alarms sounded. She let the rumble of the Hawk's engines sooth her. Found comfort in the sharp scent of aviation fuel and oil that always lingered over the hanger bay before settling her respirator into place. As the engines warmed up, Jay closed her eyes a moment, waiting for Deeley's voice to sound in her earpiece. By the time they were given clearance to taxi out to the runway she had gotten her balance. She reached back with her left hand and tapped Granddad's bell, then toggled her comm.

"You set?"

Silence. What was he doing, napping?

"Panski? Are your systems green to go?"

"Green to go, captain."

"Okay, roll her out nice and easy. We're slated for runway ten-alpha."

"Ten-alpha, Aye."

Her shoulder muscles tightened, and Jay had to force them to relax again. Something about this guy put her on edge. She didn't trust him with her back... or at it. There was a general feeling of laxness about him. As if he saw nothing wrong with cutting corners. She knew all too well that attitude got pilots killed... and not always the one taking the shortcuts.

Ten years ago she had been a raw cadet. Top of her class in flight school, the most recent in a long line of Ace pilots going back to her many-times-great Granddad... her head had been so far up her ass she'd have smelt dinner coming down if she hadn't been so oblivious. Cadet Justin Calloway had been her wingman. For the final flight exercise before graduation she had been less than thorough in her preflight. At three thousand feet, executing a hard bank-and-roll maneuver, her right rudder locked up, sending her plane crashing into Justin's. She'd been able to eject, suffering no more than a broken arm in the impact. Justin had lost his life in the resulting fireball. The accident had been attributed to mechanical failure and she had been allowed to graduate—with something less than high honors—but she knew the truth. Her friend had died because she'd been sloppy. His father, General Calloway, was just as certain and never let her forget it.

Not that she ever could.

"Scarlet Jay, please proceed to runway ten-alpha," Deeley broke her reverie, reminding her she was holding up the flight schedule.

"Going wheels up, flight control," Jay spoke across the comm. "See you in two."

"Wind to your wings, lassie," Deeley answered, as she took to the sky.

Jay grinned at the sergeant's informal hail. He was never less than regulation face to face, but over the comm he loosened up once in a while and that felt good, like a pale echo of her Granddad watching over her each time she flew.

And then they were airborne, and that faint shiver of nerves returned as Panski took up position on her wing.

Take-off had been uneventful.

Patrol was downright dull. Jay decided it was time to assess Panski's flight capability... not to mention give her nerves a rest, before she climbed right out of her skin. Toggling her comm, for the first time in half an hour, she spoke. "Panski, take lead for a bit."

Rather than simply pull ahead, the pilot executed the type of fancy, rolling dive rarely seen outside of an air show or combat and brought his NovaStream up in a sharp climb before leveling out in front of her. Jay didn't comment, merely noting the way he handled the jet, which grudgingly she had to admit was with a fair amount of skill, and just as much flash.

She watched the jet in front of her closely, noting a tendency to drift right, which Panski periodically corrected for. Hard to say if it was due to a heavy hand on the stick, or a bug in system. She made a mental note to have it checked out. Other than that, she didn't find much to fault in his piloting. He showed promise once his attitude got knocked into shape.

Jay shifted her focus to the dual-monitor set into her control panel. After all, they were out here to patrol. One monitor played a recorded feed from the previous day's fly-over, the other was a real-time image fed to the screen by high-powered surveillance cameras mounted to the exterior of the fighter. Together they allowed those on patrol to note subtle alterations that might signify a move by Dominion forces.

No Man's Land was quiet today, not even a rabbit sticking out its pointy teeth. Their flight took them over mile after mile of low scrub and the occasional sapling that hadn't been routed out yet. Other than the patrol road to their right, running along the edge where the border met the DMZ, there were no other defining features. The monotony left her with little to occupy her mind, which, left to its own, dredged up an old bone to worry at: Calloway and his efforts to basically ground her flight. His official position was that new pilots needed skilled veterans to acclimate them to the reality of combat on the line. Jay had it from trusted sources that his not-always-private stance was that women didn't belong in the cockpits of fighter craft. That was her fault, based on that one ill-fated flight, but it colored his opinion of female pilots across the board. Never mind that their physiology made them better suited to pulling high-g's, allowing them to execute maneuvers that caused their male counterparts to black out. Or that their fine motor control gave them the delicate touch modern aircraft demanded. And forget about the fact that their ability to multi-function and their utilization of both lobes of their brain aided their adaptability under high-stress situations. None of that mattered. Not in the shadow of his son's memory.

From that point on, Calloway wasn't just old-school... he was ancient-school.

And there wasn't a thing she or the Morrigans could do about it. Not without damaging their careers. Nothing pissed her off more than having no viable recourse. What was more, she had to remember it wasn't the greenies' fault. It was so easy to let the situation color her responses to Panski and the new pilots in general. Not a good habit to get into.

"Variation in terrain," the computer called a sudden disparity in the camera images to Jay's attention, distracting her from her thoughts. She glanced at the screen. It was difficult to make out what was there; she would have to make another pass.

"Hey... Flash,"—it suited him much better than Panski—"I'm circling back to investigate an anomaly."

A moment of dead air, then he responded, "Acknowledged, Scarlet Jay."

She banked left into a turn that brought her skimming over the terrain they'd just covered, using the digital zoom to capture the landscape below to document her report. The anomaly appeared to be a camouflaged perimeter sensor that had come partially uncovered. The sensors were used to alert of aerial movement over an area. She didn't recognize the design, which pretty much meant it was Dominion. The question was: how many were there besides this one, and had their patrol already been tagged?

With the intel secured, she guided the Hawk back into wing position, only to discover the patrol road was to the wrong side of them. They weren't just drifting slightly; they were half a klick into the DMZ.

"Pilot, we are off course," Jay spoke across the comm. "Correct your heading and return to Allied airspace."

"What the hell are you talking about?" Panski responded. "Heading confirmed as 03-niner... ma'am."

Being informal was one thing, but he clearly forgot he addressed a superior. She let it go. They had bigger issues at the moment. "Radar engaged," the computer announced. She glanced at the screen; there was the faintest ghost on the very edge of her radar, not even strong enough to consider a blip, but also clearly not stationary. *Probably nothing,* she told herself with one eye still on the radar. That uneasy feeling returned.

"Forget about your instruments for a moment," she instructed him. "Calculate your heading by the sun." She glanced down at her chronograph. "It is precisely 0730."

Jay waited, gave him a moment. She could see him taking visual. Across her comm came the sound of rather inventive swearing.

Before she could respond, a more strident warning sounded in her cockpit.

"Radar engaged. Radar engaged. Radar engaged. Radar engaged." Like an antique record album skipping, the flight computer repeated itself, only this was no malfunction. A quick glance down at her radar showed multiple ghosts on the display; so faint she would have discounted them as noise if they weren't advancing so steadily.

She scanned the horizon for confirmation. Whatever was headed their way was too far off to be seen. Her nerves stilled and a warm current of adrenaline flowed through her until each muscle was taut and her mind sharp focused in combat-readiness. They needed to get back to friendly territory.

"Veer off!" she ordered Panski. "We have bogies."

A hard bank left took her back toward their designated airspace. After a moment, though, she realized Panski hadn't followed suit. "Flash, veer off now, we are not authorized to engage in full air-to-air."

"I'm trying, damnit!" Jay could hear a thread of panic in his voice. "I have a systems malfunction." Glancing back, she watched as the NovaStream dipped and bobbed erratically on the currents as if the flight control profile no longer correctly registered the parameters of the aircraft.

This was much more than a simple case of drift.

"Pilot Panski, I take it you blew off the eyes-on preflight?"

There was a long moment of dead air. "Ma'am, yes, ma'am," he answered quietly, as any pilot scared shitless would.

Swearing, she banked again, reversing her trajectory.

No doubt the ghosts on the radar were Dominion aircraft, which pretty much confirmed they'd seeded the DMZ with perimeter sensors. There was no way this was in response to the one she'd spotted; the enemy couldn't have gotten airborne this quickly if that were the case. And with the NovaStream going buggy there was no way they were going to outfly the incoming fighters. She mentally assessed their resources: the Hawk had 20mm Valkyrie internal cannons and starburst missiles mounted beneath each wing, four to a side. The NovaStream didn't have cannons, but it had eight each of heat-seekers and starbursts. Not nearly as much firepower as she would like. Maybe that would last ten minutes in full engagement. Setting her comm to command frequency, Jay called in for air support and was promptly acknowledged by Deeley. She prayed the forces arrived in time. A glance down at her radar showed the ghosts getting closer, the pattern denser. It looked like they had two flights closing in. With an efficiency garnered on the frontlines of more battles than she could count, Jay powered up her weapons systems and focused her thoughts on figuring a way out of this mess.

Her gaze tracked on the thin ribbon of road below and to her left, pretty much the demarcation between the Allied border and the DMZ. It was used by their ground patrols. Right now, none were in sight. Too bad, they were equipped with mobile SAMs and maw deuce 50-caliber machine guns; that would have come in handy as ground support. Well, looked like for now they were on their own.

"Hey, Flash, I need to know if you have enough control to maneuver…" She waited for him to acknowledge.

"I think so." His voice didn't shake but the words were tight and short.

She grimaced. Not good enough. "You need to confirm. Test her out now before they're on our tail."

She breathed out a silent sigh as he wrestled the NovaStream's nose down and into a left bank, the stick fighting him the whole way. The jet wobbled as it pulled to the right against his guidance, but he was able to correct. He then reversed the maneuver with much more control.

"Okay, here's what I need you to do… see the patrol road?" He made a vague sound she took as assent. "We are going to reverse course and head full throttle back toward base and intercept with our reinforcements. That road is your marker… it stays to your left wing at all times. Understood?"

"Loud and clear, captain."

She had to respect his fortitude. No matter how he came across before this, under fire, so to speak, he was holding up better than some veteran pilots she'd flown with. In theory, once they were over Allied territory they were safe. Jay wasn't holding her breath on that. The Dominion wasn't known for playing by the rules.

"I've reported our situation. Our job now is to hold our own until our backup arrives. Get your weapons systems armed." As she spoke, she flipped the master switch for her own cannons and armed her missiles.

Panski's muttered "Acknowledged" spoke volumes through gritted teeth. She could hear the strain in his voice. Her own gut was in more knots than a fishing net as she watched over the limping NovaStream. Flashbacks from a decade past sent a shudder through her. Blood pulsed like a drum in her ears, for the moment louder than the engine roaring at her back as she held her breath, her full attention locked on Panski. The NovaStream bucked hard as it sliced through a thermal. Jay gasped and the same sound echoed from the other cockpit. There was a sour taste in the back of her throat.

"Pull up!" Jay called out. "Keep that bird in the air!"

"All respect, ma'am," the pilot snarled, "I'm fuckin' trying!"

Scarlet Jay held her peace after that, sending up Hail Marys and shadowing the craft from two hundred feet above his flying altitude. He got the NovaStream pointed the right direction and both of them put on some speed.

"Hey, Deeley," she hailed flight command once more. "I don't particularly want to be the only girl on the dance floor. You have an ETA for me?"

"Air support is wheels up and on the way, full burn. They should reach you in T-minus-fifteen minutes... but between me and you, Calloway ain't happy, says...."

The sergeant's words cut off abruptly and there was the sound of a sudden commotion coming over the comm, followed by a familiar voice. "Corvidae! No screwups this time."

Scarlet Jay clenched her jaw on what she wanted to say to the old bastard. "Duly noted, sir."

"I mean it!" Calloway snapped. Rage burned through the words whereas he had always been cold and abrupt with her before. "You better bring that pilot back alive with all his bits still where they belong or you're through, acknowledged?"

Hostility came across the line in scorching waves. That was when she was forced to admit to herself, somewhat shamefully, that outside of receiving orders, she had never spoken to him, never approached him as Justin's father. For the past two months she'd taken everything he'd heaped upon her but she had never said what needed to be said. And this might be her one and only chance. The comm wasn't exactly private, but it would have to do.

"General Calloway," she said quietly and with absolute sincerity. "I deeply regret the loss of your son, I was careless… stupidly so, and I cannot tell you how sorry I am that I was not the only one to pay for those mistakes." She purged ten years of guilt, but she didn't lie down and offer him her throat. Her tone took on a bit of steel as she continued, "I know that can never be enough, but as my flight record will attest, I am no longer that cadet, I have learned from my mistakes and I *have* paid for them more than you can ever know."

He sputtered in response…likely preparing to yell; she didn't give him a chance.

"All due respect, sir, I have to go so I can concentrate on not making new ones."

She flicked the comm to short-range only and put the General from her thoughts. She likewise switched off the Hawk's verbal address system. Things were about to get hairy. She couldn't afford the distraction.

"Um… Jay…" Panski's voice cut in.

"Go ahead, Flash."

"Either my radar is acting up too, or we have trouble coming in at ten o'clock."

Jay glanced at her radar for confirmation. "Damn! They've circled around to cut us off!" She considered their options: cut deeper into Allied air space and pray they didn't follow, stay on course to the base and try and outrun them, or opt to engage and try and buy some time for backup to arrive. "How's the Nova responding?"

"She's fighting me," he responded. "I can strong-arm the stick, but I can't throttle above 400 knots or she shimmies like crazy."

That left them only one real choice, to face the enemy. "Okay… work it the best you can. Go for evasive maneuvers, and only take the sure shot. Keep your heading toward base as much as possible; I'll run interference and do what I can to take them out."

"Acknowledged." He saluted her from his cockpit and she had to grin as she returned it, then, firewalling the throttle, she took it to the enemy.

It had been months since she'd seen close-in aerial combat. Her chin dropped and her fangs were out as she rushed to engage the lead element. She clawed for altitude as she closed the distance. The ghosts on the radar blossomed into full blips, sending warning lights flashing through the cockpit; her eyes narrowed in response, but she kept her gaze focused on the sky outside her canopy and at her six. Below her, just above the cirrus deck, she could just make out the needle-like profile of four Dominion Hyperwings, advanced remote drones that had evolved considerably from the old Predator technology.

"Come on, Gomer... bring it," she muttered under her breath, unconsciously falling back on the slang learned at her Granddad's knee.

No doubt these were just the advanced scouts. Somewhere in the atmo were fighters headed this way. They had to take the Hyperwings out before the enemy reinforcements arrived, or she and Panski were done for. Two of them broke off and headed for the NovaStream. The other two came at her from split vectors.

"Flash, deuce bogies headed your way!" Jay had just enough time to call the warning to Panski and then she had no more attention to spare. A hail of lethal artillery came spraying toward her, lit up by the flare of tracer rounds.

She swore with enough heat to blister even her Granddad's ears as she jinked to the right, then dipped her wing to the left and rolled the Hawk, diving for the deck. Working the stick, she pulled up into a steep climb, scissoring across the nearest drone's flight path, trying to come in behind it. Every time she tried to get a lead on one of them, the drones reversed, spoiling her aim.

"Come on, already! I wasn't serious about dancing!"

Scarlet Jay came down in a screaming dive and broke off sharply as she worked the Valkyrie's radar controls, furiously trying to get lock. And then she had it; the drone off her right wing lit up as she came around in a tight turn. Jay depressed the trigger on her cannons and crowed as incendiary ammunition devastated the rear half of the craft.

The Hawk soared through the flack as the debris rained down on the DMZ.

"Boola-Boola!" Jay yelled in triumph, though the comm would not carry the "kill" to command.

From off to her right, strafing fire dimpled her canopy and Jay reflexively ducked in her harness. "Shit!" A quick glance through the canopy showed a bit of smoke trailing from her right wingtip, but she saw no sign of fire.

Before it could fire again, Panski buzzed the attacking drone close enough that the wake from his slipstream sent the craft into a dip, ruining the targeting lock. He then executed a hard bank and roll to evade before arcing away. The drone veered off to follow.

Her teeth bared, Jay yanked the stick in tight and slammed the throttle into full burner, booting the left rudder, sending the Hawk into a 135-degree slicing turn. The damage to her bird pissed her off. She closed on the pursuing drone, flying in close, then let loose with a starburst when she had the enemy craft square in the cone of vulnerability. A scan of the sky and Panski's thumbs up were confirmation he had taken care of his two as well. Her grin felt good and vicious, as she returned the gesture, but their triumph was short-lived.

The cockpit lit up like Christmas as the radar flashed both red and green, alerting her to incoming enemy aircraft closing fast and friendlies just pinging at the edge of the radar. It was a race now, one she was afraid the Dominion pilots were going to win; yet she dare not comm the rescue fighters. Right now they were beyond enemy radar range. If she made any attempt to communicate it could very well be intercepted, robbing her side of the element of surprise.

She didn't know what the Dominion was after, but she was here to see they went home disappointed... if at all. Estimating the approach vector and speed of the enemy craft, she took the fight into the vertical. The Gs were crushing as she whipped into a steep climb, bringing the Hawk to 12,000 feet. She held it a moment, then stomped on the rudder to get the nose turned back down.

The dive took her right through the center of their formation, scattering the squadron of Boru 47-Vs—the Dominion's delta-wing fighters—sending one careening into his wingmate. Panski came in from below, only a little unsteady, and took out another with a starburst missile. The fireball surely lit up the sky. Jay couldn't say, though, she was too busy watching the ground rush toward her. With every muscle straining she fought the stick, leveling the bird a bare two hundred feet off the deck. She laughed with the rush as she climbed back up to engage. With backup approaching they no longer needed to conserve their ammunition. She and Panski harried the Dominion fighters, dipping and diving among them like crows tormenting a hawk.

The old girl took damage, but nothing crippling. In fact, now that the pressure was off, Jay was having way too much fun. One of the Borus veered off, turning tail back to base with one engine trailing a plume of thick, black smoke punctuated by periodic shooting sparks. She'd sent at least one more crashing to the deck with a starburst. There were two left, both of them hard on her tail, and then her luck ran out. A warning klaxon shrieked through her earpiece. At least one of the enemy fighters had lock on her Hawk.

"Crap!"

The Hawk's engine screamed in protest as she rolled hard left and pitched down. As she did, she hit the chaff release on the stick, launching a cloud of debris in her wake to break up the radar lock.

"You aren't good enough to take me down, Demon," she taunted, though there was no way the Dominion pilot could hear her.

As she powered away, her gaze darted down to the radar. Whoever was coming to their aid was nearly here. She set her heading for intercept, with just enough wobble and limp to give the enemy pilots the impression she was having difficulty. All the while, she lured them closer to the kill zone. No telling who command had sent on the rescue run but they were fresh and presumably fully loaded. Daring a second glance she made a quick count and whistled long and low as she counted ten Allied jets coming in fast. By now they had to be pinging the enemy radar.

There was no way two lone Dominion pilots would engage such an overwhelming force over Allied territory. Jay anticipated they would cut out and run away.

She was wrong.

"On your six!" Panski called out over the short-range. Jay craned her neck for visual confirmation through the cracked canopy. The remaining jets were closing fast working furiously to gain target lock.

She must have pissed them off.

Jay dipped and bobbed and spun off for all she was worth to spoil their aim. She took the Hawk low, blending in with the ground reflection, using every trick she knew to pull ahead. Cannon fire and missile impacts chewed up the terrain. The Hawk shook with half a dozen impacts but somehow held together.

And yet, no matter what trick she pulled she couldn't shake them.

"Take it vertical," Panski called out. Going with her gut, she instantly obeyed, yanking back the stick and giving the Hawk full throttle, she shot up into the lightening sky mere seconds before two of Panski's heat-seekers flew up the tailpipes of the Boru fighters.

"Way to go, Flash," she called over the short-range as she brought her craft back down, banking wide and circled above the NovaStream, noting the fresh battle scars dotting the fuselage, taking in the burning debris from enemy aircraft scattered far and wide below. She considered the other pilot, the way he stepped up to the fight; not hotdogging it, but working as a team. A smile tugged at her lips. She had to admit he didn't have all that many rough edges left to buff.

"Hey, let's get that bird back to base and figure out what's wrong."

As she set her heading to intersect with the approaching friendlies, she reengaged her long-range comm and hailed flight control. "Scarlet Jay to command," she reported, the words heavy with satisfaction. "The party's over, and we're coming home."

IMMUNITY PROJECT
Ann Wilkes

'VE GOT A FENCE DOWN, KARNA CONTINENT. DELTA SETTLEMENT, TRANSMITTER D14," said Donard. "It must be hardware. Damage to the transmitter itself. Diagnostics aren't picking up any malfunction, but it's not transmitting."

"Any sign of activity outside the perimeter?" asked Ella.

Donard rubbed the back of his neck. "I'm picking up four people on the infrared."

"Crap!" She bit her lip and drew herself up. "Come in shallow from the East and set us down as close as you can to the main junction, but first send a data stream to HQ."

Donard heard her heave a sigh as she left for the bunkroom. His heart sped up. He'd never had to land on Kradon. He'd heard stories about teams who wound up having to extract or exterminate Kradonians to safeguard the project. Donard had taken the job hoping to raise credits fast to buy his own ship. He felt like a sell out, helping the Allied Human Worlds Directorate experiment with the Kradonians. His gut wrenched and he began to sweat.

To: AHWD IPA At: 2498, 11.04.06:32
From: IPA Solar Sprinter, Mirage in orbit of Kradon.
Malfunction detected in psionic fence transmitter D14, Karna continent. Source of malfunction is local. We are landing for repairs and recon.

He hit the send button and fastened his landing straps.

The engineer, Charney Jonis, came in already dressed in Kradonian garb and deposited his muscle-bound mass in his flight seat and strapped in. "You may get more action than you bargained for, mate. Just keep cool and you'll be all right."

"Just shut up and let me fly this thing."

"Sorry. Truth be told, I'm a bit nervous."

Donard grunted. He had to concentrate on the controls. He heard Ella strapping in for landing behind him. Ella knew better than to talk during a manual low-fly. Donard brought the ship down behind a hillock, within a kilometer of the Delta perimeter, near the main junction box. With a gentle shudder as the thrusters disengaged, the sprinter settled onto the sandy surface.

"Smooth. Good job," said Ella as she released her straps. "Get suited up on the double."

"Yes, sir."

Donard went to his bunk and pulled cotton drawstring pants from his footlocker. The rough weave scratched his skin. He grabbed a sensiderm undershirt from one of his drawers. He had just pulled it over his head when Charney came in like a bulldog following a scent. His broad shoulders and heavy jowls rounded out the effect.

"What do you think you're doing?" he asked.

"Getting dressed. What does it look like?"

"You know the regs. Lose the sensiderm. Don't want the Krads to get suspicious."

"Yeah, yeah. So instead of the synthetic undershirt, they'll see a guy dancin' around 'cause he's itching to death." Donard jerked off the undershirt.

Before they left, Charney strapped a slender tool belt around his waist under the loose tunic and taped the thumb-sized Memory Eraser to his leg just under his knee. Ella looked Charney over, making sure no bulges showed.

"Rad levels within specs," Donard said. "We're good to go."

As they passed through the hatch, Charney hit the palm reader to close the door. When it sighed back into place, the holoflage engaged and the ship began to shimmer like air over oily tar on a hot day and vanished from sight.

They headed for the main junction box of the psionic fence network. Donard felt a growing unease as they neared the perimeter. Knowing the fence artificially induced their anxiety did nothing to lessen the effect. Donard battled the psionics and his guilt for being involved in the project.

Charney squatted near a fake boulder, turned it over, and started running diagnostics while Donard and Ella stood back, scanning the area for Krads wandering the countryside.

"It's not reading D14. Probably a localized short. Might have been gnawed through by a rodent."

"Let's hope," said Ella.

"Always," said Charney. "I have to turn off the whole network to fix the short."

"This project is 205 years old. Let's see to it that it makes 206. If we're spotted, stick to the script. They're sickly, but they outnumber us, and if they find out the truth..."

They knew how they'd feel if their distant cousins, people they trusted, *their allies,* had kept them isolated and sick instead of rescuing them. The Directorate had sedated the Kradonians who survived the Praktorians' orbital nuclear attack, rounded them up into six settlements built over kappa radiation generators that the Directorate had inserted, and held them there with psionics while the rest of their planet healed itself.

Immunity Project teams had been sent to Kradon twice a year to deliver custom-made phages into the water and air of the settlements to breed a race of humans resistant to kappa radiation. Ostensibly, for human expansion across the galaxy to prevent humanity from being wiped out because of our concentration in one area. Most AHW citizens who were privy to the existence of the project suspected a different agenda: the conquest of the Praktorian worlds simply because the Praktors weren't "human" enough.

"Okay, the fences are off. Stay sharp," said Charney.

"D14 is three klicks south/southwest," said Donard.

Ella and Charney took the lead.

After half a klick, they stopped and Charney pointed at something to their left. A little girl lay prone in the dirt by an outcropping of rocks. She wasn't moving.

"We'll get samples for medical on our way back. We need to get the fence repaired," said Ella.

"She could still be alive!" To the mission, that made no difference. They were mandated to let them die so long as enough survived to test the gene modifications and improve the kappa immunity. But to see a poor helpless girl lying in the dirt....

"That fence comes first. The whole project could tank if we don't get it fixed right away." Something in Donard snapped, and he took off across the field.

"Donard, stop! Stop!" Ella hissed at him, not raising her voice lest the other wanderers were close enough to hear.

Donard didn't slow down, and she and Charney gave chase.

Donard knelt beside the girl and gently rolled her over. She looked about eight years old. Blood pooled next to her leg and trailed from the edge of a sharp rock. It was fresh.

"You idiot!" Ella had that look. That 'I'd-like-to-kill-you-with-my-bare-hands' look.

"It's not the radiation or a bad bug."

"That makes no difference, and you know it."

The girl didn't seem to be breathing. Donard listened to her chest and checked her pulse. Her breaths were shallow and her pulse, weak.

"We have to get this bleeding stopped," he said. "I need cloth for bandages." He tried to rip the bottom of his pant leg, but since it only looked like homespun, it wouldn't tear. Donard pulled off his shirt and wrapped it around the girl's leg as tight as he dared. She stirred but didn't open her eyes or speak.

"Terrific!" Ella spat.

"What? She's not dead," said Donard.

Ella gestured for him to come away for 'a word'. He got up and followed her ten paces from the girl. Charney came too but kept one eye on the horizon, looking for the other Krads.

"You're putting the whole Project in jeopardy," said Ella. "What now? Are you going to nurse her and tell her who we are and what we're doing here?"

"We can't just leave her to die. What about the ME?" Donard asked.

"It isn't very reliable. Her memories could resurface or it could leave her as blank as a newborn."

"I can't leave her. I won't." Donard stared Ella down.

"If you screw this up for us," she jabbed her finger at him for emphasis, "I'll do more than just report you. I'll kill you," said Ella. "Get her back to the ship and patch her up. We'll dump her close enough to the settlement to be found. Hurry, before we find someone else or vise versa."

Halfway back to the ship, Charney offered to carry the girl the rest of the way. Donard accepted and hoped it was a gesture of support. Just as Charney hoisted her up to his shoulder, she came around.

She whimpered, rubbed her eyes, and opened them, probably expecting to see her dad holding her. Then she yelped and pushed away from Charney, who had her in a fireman hold.

"Who are you?" she cried, still struggling to get free.

"Hi, sweetie. I'm Charney. We're going to make you better. Your leg's hurt."

"I've never seen you before," she said while looking around at Donard and Ella and her surroundings, her blue eyes wide with fright.

"What's your name?" said Ella in a syrupy voice, "I'm Ella and that's Donard."

"Coree. My tiva's that way. Where are you taking me?" Now she sounded more defiant than scared. Even a small child could see through Ella's act.

"We know," said Ella. "We're going to take you to our camp where we have herbs and bandages to make you better. Our camp is closer than your tiva. We'll fix you up and then take you home. How's that?"

Coree nodded. She must have picked up on Ella's tone and figured it was a rhetorical question. She laid her head against Charney's chest and fainted again.

When they neared the vessel, Charney nodded to Donard, who went ahead to the ship. Donard looked back to be sure the girl was still turned away, reached for the door and felt around for the palm reader. The door slid back into its recess in the bulkhead as the ship shimmered back to visibility. He entered and let the door close behind him, re-initiating the holoflage.

Donard grabbed a field med kit off of a shelf, extracted a tranq patch and ran to the door. He took a deep breath. He hoped Coree was still out.

Charney stood outside the door with her. Blood dripped from the makeshift bandage into the dirt. Donard placed the patch on her neck.

"I'm going to turn the breaker back on while you two deal with her." Ella spun on her heel and left.

Charney brought Coree inside and placed her on Ella's bunk. They'd need room to work and the other two bunks were stacked.

"Why didn't she have you go?" Donard asked. "Think she's concerned you might bring home a stray as well?"

"That was a pretty stupid move. Ella's right. She'll tell her folks about us. They'll be more than a little curious. And that Memory Eraser..." Charney shuddered.

"I couldn't just leave her there. Watching from the ship is one thing. Close up is different." He removed the bloody shirt.

"Here." Charney handed him a metal basin and some disinfectant wash.

"Thanks." He placed the basin under the girl's leg and handed Charney the shirt. "Doesn't this whole project ever bother you? The Kradonians? We should have just rescued them."

"A little late to start questioning it now, isn't it?"

"I've just been thinking..." Donard said as he irrigated the wound.

"Doesn't matter what we think. We have a job to do and we do it. Nobody consults us when they make these decisions and it's best not to dwell on it," Charney said, handing Donard antibiotic gel and a liquid-suture syringe.

"But we treat them like specimens, damn it. Have you ever met any of them before now?" Donard asked.

"No. Don't forget that if it weren't for us, they'd all be dead long ago. And serve them right, too, for letting the Praktorians use their nuclear weapons against them."

"Yeah. But that was their ancestors. Not them. Think she needs plasma?"

"Wouldn't hurt," said Charney, "but it'll take too long. We could have been back in orbit by now."

"Let's give her a pint. I'll be fast."

"You can't make the IV drip any faster. Better not. I don't think she lost too much and it's stopped now. Let's just get this over with."

Donard said no more as he applied the suture. He heaved a sigh as he rose and picked up the mess.

Charney grabbed fresh bandages of the "homespun" variety. "We better cover the wound with these. They haven't got liquid-suture anymore."

"Yeah. They don't have squat *anymore*." Donard got up and washed his hands in the micro sink.

"I may not agree with the Directorate's policies all the time, but I play it their way so long as the company transmits the credits to my account."

"All done?" asked Ella as she entered the bunkroom.

"She'll be fine. What now?" Charney got up to face her.

Ella didn't answer him. She stared at nothing in particular, her jaws set and a muscle in her cheek twitching.

What's she plotting? Donard wondered.

"We'll take her with us," said Ella, "and leave her just inside the perimeter once the fence is repaired. Make sure she stays out for a couple of hours, Donard. We still have three more Krads out here somewhere."

"What about her memory of us?" said Donard.

"When she tells Mummy and Daddy about us, we'll be initiating pre-launch. We'll leave them with a mystery. They'll hand down the story of the angels that helped a little girl. The sooner we get the system fixed and get out of here, the better.

"We'll bring more tranq patches and the ME. They'll be plan B. We can tranq and wipe an entire search party if it comes to that. Don't worry. She'll be fine."

"What's plan C?" Donard regretted the question as soon as the words left his mouth. He knew plan C. They'd kill the entire search party, get samples for Medical, and dispose of the bodies. And he would be responsible for the swift decline in viable test subjects. He hated himself for even considering how any of this would affect him. He wasn't the one being deceived, tampered with, and destroyed.

Ella flashed her 'don't-ask-stupid-questions' look.

Donard gave Coree a sedative shot and peeled off the tranq patch. Donard picked her up and carried her cradled in his arms. They left the ship in silence. At the junction box, Charney turned off the breaker again and they headed for the transmitter. Donard had just spotted the yellowing evergreen tree that housed the transmitter when he heard voices calling Coree's name from his left.

Two adults and an older child were searching the area. They couldn't reach cover in time.

One of the adults, a man, spotted them and called out. "You there. Is that Coree? Is she okay?"

"Yes. She's cut her leg," Donard called. They walked in the direction of the search party.

"Coree!" the other adult, presumably the girl's mother, cried out as she ran the rest of the way toward them, her long, blonde hair trailing behind her. She wore a gauzy white shift. Donard stared. She had all the right curves in all the right places.

"Oh, baby, are you okay?" The woman's pale face creased with worry as she reached for her daughter. Then she saw she wasn't moving and scanned the faces of her rescuers.

"Who are you? What have you done to her?" she shouted.

"Mommy!" Her mother's voice had wakened Coree.

The woman took her from Donard, never taking her wary eyes off his.

The girl locked her little arms around her mother's neck. "They fixed my leg. I hurt it on a lava rock. See?" She held out her leg.

The other Kradonians approached. "Who are you?" asked the old man. "Where have you come from?"

"My name is Ella Brolen and this is Charney Jonis and Donard Terrellen. We've traveled over the mountains. We heard stories of another settlement this way. Our camp is a couple of klicks back."

The man scratched his red beard and looked at them as though sizing them up.

"How many people live where you come from?" asked the boy.

"Not many. There are only twelve left now that we're gone. And some of those may be dead by now," Ella said. "What's your name?"

"Joshen," he said, looking at his feet.

The woman stopped kissing and hugging her daughter and looked up at Ella. "My name is Cheela. And this is my father-in-law, Bave. Thank you for seeing to my girl's wound. Have you eaten? You must come with us."

Bave continued to glare at them. "Over the mountains, you say? Your accents surprise me. Your *existence* surprises me. We haven't had a visitor in… in… well, longer than I can remember. Way before my father was born, I can tell ya."

"Our speech has been influenced by the migration of the Colna mountain people," said Ella without hesitation.

"Must be pretty cold in the mountains. Where's your winter cloaks?"

"Back at our camp," Charney said.

Bave nodded. He still didn't seem convinced. "You'll be wantin' to get your things first, I warrant," he said.

"Oh, no. We can grab our bits and pieces later. We're rather hungry, as a matter of fact," said Charney.

"Of course you are," said Cheela, and to Bave. "We've been gone too long. People will worry. Carry your granddaughter, would you? She's too heavy for me." Cheela gave Coree a kiss on her cheek before Bave took her.

Donard was relieved to find out that the grizzly, red-headed fellow was not Cheela's husband. But what was he thinking? What did it matter? "That's a beautiful girl you have there," he said to Cheela. "How old is she?"

"Thank you…?" Cheela looked at him quizzically.

"Donard. Donie, you can call me Donie," he said. He felt a silly grin creep into his face.

"She'll have seen eight years in a matter of days. Do you have children?"

"No. My wife and child died years ago." He looked over at Ella. She pierced him with her 'stick to the mission' warning face.

People working in fields, orchards, and vegetable gardens stopped their work and followed them to the settlement. About a third of them had obvious deformities. Some had three arms. Others had one. The faces. Donard gulped and tried not to stare. Three eyes here, no eyes there, half a face, bulging purple tumors.

A young woman with a swollen belly walked right up to Cheela. Donard couldn't tell if she was pregnant or malnourished. "Cheela, who are these people?" she asked. "Where have they come from?"

Others echoed her questions. A few of the children approached the strangers and stared up at them. A small boy, with a growth on his shoulder too hideous to look at, reached for Ella's hand. She shrank back before forcing a smile and taking it. The boy beamed at her as though she were his long-lost mother. Ella's face flushed and she looked away. Donard wondered if that was a miniature, conjoined twin on his shoulder.

"Give 'em room you li'l uns. They're from across the mountains and we're gonna feed 'em. Go about yer business, all o' yez." Donie could see that Bave decided it wouldn't be a bad thing to be the keeper of the strangers. Might gain him some bragging rights.

They passed a cemetery. So many graves for such a small enclave. Many of them were packed so close together he wondered if they cremated their dead. Or maybe they were the remains of infants and small children.

A couple dozen tivas were carved into a low hill. Cheela's was in the middle of the row, a bit smaller than most. They ducked through the doorway, the thatch on the roof scraping their heads as they passed into the one-room abode. The floor was hard-packed dirt, possibly with baked clay to keep it firm. A single oil lamp, suspended from the low ceiling provided the only light. No windows. Their homes were built with insulation in mind, not aesthetics. The rear of the tiva recessed into the rock; a cave. It smelled of rotting vegetation, wood smoke, and peat. Two beds, a small pallet, and a table with three chairs made it look even smaller.

Bave lit a fire in the hearth and then dusted his hands on his tunic. "So ya say ya been journeying for months? Not seen any other people or signs of civilization?"

"Some ruins," said Ella. "A skeleton or two but not a living soul anywhere. Not many animals, either."

"So do ya think there's any more settlements on Karna? Ever had any visitors where you are?"

"Not a one. Old Ogden, he's forty-five or so, said that two men and a little girl came there when he was little and stayed. No one else remembers them. He said they were dying when they arrived and only lived another year. Ogden's been dead ten years."

Donard drew in a breath through his teeth. Ogden was Ella's cat. She was way too good at lying.

Cheela swept her golden hair up on her head, fastening it with a string. She had no outer ears whatsoever. That's not so bad, Donard thought. He wondered if that was the full extent of her mutation. She fetched vegetables from a recess in the cave wall, a cutting board and knife from a shelf high over the fireplace, and sat at the table to chop the vegetables.

"Donie, could you bring me the wooden bowl from that shelf by the fire?"

He handed her the bowl, smelling the sweet smell of yeast emanating from under the cloth that covered it.

Donard admired the soft lines of her nape, punctuated by strong muscles, as she kneaded the dough and formed it into a loaf. She placed it in a small, cast-iron chamber under the fire grate and set the pot to boil with water from an urn in the corner. She wouldn't look up and meet his gaze, but her movements seemed forced and unsure, as though she knew she was being watched.

Charney sat on the floor with Coree, looking at her collection of colored stones.

"These vegetables," Donard said. "They are some kind of root, aren't they? What do you call them?"

Cheela looked at him like he had sprouted an extra head. Then she took a deep breath and continued chopping. "Is your climate so different? I thought doba roots grew all over Karna. You've never seen them before?"

Donard flushed and his mouth went dry. "Uh. Well, we have something that looks a little like that. They're a darker brown and smaller. We call them laoda roots. Maybe both had a common origin before the Great Waste." He hoped he sounded convincing.

Cheela just nodded. Donard wondered if she didn't believe him or just didn't like to be reminded of the Great Waste.

During dinner Cheela told them the tiva had been in her father-in-law's family for generations. Klive, her husband, had died a few years before. "Joshen works in the grain fields with his grandfather, while Coree helps me around the tiva and in the garden." Cheela's face clouded over. She looked far away and mournful.

"What's your village like?" Bave asked Ella.

"It's smaller. We live in huts that we have to replace every few years. We get together for a common meal once a day. The cooking, gathering, and hunting duties rotate between us. Cross-training is essential with our high mortality rate."

Donard gulped. If he didn't know her, he'd believe her. But she made him nervous. She continued to give long, detailed answers to Bave's questions rather than changing the subject as he and Charney had. She seemed to enjoy acting, like it was some kind of game.

"Thank you for your hospitality," said Ella. "We'll have to get back to camp now. Perhaps we can talk again in the morning?"

"You're welcome. But please, you must stay the night. You don't want to walk in the dark to a bedroll on the cold, hard ground."

"We don't wish to impose. We only ask for a torch from your fire and we'll be on our way," said Ella.

Cheela looked at them with suspicion, but replied, "Of course. Bave will prepare one for you. You will be back tomorrow?"

"Sure. We'd like to talk with your neighbors and maybe take some seeds with us."

"Why must you continue to journey? Do you expect to find a better place further east?" Cheela asked.

Ella sighed. She looked about as though searching for the answer. After ten long seconds, Charney opened his mouth to answer, then Ella beat him to it. "We're not sure. But we have to know. We'll return at midmorning."

Bave harrumphed and scratched his beard before fetching their torch. Cheela's jaws were set, her eyes dull as she stroked Coree's hair. Coree clung to her mother's tunic, her bottom lip protruding in a pout.

The crew didn't speak until they reached the edge of the settlement. Donard wrestled with thoughts of sabotage. Of undermining the project to save Cheela and the others. How could he be part of this?

When they reached the transmitter, they slowed their pace. Charney pulled off the cover and hunted for the faulty connection while Donard held the light. "I've got it. I'll have to switch out this connector and solder the assembly back in place. Might take a while."

"Let's get that damn fence mended and get out of here." Ella paced and darted her eyes around, watching for Krads.

Donard yawned and handed Charney the wrong tool.

"Just go ahead. I've found the problem. I can take it from here," Charney said.

"You sure?" Ella asked.

"Go on," Charney said.

"I'll stay and help, if you don't mind," Donard said to her, "He still needs someone to hold the light."

"Make it quick, boys," said Ella over her shoulder.

"You think we'll be okay after that lengthy exposure?" Donard asked when Ella was out of earshot.

"We'll be fine. Just follow decontamination procedures and you'll still have little Donies and Dollies to your credit one day." Charney's tone had turned nasty.

"What's eating you? We're home free, now," said Donard.

"Just a little rattled from seeing them... their deformities, their ignorance."

"Yeah. That's what I was trying to tell you."

"Donard, just shut up and let me work so we can get the hell out of here."

Donie held the light and his tongue. His thoughts turned to Cheela. So beautiful and fragile. He fixed the image of her alabaster nape in his mind as he crouched there in the cold.

"That'll do it," said Charney as he stood up with a creaking of joints. "Now to turn the fence back on and get out of here. Deradiation chamber, here we come."

They trudged to the junction box in silence. Donard was feeling a bit queasy from the radiation. When they got to the ship, he had to run to the bushes to hurl.

"You okay?" asked Charney.

"Yeah, yeah. Just give me a minute."

"Don't be long."

Donard could hear Charney fumbling around for the palm reader and then the door sighing open and shut as he leaned over with his hands on his knees creating a vile puddle of partially digested home cooking.

Coree couldn't sleep. She lay on her pallet, looking up at the ceiling. What if the strangers didn't come back the next day? Her leg didn't hurt at all anymore. She wondered if they were angels. Momma had said angels could look like people and that's why you should always treat strangers with love and kindness. She didn't know what a stranger was before today.

She waited until she heard her mother's breathing become steady. Grandfather had already been snoring for half an hour. She got up, checked the bandage on her leg to make sure it wasn't red again, and slipped into her shoes. She grabbed her cloak off its hook by the hearth and holding her breath, tiptoed to the door. It creaked when she pulled it shut. She cringed and waited to be sure her family still slept.

She scanned the hillside, trying to find the track she had taken to the rocky field. She had only been there two times before. The strangers had brought her back from left of that field. If they had walked in a straight line, finding their camp should be easy. She walked for an hour before she rested. She couldn't see her settlement anymore. Her skin began to tingle and she became suddenly terrified of nothing in particular. She felt a deep longing to be home in her tiva with Mother and Grandfather. No one ever came out this far from the shelter of the tivas. She willed the fear away. She learned to do that with the nightmares. She thought everyone could.

All the bushes started to look the same. She climbed a hill to get a better view of her surroundings. She saw movement to her left in the bushes on the brow of the hill. A bright light appeared from behind the bushes. The beam of light came from what looked like a metal tiva. A man stood in the doorway. As she watched, the light vanished as the door slid shut and then the man and the metal tiva were gone. As if it had never been there. Coree wondered if that was the way to heaven.

Once her eyes readjusted, she crept toward the bushes where she had seen something move. A man stood up from behind the bush, wiped his face and looked up at the stars. It looked like Donie. Coree had been holding her breath so long, she gasped for air. She didn't mean to make a noise. He turned toward her.

Coree knew she'd never be able to make it back alone. She stood upright and called, "Donie, is that you?"

"Coree! How did you get here?" He hissed in a low whisper.

"I'm sorry. I followed you. Are you an angel?"

"Coree, you shouldn't be here. It's not safe."

"What do you mean? You fixed my leg," Coree's eyes searched his face.

Donard stepped toward her, holding out his arms.

She ran to him. So trusting. He picked her up and hugged her. He would have to deprive her of her memory... or worse. He bit his lip and held her tight.

"Donard," Charney called from behind him, "we've got to... what? Who's that?"

Donard turned around, still holding Coree close.

"Oh, no! That's the turned torpedo. It's ME time," said Charney.

"No, we can't. I won't."

"We can and you will. No sentimental crap. Just get her in here," said Charney.

Donard felt Coree tense. He rubbed a hand lightly on her back to soothe her. He thought again about sabotaging the project and staying. But it was just an idle, impulsive idea. He wasn't immune to the radiation. He'd die of exposure in a few months if he left the enclosure right then without treatment. How could he get the treatment and get away? Was he really thinking of staying? He couldn't save himself, much less Coree. Then he thought of Cheela, her mother.

Ella's appearance halted the wild thoughts thrashing about in his mind. She held a laser pistol down at her side. "Donard, you need to bring the girl. Now."

"What if it doesn't work? What if she still remembers? Or remembers nothing at all?" he asked.

"We've moved beyond that contingency. To *extraction*. The infrared is picking up two others coming this way. We need to leave."

The ship didn't have the life support for another person. The girl would be brought back to HQ as a 'specimen.' Donard set Coree down and moved her behind him.

"What's she talking about? Donie... Donie..." She tugged at his sleeve.

"Don't worry," he whispered to her. "I won't let anything happen to you."

Charney had closed the gap while Donard's attention was on Ella. "Let me take her," he said, "You know it's for the best. Don't frighten her."

Two anguished voices called out Coree's name from the other direction. The Kradonians were fighting the psionics in their desperation to save her. Coree wiggled out of Donard's grasp and ran toward the voices. A flash of light. Coree screamed.

His blood running cold while his anger raged, Donard looked in the direction of the scream. Coree was still running. He let out his breath. Another flash and she screamed and fell face down in the dirt. Donard wanted to run to her but knew it would be too late. Instead he barreled toward Ella as Charney stood there in shock. She pointed the gun at Donard. Steadied it with her other hand. She would have to kill him. He had already started his charge. No turning back.

She narrowed her eyes, tensed her shoulders. He came at her, arms up. She hesitated. He knocked the laser pistol out of her hands and rammed her in the gut, pushing her into the hull of the ship with a thud before she could react.

"You can't, you bastard," she said.

She struggled against his grip. Donard socked Ella hard in the jaw and spun around to Charney, who leaned sideways of Donard's thrust and grabbed his arm just above the elbow, using his momentum against him to throw him to the ground. In one final push of strength, fueled by desperation and rage, Donard broke free and roundhoused Charney's jaw. Donard heard it shatter as the man 'arghed' in pain. Charney's hands went instinctively to his injured jaw and Donard took his opening, landing a powerful blow to Charney's gut. The man keeled over like a felled tree, his eyes rolling up into his head.

Donard turned to see Ella crumpled against the hull of the ship, her head lolled forward. He ran through the open hatch and grabbed tranq patches. He looked for a few tense seconds at the torapital. The drug they would have used on Coree. Like putting down a sick dog. He almost grabbed that instead. Angels indeed.

He knelt over Ella and applied a tranq patch. He ran to Charney with the other patch as Cheela and Joshen came around the very bush that had concealed Coree. He slapped on the patch before straightening up.

Cheela, seeing her daughter lying with her face in the blood-soaked dirt, screamed and dropped to her knees by her side. Joshen looked around for his sister's attacker.

"I'm so sorry," said Donard "I tried to save her. God help me, I tried."

Joshen looked older than his years as he advanced on him. Donard wanted to let the boy beat him to a pulp. He deserved it. But his survival instinct wouldn't allow it. He blocked his blows easily. Joshen wasn't a trained fighter. Donard got him in a headlock.

"Joshen, I don't want to hurt you. Ella killed your sister. I've subdued her and Charney. Please, let me explain. I'll tell you both everything. I don't care anymore. But if you fight me, you'll never know the truth. Will you calm down and let me explain?"

Joshen nodded.

Donard released him. He took a deep breath and explained the unexplainable, inexcusable truth. Cheela held her daughter's head in her lap and stared at him with hatred, tears coursing down her cheeks.

"...there's no radiation outside the perimeter of your village. The reason you never venture far from it is that we have placed an invisible fence around it that causes anxiety. It makes you scared to leave. Once beyond it, you can go anywhere."

Cheela set her daughter's head down, charged Donard and slapped his face. "You mean to tell me that your people have been using us for centuries?" Her voice ran up the scale as she shrieked at him.

"I'm sorry. I don't know what else I can say."

"You're animals. Vicious, obscene animals. How could you?"

She raised her hands to pound his chest but this time Donard grabbed her arms. She remained fixed there with his hands around her wrists. She gave him a searching look. Donard's stomach began to lurch again, reminding him of his need for treatment.

"The project is working. Your people are getting better. I'll die without treatment. There's a machine on the ship that can reverse the effects of short-term exposure. I don't deserve to live after what I've allowed myself to be party to, but I can't help you if I'm dead.

"They'll come for us in another ship. You'd have to hide, be on the run all the time. But you'd live and thrive."

Cheela didn't speak. Her brow wrinkled and her lips pursed.

"What are you thinking?" he asked as he released her.

"What if your help creates more problems than it solves? We can't defend ourselves against the Allied Human Worlds. And how long can we hide from them with their sensors sweeping the planet?"

Donard felt dizzy and his extremities tingled. He felt the blood rushing out of his face.

"Donard?"

"I need to get treatment. Can we talk about this after?" He stumbled to the ship. Cheela and Joshen followed him.

"What about those two?" Joshen asked.

"I tranqed them. They'll be out for an hour yet. We should probably tie them up before then."

Joshen looked at him with wide eyes and gulped.

"I'll do it. Just let me get my treatment first."

Donard stepped into the chamber and nodded to Cheela to flip the switch he had shown her. The treatment would take twenty minutes. He had time to think. And Cheela and Joshen would have time too. To look around the ship. To learn that what he said was true. Not that they had any reason to doubt it.

Donard watched from the glass chamber as Cheela sunk to the floor and sobbed.

Cheela played out various scenarios in her head. She would not let this stranger decide her fate or the fate of her people, no matter how good intentioned he appeared. *How hard could it be to fly their ship? Donard had said it only had life support for three. Ella and Charney would die if they remained on Kradon. But Ella had killed Coree, so what of it?*

Cheela wanted to take her demands to the enemy. Not wait for them to get there. But her people needed to know the truth. They couldn't hope to win a battle with the AHW, but they could remind them that they weren't specimens in a lab.

She got up, wiped her eyes, put her arm around Joshen, and brought him outside. Her rage and grief was pulling her apart. She stared with glazed eyes at the two unconscious conspirators.

"Now that we know what we're up against, we can fight back. We may not win, but it won't be as easy for them now. I need you to convince our people to leave the settlement. I'll go with Donard and try to convince theirs to leave us alone."

"No! You can't! It's too dangerous! They won't listen to me. You should stay. Let me go."

"Joshen, you're a man now. Be the leader I know you can be. Do this for your sister. I'll destroy the fence and you can bring the people here to bury her. That will make a good start. But first, tie Charney up and get him inside. Donard may need him to fly the ship."

"What about Ella? She killed Coree!"

Cheela walked over to Ella's inert body and extricated the weapon from her stiff fingers. Then, with shaking hands and pounding heart, she blasted Ella right in the chest. Turning to Joshen, she said, "You won't have to worry about her."

She couldn't show weakness and expect strength from him. She walked over to the panel that Donard had indicated when he told her about the fence. She opened it, stood back, and fired the pistol. Flames and sparks belched from it. She saw her son in her peripheral vision, stopping momentarily in his work of tying Charney.

She knelt again at the side of her daughter and held her cold stiff hand. "My sweet Coree. I must be brave like you." *I knew there was something wrong about them. Why couldn't I have been the one to follow them?* Tears dripped onto her daughter's blood-matted hair.

Cheela stood up, straightened her skirt, and took her final steps on her world, toward the instrument of her people's suffering. Joshen looked determined and older as he came out of the ship, having deposited Charney. She put her hand on his cheek and brought him close and hugged him. She had to resist the urge to tell him all the things welling inside. There wasn't time. She kissed him on the cheek, squeezed his arm. She lost Coree. Now she may never see her son again. Loss came through every family on the planet. But to give him up was the hardest thing she'd ever do. Harder even than killing.

"I know I'm asking a lot of you but you must convince the others to split up and go four different directions as far from here as they can."

"Be careful, Mom."

"You too. Now hurry. I love you." She closed the door before he could reply.

Donard banged on the glass and demanded an explanation. The deradiation cycle could not be interrupted. She collapsed into a chair and, with no expression at all, watched him. Hot tears rolled down her cheek. She could feel her jaw muscles tense. She still wasn't sure he'd go for this plan. She hoped those looks he had given her at home meant that he had feelings for her. She wasn't sure she thought much of him. But after Coree's death, she wasn't above using him.

IN THE MIDDLE OF NOWHERE
Laurie Gailunas

WENDY "KIT" KITLING THOUGHT SHE WAS MAYBE GETTING THE HANG OF THIS whole pacifism thing. She no longer dove for cover with every loud bang, no longer reached for a holstered weapon every time she heard a quiet sound behind her. She'd moved on from her life of loss and revenge.

So when the two-way radio crackled to life, she felt no premonition of doom, had no inkling today would not be like every other day on the colony world of New Hope.

Only a few people had shown up for clinic hours. One of the farmers, Sylvester Mott, arrived with a rapid pulse and purpling insect bite on his arm, his wife Helen with him. Alicia Mina and her infant daughter, Cissy, both had coughs and elevated temps. Marianne Simpson had tripped over a well cover and cracked her right ulna.

Kit was loading a cart with casting materials when the call came.

"Kit, it's Max Stimpel." The mayor and security chief. "We got a ship in orbit that worries me. It won't answer our hails, won't acknowledge anything we say. I've ordered everyone into bunkers at the Meeting House. A team is on its way to help evacuate the clinic, get all of you over here."

Kit grabbed some towels for the cart. Casting was messy business. "If there's no comm, maybe there's no ship," she said into the radio. "How do you know that obsolete tracking system of yours isn't sending a wrong signal?"

"This isn't a rogue signal, Kit. Too many details in the data. Start getting your patients ready."

"Isn't this a little dramatic for just a silent, orbiting ship?"

Max hesitated. "The ship's a Shark design."

She sucked in a gasp and dropped the towels onto the cart.

Denise, the nurse, looked up from her charting, eyebrows raised.

Kit cleared her throat, managed to swallow. "But we're as far from Sharks as it's possible to get. That's why I came here."

"I know, Kit, I know," Max said. "I'm hoping, I'm praying, that it's just some human who got their hands on a Shark vessel and is dumb enough to use it."

The door squeaked open and Kit tensed, but it was just four men huffing and puffing from running over.

"I think the evac team is here," Kit said.

"Yeah, good. Get your people over here as fast as you can." The radio clicked and Max was gone.

Kit turned to face everyone, but found she couldn't explain what was happening, couldn't even say the word "Shark." One of the evac guys, Ricardo Mina, hugged Alicia and Cissy, his wife and daughter, and did the explaining. His fear showed in the tight control of his voice and words.

Kit's training as both medic and warrior came into its own as she organized work teams to prepare her patients for transfer to the bunkers. She personally took charge of the two confined to beds.

There was Crazy Jimmy, a regular visitor to the clinic. Yesterday he'd neglected his enzyme metabolizer supplement once again. In the ensuing dizziness, he drove a tractor into his mother's hover scooter as she headed for town. Kit had casted his broken ankle, but was keeping him on an I.V. a few days while she got his enzyme levels stabilized.

His mother, Nan Korlinski, lay in the bed next to him with a head injury from the accident, sedated and quiet.

The little six-bed ward crackled with fear as they worked, and Crazy Jimmy muttered about the end of the world. He had a sixth sense about things, so when his voice cracked and stopped, everyone went quiet for a moment, watched, waited.

Jimmy rolled and shook the side rail, trying to get out of the bed. "I have to pee."

"No, no, Jimmy, stay there!" Kit dashed across to his bedside. "Come on, man, stay in the bed. Denise is bringing a float pallet over for you to ride to the Meeting House."

"I have to pee before the monsters come."

"That's fine," Kit said. "Let's get you onto the pallet and I'll get you something to pee in."

Kit leaned over the pallet—a long stretch for her, the most petite woman in the colony—and helped him scoot over. She settled him with a urinal under the sheet, but didn't draw the curtain around him. It was best to always keep Jimmy in plain view.

As Denise and Kit un-tucked sheets around his mother and prepared to lift her onto a float, Denise said, "Are you going to be all right, Kit?"

Kit snapped her head up. "There might be Sharks orbiting our planet, and you're asking me if *I'll* be all right? Denise, none of us will be, if it really is Sharks."

"Yeah, but, you're the only one who knows what that really means." Denise unhooked Nan's I.V. pump and reached over to hang it on the pallet. "The rest of us, we grew up here. Everyone I know, except you, is Quaker or Mennonite or something. Nobody has ever been to war. We've never seen what Sharks can do. I've never even seen a real one, just pictures."

"Well, they're gray, and kind of short, like me," Kit said. "And they're not really a fish, they're marsupials. Oh, and the slits in their necks? We call them gills, because that's what they look like, but they're actually nostrils for air. That's where you want to punch, or stab, if you're cornered. Either there, or the nose. Or both if you live long enough. And do your best to stay away from those jagged teeth of theirs. Really, really nasty stuff."

Denise stared at her for a moment, trying to take in what Kit just said. "Somehow I don't think seeing people bloody from an accident is the same as seeing them bloody from violence."

Kit's memory flashed...*hiding from Sharks behind a fence...her sister's head exploding, splashing against their mother before she too collapsed... Kit's vow of revenge...*

She forced in a deep breath, pushed the memory away. "No, it's not the same."

"What I was getting at," Denise said, "was that I think this is harder for you than the rest of us. So hang in there, OK?"

"Yeah, I'm hanging. Now let's get Nan moved."

Kit had the evac team pile a third pallet with towels, bandages, suture kits, I.V. pouches, and other supplies for the bunker. She loaded her pockets with the nano-injector and med vials she'd need for these patients in the next couple hours, plus a few extra vials of sedatives. No matter who the mystery vessel belonged to, some people were going to panic.

Denise joined her and started stuffing her own pockets with meds. "Kit, what do we do if it really is Sharks, and they come down here?"

Kit looked up at her. "Then we do the only thing you can do with Sharks. Fight or die. Or fight and maybe die anyway."

Denise's face went still. "You're in the Caritas Unity now, Kit. You know we don't fight."

Kit turned away. "Then I guess we'll just die."

As Denise and Ricardo lined up the pallets in a convoy, Kit decided to throw a cast on Marianne Simpson's arm. It would just take a moment, she had the materials all set up, and it would make the woman more comfortable.

"All right, Marianne," she said, "let's get that arm in a cast so you can get over to the Meeting House with everyone else."

"Is it going to hurt?" the young woman asked.

"Not much. I don't need to set yours, just cast it." Kit held up a foil packet, about the size of her outspread hand. "See? Immobilization foam. Put your arm in this little trough here, like this. Once I open the pack and pour it over your arm, the foam expands and hardens instantly."

Kit started to open the pack when a scream erupted from the front of the building, a scream that stopped mid-breath. The radio chimed for attention just as the doors bashed open.

Kit was on the other side of the room. She ducked behind a bedside curtain that offered no protection except a short-lived invisibility, and peered through a gap.

Two gray creatures, males wearing only blue shoulder pouches, leaped into the room. How the hell had they snuck to the surface like this? That damned tracking system.

Both Sharks started shooting heat darts, thin projectiles with a tiny explosive compound that also released a high-voltage current on impact. The current followed the major blood vessels, the path of least resistance, searing and destroying as it went. It usually grounded through the feet, unless the person was touching some other grounded object. Then it was the hands that fried. Lucky victims died instantly, their hearts overloaded by the electric charge.

Denise gurgled and crumpled, one of the lucky ones.

The colonists froze and stared. In the brief moment before their brains processed the scene, blood spewed from the mouth of Nan Korlinski.

Crazy Jimmy pulled his full urinal out from under the sheet. Kit had forgotten all about it. He hurled it at one of the Sharks, and the little bomb hit it square in the face, surprising it, disrupting its aim for a moment. Maybe Jimmy wasn't so crazy after all.

The clang of impact and urine dripping off the Shark's shoulders galvanized the stunned colonists. The room erupted in a pandemonium of screaming and running; a few made it out the door, some crawled under beds, Sylvester dove at a Shark's knees and got his brain fried for it.

Three years of Kit's pacifist training shattered and her warrior conditioning flamed into action.

She bit a tiny hole at the top of the packet still in her hand, and threw it like a grenade. The hole blew wide open when it smacked against the creature; white casting foam spilled across his shoulder and arm. The Shark blinked in surprise as his arm holding the heat gun froze in its fully extended position. Enough splashed against the gun to block its firing mechanism.

The second Shark turned and broiled Jimmy.

Kit grabbed another packet of foam, ripped it at the seam and hurled it at him, this time aiming for the face. The hole was too big, though, and foam spurted out as the pack sailed across the room, hardening the moment air touched it. Irregular white blobs tinkled to the floor like marbles falling on tile.

Enough hit the Shark's face to make it mad, but by then Kit had another pack ready, with just a tiny slit. She threw it just as the Shark turned his heat gun toward her, the foam busting open full in his face.

Bingo. Blinded Shark. Another throw blinded the other Shark.

The two creatures careened around the room, each trying to scrape the foam off his face. The one with the working gun fired blindly at the same time; maybe he'd accidentally shoot his comrade.

The baby screamed, a sudden, high-pitched wail of pain. From her mother and father came a lower-pitched shout of disbelief.

Kit grabbed a few more foam packs and dashed toward the blinded Sharks, dodging a couple of dazed colonists crawling on the floor.

With a front snap kick, Kit knocked the one functioning heat gun from the second Shark's partially webbed hand. He whirled, trying to find the attacker, but before he could find her, Kit slapped her foam packs against his shoulders, which were the same height as hers. His arms froze into place. She ducked quickly when he turned to bash her head in.

Like a gunslinger reaching for holsters, she pulled two more foam packs out of her pockets, nicked the seal, and crushed them against his hips.

This time she didn't pull her hands away fast enough; a blob of foam sealed her left pinkie and neighboring finger together.

A few more packs on the lead Shark kept him out of the way for a few minutes.

The two Sharks hobbled around, their sputtering invectives muffled by the sloppy casts over their heads and joints. Kit scooped up the heat gun she'd kicked away. It was empty, but she tucked it into her waistband.

Whimpers of fear sounded from around the clinic; Helen Mott crawled out from behind a waste barrel and scuttled out the door. The room smelled of the acrid effluvia of death excretions and the unmistakable stink of charred flesh.

Kit used her right hand to try and break the cast off her fingers, but the hardened stuff was stronger than plaster or fiberglass. A Shark's dense musculature would crack through it before too long, though. She'd only slowed the creatures down, not disabled them.

A new series of screams sounded from outside.

Kit wouldn't be free to help the people in here or out there as long as these Sharks were alive. She remembered from her medic days caring for POW's, that Shark metabolism had a different electrolyte balance than humans; they required more sodium and less potassium, so fatal hyperkalemia was easy to induce.

In the med room, she wrenched open a cabinet door and pulled out the potassium chloride. Three bottles. She loaded a twenty cc syringe and attached a long, old-fashioned needle, which was more direct than a nano-injector.

It was going to be tricky jabbing a big needle between the ribs of a moving target. Kit sidled up to each Shark, matched their motion and stabbed. She got one on the first try, and shot the deadly potassium straight in, as close to the heart at she could get. The other Shark needed two tries.

The effect was highly gratifying; in less than a minute their hearts stopped. Each crashed down in a satisfying, final thud.

"Are you hurting them?"

Kit spun around. Marianne sat on the floor under a bed, holding her broken arm against her chest, her other hand clutching the lifeless hand of her husband.

Kit couldn't tell if the woman was concerned for the Sharks, or if her pacifist upbringing had shattered and she wanted the Sharks hurt.

"No," said Kit, "I'm not hurting them." It was true. Sudden cardiac arrest did not hurt, it was the resuscitation that was a bitch. And there would be no resuscitation for these two. "I'm just sedating them so they can't cause trouble." (Oh, they died? Oops.)

Kit searched the dead Sharks for charge pods for the gun. In her assault with the casting foam, though, she'd covered their ammunition pouches. She tried reaching underneath the casts, but the foam had adhered directly to the Shark's skin. She could cut the damn things out, but that would take a while and she didn't have time right now.

She did a rapid triage of her patients.

Marianne had no further injuries.

Crazy Jimmy was, amazingly, still alive and gasping shallow, moaning, breaths. His right hand had exit burns, from where the heat dart's current flowed out of his body. He'd been on a float pallet, hovering with nothing to ground him. He must have been touching a piece of furniture or something and thus let the current run its course. Poor Jimmy.

Kit knew he would not survive long enough to get to a burn center off-world, and even there would probably not survive. With a lump in her throat, she pulled out her nano-injector of sedative, set it for a high dose, and pulled the trigger. He'd at least be comfortable while he died.

Wiping her tears, she moved on to the next huddle of people, on the floor behind a supply cart. Ricardo Mina, his wife, and baby. When Kit called Ricardo's name, he rolled over and looked at her with haunted eyes.

"Cissy's dead," he said.

"Let me see."

His wife lay, unmoving, next to him. When Kit reached to take the silent baby from her arms, Alicia's eyes flew open and she locked her arms tight, holding the baby close. "You can't have her!" the woman screamed. "She's mine, and you can't have her."

Ricardo spoke quietly, tried to calm her, get her to let Kit examine the baby, but Alicia just screamed louder and held on tighter.

But Kit didn't need to examine the baby, it was obvious she was dead. She tapped Ricardo's shoulder, shook her head. "Are you injured?" she asked.

"No. Alicia and I weren't hit."

"All right." Kit stood and took a final tally. Little Cissy, Nan, Marianne's husband, Denise and Sylvester, dead. Four surviving humans. Five including Jimmy, but he wouldn't stay on that list very long. The others had made it out the door, condition unknown at this time.

Kit picked up the radio and tried calling the Meeting House. No answer. She tried other frequencies, but still got no response.

Was everyone dead? Underground in the bunker?

Up until this moment, she'd been in action, her mind busy with staying alive and trying to keep others alive. Now she surveyed the clinic, and the debris of everything she'd worked to create these past three years.

Not again. Please, dear God whom the colonists all pray to, please don't take everyone away from me again.

When Kit was sixteen, Sharks had slaughtered her family and most of her frontier world. When she was seventeen, she'd joined the Casimir Space Command so she could learn how to hunt, fight, and kill Sharks. She was very good at it, patrolling the frontier worlds with her unit. Until it was wiped out. Until her quest for revenge overwhelmed her while interrogating prisoners.

That was about the time the more populated human worlds, safe and cozy far from the frontier, voted the Caritas Unity into ascendance. Anti-war, anti-violence, anti-Kit and the death of prisoners.

But by then Kit knew that violent revenge didn't bring anyone back, didn't make anything right, didn't heal the wounds of her soul. She explained this at her court-martial. She'd had enough. She didn't want to fight any more.

The powers-that-be chose someone else to parade through the media as the face of evil violence. For Kit, an unpublicized sentence of five years' probation—no killing—on New Hope.

The most pacifist colony of them all. A community based on love, acceptance, non-violence. The kind of home she'd once had.

For three years, it worked.

Well, it was ruined now. People she loved were dead and she'd violated her probation. Prison was probably next.

So, she might as well make a clean sweep and kill every Shark she could find and safeguard any people who were left. Go out in style.

Kit pulled out a cast cutter and freed her stuck fingers. Thankfully, the foam didn't stick to human skin the way it did Shark's. She stuffed her pockets with foam packs and, looking around, noted the scalpels. She grabbed all six, still in their padded, sterile packs, and squeezed them in with the foam. She still had the nano-injector, syringe, and meds.

She told the survivors to stay hidden, and went to see if anyone else was still alive.

It was late summer on New Hope, the air heavy with heat and yellow dust and the tang of eucalyptus shrubs. The dirt street in front of her was quiet. Too quiet. Where were the rest of the Sharks?

She ducked across the street, but no one shouted, nothing shot at her. Trying to stay invisible, she made her way toward the Meeting House.

Reaching a corner, she peered around it from behind a sheltering house. A Shark sauntered toward her half a block away, feathery blue fronds below the gill-like nostrils. A female.

A long rope of pearls draped around her neck, with a typical Shark bandolier underneath. Wads of jewelry and silk scarves sagged from the loops that should have held spare charges. Obviously the Shark had helped herself to Alline's Ladies Apparel.

So, these were just a bunch of raiders on a smash and grab. Shark military only used males. Females did, however, learn basic fighting skills, thinking it would imbue sons with ferocity while still in the pouch. And those skills could be formidable. Kit saw no visible weapons on the female, but there would be some, somewhere.

Kit burrowed into a hedge, ignoring the sticks poking her back, hoping the eucalyptus smell covered her sweaty scent. She fingered the half-filled potassium syringe in her pocket.

The Shark crossed right in front of her, oblivious, simply out for a stroll to do a little looting, enjoy the sunshine, kill some humans.

When it was three steps past, Kit pulled the syringe from her pocket and sprang from the hedge, stabbing the needle into the Shark's neck.

When the creature screamed and twisted to see its tormenter, Kit felt the needle snap off. The Shark reached for her, but its hand tangled in the pearls, slowing it enough for Kit to pull out her bandage scissors and stab them deep into one of the gill-like nostrils.

Kit yanked her hand out and ran like hell, ducking through a wooden gate and behind the hedge. She peered between the branches, breathing hard, as she wiped blood and mucus off her hand and scissors.

The Shark was already down, still and silent.

Kit waited a few minutes, but the creature did not move and no one came to investigate. She edged up to it, cautious, alert for trouble.

The Shark lay with bloody bubbles of its final breaths clustered, unmoving, around the stabbed gill.

The flashback flicked in an instant: *another time, another Shark, bloody bubbles oozing from the prisoner's gills as it struggled for air, its final breath spent on calling to its god.*

No, no, no. Not here, not now. Kit took a deep breath, trying to steady herself.

She reached down and pulled the strand of pearls off the creature, plus the bandolier of stolen trinkets. If other Sharks came looking, she didn't want them to help themselves to the loot. She tucked them under the hedge; later she'd tell Alline where to find them. If there was a later.

Kit searched the body for weapons, finding a short eating knife in a red scabbard and (yes!) a Kappel Snake dart.

Slim, pointed, about 10mm long, it was a handy little dart in its own right. But once it impacted flesh, a hundred fractal threads emerged, each wriggling like a little snake to rip apart everything in its path. They also acted as flagella to pull the dart in deeper until it ran out of power. It could turn a limb to mush in a few minutes.

Kappel sheathes came with a fingerprint lock to prevent anyone but the owner from opening it, and to keep it from activating by accident. The lock on this one, probably stolen in some raid, was cracked.

Kit opened one of her scalpel packs and placed the sheathed dart in the padding. With great care, she slid it into a thin pocket designed for scissors.

She scanned the street. Nobody. No Sharks, no humans, a landscape devoid of all life.

She eased around the corner and faced the town square. The Meeting House sat on the far side, the largest structure in town built of local, pale yellow stone. She skirted the periphery of the square, and just as she climbed the three steps to the Meeting House, the door opened.

"Get in, quick." A human arm pulled her in and slammed the door behind her.

It took a moment for Kit's eyes to adjust to the indoors.

Tom Miller, who ran the machine shop, glared down at her. "You could have been killed. There's Sharks."

"I noticed."

"What were you doing out there?"

Kit slid past him. "Trying to get here."

The Meeting House consisted of an assembly room, big enough for two hundred people to sit comfortably, and a labyrinth of smaller meeting rooms. Today the large room smelled of sweat and coffee. A dozen men were there with net guns, watching through the windows and manning radios.

At least somebody else was still alive. Kit could have cried, but didn't have time. She moved over to stand beside Max Stimpel, the mayor. A large, burly man with black hair and beard, some people called him Bear. But never to his face.

"Who else is here?" she asked.

"We got about a hundred folks down into the bunker," Max answered. "And you're right, that tracking system isn't worth the price of scrap metal." He told her the ship had originally landed on the other side of town, then moved near the ethanol plant. Patching together radio reports, it looked like three Sharks had gotten off first, then another two at the plant.

So Kit still had two to hunt down.

"I met those first three," she said. "Two in the clinic. One on the way here, a female. That's good, means they aren't regular military."

"You met them?" Max narrowed his eyes. "If you're still alive, where are the Sharks?"

"I, um, left them immobilized and...sedated." Kit wasn't ready to explain the fatality of that sedation, not until everyone was safe. She hurried on before they could ask about it, and told of the attack on the clinic. A quiet moan rippled through the room when she reported the list of casualties. "I tried to radio you, but didn't get through," she said.

Max rubbed the back of his neck. "Yeah, it's been a little crazy here, with all the outlying farms trying to call and jamming things up. We did try to warn you when we saw they'd slipped through, but no one answered at the clinic. We thought..." His voice caught. "Well, let me just say I was real happy to see you walk through that door. Glad at least some survived."

He cleared his throat. "We got a call from one of your evac guys after he ran out. He holed up at the post office, got through to us on the radio. He didn't think anyone at the clinic would still be alive."

"Yeah, well..." Kit looked at her toes. "So what do you plan to do next?" She had her own ideas, but wanted to know what Max had to say.

"Wait 'em out," Max said. "Come look out this window."

She crossed to the back of the room with him. Tom Miller followed, along with Tom's teenage son, Samuel.

Max had the sense not to outline himself in the window, but kept behind the shadow of a curtain. "Look out here. The Sharks are over at the ethanol plant, looks like they just want to re-fuel. We can afford to gift 'em some, so let's leave them be and maybe they'll leave us in peace."

The plant lay three blocks from there, but even at that distance Kit saw two Sharks roll a fifty-gallon drum out of the plant's loading doors.

"But, Max," she said, "Sharks don't fuel their ships with ethanol."

He looked out the window, puzzled. "Then what are they doing?"

"Looks to me like they're after booze," Kit said.

Samuel's face lit with interest. "You can get drunk on ethanol?"

Max scowled. "Hush, Samuel. Well then, Kit, we'll just hunker down till they drink their fill and leave."

Kit turned to face him. "No, Max. If we let them leave with the ethanol, they'll set this up as a regular stop any time they're thirsty. These are just pirates, out to find whatever catches their fancy. But eventually their military will notice. And from here they'll expand to other human worlds—"

"Yeah, yeah, we get the point." Max crossed his arms over his barrel chest. "So what are we going to do that won't get us killed?"

"You can help me immobilize the Sharks," she said, "take them prisoner. Can we get a Caritas security team to come pick them up?"

Max nodded. "Yeah, we already called and they're on their way. Soonest they can get here is tomorrow afternoon. So what do you have in mind before then?"

"First we have to disable their ship so none of them can sneak off." Kit pulled a packet of cast foam from her pocket. "I could use these to block the air intakes of their ship, then they can't lift off. But I only have six packs left. We'll need something else to slow the Sharks down."

"We're pretty good with these net guns," Max said.

"Are you willing to go out there and sneak up on them to get in range?" Kit asked.

Samuel's hand shot up. "I am!"

Max and Tom Miller both glared at him and said, "Hush, Samuel."

Tom lifted the foam packet from her hand and inspected it. "We could get the fabber at the machine shop going on this, make more. As a backup for the net guns."

The fabricator! She hadn't even thought of it. "Isn't it just programmed for metals?"

"It has wider parameters than that." Tom and his son Samuel murmured between themselves, wondering what to enclose the liquid foam with (an impermeable membrane they used to line water conduits) and how to make an airtight seal(fishing line).

Tom looked up. "Yeah, we can have another dozen or so in half an hour, I think. You coming with us?"

Kit tapped her foot, thinking. "As far as the shop, yes. I can go that way to the plant. Then I'll leave you to it while I disable their ship."

"Sounds good." Then Tom looked her right in the eye. "Miss Kitling, I will unlock the shop, I will program the fabber for this stuff, my son Samuel and I will make it," (Samuel nodded so hard his neck must have hurt) "but only on one condition."

"Which is?"

"I'm not going to slow these Sharks down just to make it easier for you to kill them."

"Of course I won't murder them," she said.

Max stepped between her and Tom. "And our definition of murder is any killing. So no executions, no accidents, no deaths. You were sent here to learn how to live without violence, and I can tell by the fire in your eyes and the set of your jaw that you're not thinking peaceful thoughts right now. So unload that gun and other weapons and leave them here."

"Why, so you can use them?" she snapped.

"No, so you can't."

Kit wanted to step back, get some space, but was caught between the two men. "Max, I still don't think you get what's happening here. I've seen you fight forest fires and you went after that rampaging bull, for which I had to stitch you back together. You're a brave man, but until today you've never seen a Shark and never had to survive one."

Max paled. "Kit, come over here where we can talk in private."

They retreated to a back corner, where Max said quietly, "No one knows this, but I read the transcript of your trial."

Kit sucked in a breath.

"Now, I may be pacifist, but I also try to be a realist," he said. "I know what happened to your family, and I know what happened to your platoon. And maybe getting those prisoners to talk saved lives. Now some of the people here, like the Buddhists, think *any* killing is evil. My mind is divided on that. But I have no doubt that killing a foe you've already vanquished is evil, and I will not be party to it.

"So, again, we'll help disable the Sharks and their ship, but not just to make it easier for you to kill 'em. You have to promise me that you will honor our help. If you don't promise, we'll have to keep you here and take our chances."

Kit glanced at the door, considered running out with the weapons. But too many men stood between here and there, watching. They would no doubt grab her if she tried to bolt, or even use the net gun.

She was out-maneuvered. Sharks in full battle array were easier to deal with than righteous pacifists. Well, one step at a time. Disable the ship, get more foam, and figure the rest out later.

"All right, no killing." With a scowl, she pulled out the Shark eating knife, the scalpels, even her bandage scissors, and set them on a bench.

Max insisted she also leave that lovely heat gun, despite her protests that it was empty. "If it's empty, you won't need it. Set it here with these other things."

He handed her a net gun, which she checked to ensure was loaded. He also gave her a two-way radio and told her to stay in comm.

Kit followed Tom Miller and his work team out the door.

She hadn't mentioned the Kappel Snake dart, tucked in its little pocket and covered by her tunic.

And so, with a little secret lethality, Kit set off to do some hunting.

Late afternoon made for long, dark shadows, easier for getting through town without any Sharks seeing them. They made it to the machine shop without incident, and Kit left Tom, Samuel, and two other men to work the fabricator.

She was halfway to the ethanol plant, only one more street to go, when she found more human bodies.

Three lay on the road in the shade of a huge tree, two men and a woman. As Kit already knew from their stillness, all were dead. Kit rolled the woman over, and bit back a low moan.

It was Agnes Danielson, the first person on New Hope to treat Kit with any degree of warmth, to be a friend, to laugh and chat and bring cookies. This kind and generous person, a pacifist in the best sense of the word...

Kit's promise of no killing wavered.

A fly (similar enough in form and function to an Earth fly to get the name) landed on Agnes's cheek. Kit swore and brushed it away.

A pile of small sacks lay scattered on the ground next to the bodies. Kit poured their contents onto the dirt and used the sacks to cover the faces. "I'll come back for you," she said. "But first I have some business to take care of."

Kit stood, her lips and eyes tight in determination.

There was a scraping sound behind her. Kit whirled, stepped deeper into the shadows, crouched. She pulled out the wrapped Kappel dart.

"Kit?" a girl's voice said. "Is that you?"

Kit stayed in the shadows. "Yes. Who are you, and where are you?"

"It's me, Lacy Danielson." One of the high school girls, a cute, redheaded tomboy. "Oh, thank God, someone is here. I'm coming down." Her voice quivered with fear.

A large tree rustled as Lacy descended. Similar to an elm, its drooping branches extended all the way to the ground, making a good place for a terrified girl to climb and hide. How much had she seen?

Lacy landed with a thump and ran, throwing her arms around Kit in a tight, trembling hug, spewing out her story of terror and Sharks and guns and screams and blood and trees and why didn't anyone come for her?

Kit wasn't a huggy person herself, but didn't interrupt or push the girl away. She did watch the street, and she did wonder what she was going to do with a hysterical teenager in her wake.

Finally, Lacy took a deep breath and loosened her hold, her face chalk white, eyes red and swollen. "Are we the only ones left alive?"

"No, no," Kit said. "There's a bunch at the Meeting House, safely underground in the bunker."

Lacy started to cry again, a quieter cry of grief rather than fear. "They came when we were leaving. I was staying here with Aunt Agnes, and we were leaving. We were going to the Meeting House, like Mr. Stimpel said to." She hiccupped. "And I was slow, and Aunt Agnes and Uncle Peter already came out the gate but I was still in the yard, and the Sharks came, and they didn't see me..." Her face crumpled.

Kit grasped the girl's elbows. "Lacy, listen to me." When Lacy didn't look up, didn't slow her crying, Kit grasped Lacy's face in her hands. "*Listen* to me. You've endured a terrible thing, but the important part for right now is to keep us both alive. I need you to go to the Meeting House—"

"No." Lacy abruptly stopped crying. "Not unless you're coming with me. I want to stay with you."

"But I'm going the other way, and—"

"I'm coming with you."

They verbally sparred for a minute, until Kit decided it would be faster and easier just to take the girl with her. And maybe it would be safer. Who could tell on a day like this?

Kit called Max on the radio, told him Lacy was alive and with her, but Agnes and her family were dead. He sounded both sad and relieved, and said he'd tell Lacy's parents. He also told her there was no further sign of Sharks in that part of town, and Tom now had a dozen foam packs ready. A team was on its way to the shop to pick them up and join her at the plant.

Kit and Lacy made their way to a maintenance shed outside the ethanol plant. The Shark's ship lay halfway between the plant and the shed, the front of it about twenty meters from them.

It was an old military launch, a model decommissioned years ago. The engines used air when in atmosphere, so three intake slits lay on each side of its prow, each about 15 mm wide, 40 mm tall.

The two Sharks—per Max's count, these should be the last two—weren't visible. The plant's loading doors stood open and Kit could hear them talking inside, their voices thick with inebriation. She wondered if their metabolism could handle the 200-proof ethanol the plant made, or if they'd already diluted the stuff.

Kit handed Lacy a foam packet. "OK, you wait here. Don't let a Shark see you, but if he does, throw this at his face. It will blind him long enough for you to get away. And if anything happens to me, you run back to the Meeting House."

Before Lacy could answer, Kit ran to the shuttle in a shambling crouch. She nicked a foam pouch and, keeping it pinched closed, reached deep into the intake port. She let go and pulled her hand out fast. Some of the foam smeared on her hand, but not enough to impede movement. She plugged a second slit. A third. She ran to the other side and stuffed in her last two packs.

She turned to run back to the shed, and there was Lacy, running toward her.

"I told you to stay hidden," Kit hissed.

"I heard something by the shed," Lacy whispered. "I thought it was Sharks coming for me and I want to stay with you."

Voices. Shark voices from the plant. Coming closer.

Lacy squeaked and turned to run for the shed, but Kit grabbed her and shook her head. Even drunk Sharks would notice humans running across twenty meters of wide open space. Their only cover was the ship itself.

Kit turned back to the intake slits. She wedged in her foot—a stretch; the lower edge was about a meter off the ground—and hoisted herself up.

Lacy joined her with far more grace. They crouched together, hanging on their precarious footholds, out of sight of anyone behind or inside the shuttle.

Mushy voices. The thud and boom of a full barrel landing in the hold. Then silence. Kit placed her ear against the hull, trying to detect any further sound, any vibration.

All was still.

Maybe the Sharks had passed out. Maybe they'd died of alcohol poisoning. Now there was a pleasant thought, and it wouldn't even be her fault. But they'd probably just returned to the plant for another load.

She whispered into Lacy's ear. "When I count to three, jump down and run like hell around the shed." Before Lacy could respond, Kit said, very fast, "One two three, go!"

Lacy blinked, hesitated, and Kit gave her a little push. Not a wise move on Kit's part. Off balance, Lacy fell to the ground and yelped.

A Shark shouted.

"Run, Lacy!" Kit jumped to the ground and turned to face the enemy, about eight meters away. Too far for the net gun at her waist.

The Shark stood outside the loading doors, wearing a leather breastplate. This one did not look so drunk or incompetent. It made an "Aha!" kind of sound and started walking toward them.

Lacy tried to stand, but fell back with a grunt of pain, grumbling about her ankle. Kit stepped in front to shield her.

The Shark ignored the heat gun in its holster and reached for his bandolier, casual and languid, ready for a bit of sport. He pulled out a black fight disc, a wicked little weapon similar to ninja stars, and hurled it at Kit as he approached.

Kit dodged and it whizzed past. She listened, made a note of where it landed so she could go back and retrieve it later.

Six meters. Kit pulled out the netter from her waist and the Shark dove and rolled to the side.

She flicked the ejector switch to full range and pressed it, following the Shark's roll, but nothing happened. She pressed again. Still nothing.

Damn, damn, damn! She should know not to trust a weapon she hadn't loaded herself. She threw it to one side.

There was an unusual chirpy sound; a Shark laughing. He pulled out another fight disc.

Too bad about her promise to the mayor. Kit was taking this bastard down.

She pulled the Kappel Snake dart from its sheath and ran toward the Shark. He threw the fight disc, but she'd seen him raise his arm and was already dodging.

At three meters, she stopped and threw the dart. When the Shark recognized what was coming, he let out a grunt of fear and tried to leap out of the way.

The dart sliced into the Shark's thigh.

Shit. Too low. She'd been aiming for the gills.

The Shark grabbed the protruding end and winced. The threads had barely gone into action, but it was enough to carve away a section of muscle as he pulled the dart out.

Kit groped her pockets again, while flicking through ideas of how to get themselves out of this alive. She hit a KCL bottle, but it was useless without a needle for the syringe, broken in her fight with the female. She pulled out the nano-injector of sedative, glanced at it to see that it remained half full. Plenty of juice to knock this guy out.

The Shark stood, pale blood running down his leg, and flipped the fight disc from hand to hand, teasing her. He said something; Kit only understood "death" and "demon maggot," the usual Shark term for humans.

And then, barely taking his eyes off Kit, the Shark took a step to the side and whipped the disc at Lacy.

Lacy screamed and Kit leaped, nano-injector in hand. She had no time for proper positioning or finesse, just used her body as a projectile and slammed into the Shark, knocking him into the dust. His gills flared open, and Kit squirted in the full load of sedative as she rolled. It was fine with her if the bastard OD'd.

The Shark yanked out his gun but, reflexively, his hand jerked as he started to cough the irritating nano-needles out of his gills. A heat dart hit one of the ship's landing struts instead of Kit.

She kicked the gun from his hand and bashed the injector against his super-sensitive nose, then dove for the gun and scooped it up.

The Shark sat up coughing, waiting for death.

Kit's hand shook with restraint, with the effort not to shoot. "Come on, asshole, maybe I can still keep my oath. Now pass out before you tempt me too hard."

He snarled, showing a horrifying display of spiky teeth that could snap off a human arm in one bite.

"That's tempting me," Kit said.

There was a sudden shout from Lacy, a flash of motion, an explosion of white, a startled grunt.

Kit turned slightly, still keeping an eye on the Shark, but enough to see another Shark on the other side of the shuttle. That one stared, confused by the plaster carapace that suddenly hardened on his chest and arms.

"I saw it sneaking up on you," Lacy called. "So I threw that thing you gave me. But I missed the face."

Kit smiled. "Oh, Lacy, you're still a wonderful girl."

She'd only taken her eye off the other Shark for an instant, but it was enough for him to make his move.

He was half up, knife in hand.

Kit steadied the gun in her hand and...

Splat!

A blob of white foam hit the Shark's back. Another plopped on the ground behind him.

"Damn," a quiet voice said. "I missed."

A horde of teenage boys, lead by Samuel, had circled around the plant, coming in from behind. They shouted and ran forward, flinging homemade foam packets with exuberance, hitting the Sharks and plenty of other things. One pack brushed against Kit's hair and flicked hard pellets down her shirt.

Shouting and pounding and pushing, the boys tackled the two Sharks in a pandemonium of glee and muscle and testosterone.

A dozen adults, men and women both, rounded the shed with more casting packs, chains, netters, ropes and, for some strange reason, a plasma cutter.

For pacifists, they sure could be ferocious.

A Caritas ship arrived the next day to cart off the dead Sharks and two captives. And Kit. At least they didn't tie her up.

The crew kept their distance from her during the three-day journey to Koinonos, as if violence was a communicable disease. That was fine. It meant peace and quiet for Kit as she tried to sort out what had gone wrong on New Hope.

By the third day, she figured it out.

Nothing had gone wrong.

True, if the colonists hadn't insisted, she would have kept killing, wouldn't have tried less lethal force. But at the end, she did stay her hand. She was learning.

And if she hadn't been there, most of those colonists would be dead, and Sharks let loose on humanity again.

How could that be right? What she'd done, fight to protect her people, that's what felt right. That was alive, that was real, that was her.

Undue violence carried no honor.

But pure pacifism would get them all slaughtered.

She had only to find the balance.

At the Earth Liaison Office on Koinonos, a panel of jurists questioned her for days. They didn't arrest her, or restrain her movements at all, other than telling her when to come talk to them again.

After a week, they didn't know what to do with her. They could not get around the fact that, though she'd violated the terms of her probation, she had in fact saved hundreds of lives. From their increasingly convoluted questions, Kit got the idea they wished the whole problem would just go away.

She intended to oblige them.

On a bright and hot afternoon, she peered over a low fence—designed more to keep dogs out than humans—at the open landing fields of the transfer station. The air shimmered with the stink of fuel and sweat and commerce and action. She loved that smell.

Only one ship sat there, sleek in design but battered in usage. She didn't recognize its insignia and, intrigued, she entered the terminal. A man stood at the refreshment bar, pulling something hot out of the dispenser. He wore a blue jumpsuit with the same insignia as the ship.

They eyed each other, they said hello, they talked. He said he was Lt. Anthony Badell, from the Tarrasa Settlements.

"Never heard of it," Kit said.

"It's out past the Chinchou sector."

She scowled. "There aren't any settlements out there."

"There are now. Have been for two years."

"Oh." Kit looked down, embarrassed by her ignorance. "Oh," she said again, when she noticed something about his jumpsuit. "That's a weapon sheath!"

He glanced down. "Yeah. Don't worry, it's empty. Can't carry a weapon groundside in the Unity. I've got the OK to refuel myself and the ship, then I'll—"

"How is it you've got a weapon at all?" she blurted out.

"Like I said, I'm from Tarrasa. It's independent, not in the Caritas Unity."

Kit only had to think about that for a second before the implications began to unfold. "So you fight if need be? You're not pacifists?"

"We can't be, not out there. In such an outlying sector, right on the edge of human territory—"

"I'll join," Kit said.

Badell stopped, looked baffled. "What?"

"I'll join. Your military, or police, or whatever you're the lieutenant of. Are you accepting recruits?" she asked.

"Well, yes, but you should know it's pretty remote—"

"Yeah, good. I'm in." Kit grinned. "When can we get out of here?"

FALLING TO ETERNITY
S. A. Bolich

ONE OF US IS A TRAITOR.

That last, gut-stabbing message, flashed to my headset before the system went down and left me talking to dead air, seems to float in front of my eyes in letters of fire. I don't even know who it came from; just that quick, before the identifier could even display, somebody killed the whole network. So the sender is a suspect too, one of seven, and I'm stuck here in my duty pod waiting either for the Worlies to show or one of my own squad to blow us all to hell.

This day just keeps getting better.

I take my hand off the unresponsive panels. Someone has done a thorough job of cutting pod functions. They can't jam the guns; those operate independently from the central systems. But communications, scanners, the pod retract—all dead. We're stuck out here like carnival-goers on a malfunctioning Ferris wheel.

I'm tired. Even at zero gee my body feels like five hundred pounds of sand. My brain is mush. We've been here so long that watches just blur together, but even so this is overtime. I was just coming off operations watch when the alarm sent us scrambling to the pods. I lean my helmeted head against the clear observation port in front of me, wishing I was back on Earth, wishing I could rewind this day—hell, this war—wishing I could stop thinking about turning my guns on the outpost and ending the whole problem. I still have five friends in there.

I had six this morning.

One of us is a traitor. I don't want to believe it, but too much has gone wrong. Nguyen discovered the pinpoint hull breach and disabled alarm that would have bled our atmosphere quietly until three days from now we'd wake up dead. But Vronski was the one who found the main transmitter array hanging by an eyelash and fixed it, no fuss, no alarm, just another repair on a sentry outpost in dire need of overhaul. I myself fixed the galley hatch, with a wrench and a few unkind words. But maybe those weren't just age-related breakdowns. Did Hawk's pod really hang a couple of minutes ago, or is she crawling down into the station right now?

Ah, God. Home seems a long way away.

I stare down at the blue, wonderful planet below me, peering through a swirl of clouds over Africa's fat underbelly. So close. So far. I close my eyes against wishing. Okay. Leave out Hawk, "Lemme at 'em" Hawk who lost her whole family to a Worlie raid on stubborn Scotland. And Vronski. It's surely not Ski. Yeah, his grasp of tactics runs toward brute force but his whole country is starving because it joined PatForce instead of One World. It can't be Ski.

My eyes fly open. Gren. I'll bet it's Gren. I *never* liked having a machine assigned to my squad. GRN-17 is a blank-faced, creepy little—

Friend.

Gren's my friend, I tell my jittery nerves, dredging up all those quiet little memories that make a friendship. The time it showed me a better way to pack my ruck. The time it hauled my dragging ass up a space-chilled access ladder when I was so cold I couldn't cling on. The time it—

Gren is my friend.

But friendship in a machine can be reprogrammed some fine and starry night by a stealthy hand removing a critical chip from a machine programmed to accept regular "maintenance."

Oh, God. Not Gren.

Please don't let it be Gren.

Sudden heavy vibration runs like a shockwave up the fifty-meter arm of my pod. My heart rate shoots up about three hundred percent as I peer anxiously at the outpost. It looks the same, a squat round control pod connected by short spokes to the outer hex, just now sprouting spidery legs from long empty wells in each of the six faceless gray sides. Each leg ends in a fat and deadly little pod like mine. There are no blind spots in our observation of space around us. What the scanners can no longer see, we can. Any Worlie cruiser angling to fire on a PatForce free zone in our area of operations would have to elude our eyes, and our guns.

The pods look fine, the three I can see in our current defensive configuration, but—*Hoyt!* The hair starts jumping over my body. Hoyt's at ops inside, in control of every panel. He could jettison us all with the flick of a finger, blow the pods loose and—

Have to explain it afterward. All six malfunctioning at once? *Gee, sir, I don't have a clue what happened.*

The pod continues to vibrate. Finally it registers on my sluggish brain that something is happening in the outpost, and if that's so, then Dan Hoyt's in trouble: steady, quiet, Alberta farmboy Hoyt who never would have come into space in the first place if the One Worlders hadn't collectivized his folks' operation at gunpoint. I dive toward the hatch—and stop, one gloved hand on the release, the other clutched tight around the hand grip.

I'm on duty. I have to watch for a Worlie attack. We've been blinded to let a cruiser through, and below us is Africa, rich, fertile Africa where Patriot Force moved so much of our food production since the bread baskets of the free zones have been hammered so many times. Nebraska's a wasteland, Poland is starving, but hey—One World is your benevolent friend. Give us your farm, we'll run it better. Don't give it to us and we'll take it. Or burn it, as an example to the other stubborn hicks. The Worlies are not long on subtlety. But how did they get to my squad?

My hand starts to shake. I snatch it away from the hatch release and try the comms again. "Any station, this is Alpha. Respond, over."

I wait. And wait. There is not even static hiss in my ears. My faceplate remains innocent of words.

"Any station, Sergeant Keller, over."

Nothing.

I make a tour of all the ports, hunting the telltale indicators of a moving ship: the red gleam of an engine burn, the flash of its hull, the sudden occlusion of stars or a dark speck swooping down above a cloud. I see nothing, but my wound-up guts refuse to unwind. What in *hell* is that vibration? It occurs to me that my faithfulness to duty won't mean squat if the station power plant blows up. Suddenly I'm not tired anymore.

I try the scanners, just in case, but the screens stay stubbornly dark. Oh, this is so not good. My squad cannot be traitors. Ari survived the "accidental" plague that wiped out Tel Aviv. Miyoshi—it is *not* Miyoshi. We once floated around in hell together. I saved his life once. He saved my sanity afterward. It cannot be Miyoshi, but his name gives me hope. If I can get to him, I'll have a rock at my back no one will ever budge, even though we are no longer lovers. All those generations of samurai—he does not know the meaning of budge.

I touch the helmet comm and try to reach Nguyen in the next pod, fragile-looking, deadly little Nguyen with his coal-black hair and ice-white teeth and red, red heart. If anyone in the outfit is cold-blooded enough to betray the rest, it's him, but if there's any one of them I'd turn loose in a dirty fight—it's him.

"Nguyen?" I whisper. I am startled when his voice comes back, equally quiet.

"Sarge?"

"Have you got comms?"

"No. Did you get that flash?"

"Yeah. Any ideas?"

"Many." In my mind I can see his smile, friendly as a gargoyle and twice as evil. "Is your pod shaking?"

"Like a recruit. I'm going down to see what's happening. Cover me with your pulse gun."

"Yes."

Never a waster of words, Nguyen. I hang back until I see him open his exterior hatch and a white-suited arm appear before I pop my own. No puff of oxygen hisses dramatically into space; the pods are not pressurized. Nothing in here can burn if it's hit.

Except me.

I try to will the hair on my arms to lie down. Way down deep in the storage holds of my memory I dog the hatches tight on images of space-suited figures burning like medieval torches in the corridors of the *Freedom*. Firefights in space really aren't pretty. You suit up against hull breaches, you try to focus on the job, you hope you don't end up floating around watching your cruiser get decimated. You zoom the corridors past burning friends to try and do their job and yours when the shit hits the fan. You develop a love/hate relationship with oxygen. You—Oh, hell. Why didn't I just take the offer when PatForce told me I'd been through enough, that I could transfer off the line to Io and teach newbies how to survive up here? Stupid, stupid, stupid.

Pat-ri-ot. That's me.

The hatch opens into yawning nothing; the pods are supposed to be exited with the arm retracted, but the designers factored in maintenance and glitches. I grab the first handhold on the upper side of the arm, horribly aware of the plasma popgun in Nguyen's pod and his pulse pistol tracking me. One millisecond burst from either and my body will join the rest of the space junk orbiting Earth until my personal orbit finally decays, a little mummified thing in a tattered suit waving endless cheery hellos to the people I was supposed to protect. But I hand myself down grip by grip to the maintenance hatch in the empty well where the pod arm folds up, and no shot burns its way through my suit to light up the oxygen inside. I hunker down in the well with just my head in the line of fire and signal Nguyen that I'm safe.

"Get back in the pod and cover my post while I check this out. Over." He can't cover it all, but hopefully that blind side will not stay blind for long.

"Roger, out," comes his voice in my ear. I watch him retreat into the pod, and then grimly contemplate the hatch at my feet. I have not yet set my magnetized boots on it; the clunk would be clearly audible inside. I opt for stealth and awkwardly crab my way around, thinking about whizzing along in space at seventeen thousand miles an hour with no tether. It's not the first time, but I have never much cared for it, and I make sure that I punch in the correct code.

The hatch slides smoothly aside. The dark well of the airlock never looked less inviting, but the weird vibration spurs me onward. Sentry outposts are not built for anything but stolid, unadventurous orbit; their engines fire only in emergencies or for stabilization. This tremor reminds me of a cruiser at max velocity, shaking her tail off in pursuit of a Worlie raider.

I take a deep breath that hisses in my ears as I let it out, and lower myself into the airlock. The little glow-light above the controls is out, which does nothing for my nerves; I draw my sidearm with my right hand and work the controls with the other. As the outer hatch closes behind me, I try to flatten my suited-up self against the bulkhead. Anybody shooting into the airlock really can't miss.

The inner hatch slides open. Light spills in, blinding me for a second. Quickly, I dive through, putting all those hours in the weightless gym playing dodge'em to good use. The narrow corridor beyond is empty. Hoyt, if he is alive, and not a traitor, will be in the control room at the heart of this armored tub.

There is no access to the control room in this section, just a narrow gray corridor running beside the food storage and galley. I shove off toward the nearest section seal, still spurning the deck. Weightless is faster, quieter. And I do not remove my helmet, in case the traitor has played a really nasty trick and depressurized the whole outpost. If a Worlie cruiser is on the way, the suits have enough air to sustain his—her?—miserable turd life long enough to thumb a ride back to Luna Station, there to rejoin the rest of the loonies trying to turn Earth into one big happy family.

The section airlock is sealed, which just winds my guts up tighter. Laboriously, I key it open and make sure it cycles before opening the far hatch. The next section is all power generation behind blank gray bulkheads, humming quietly on my right. The sound in my helmet reassures me that there is still air in these corridors. I seal this section behind me too.

Beyond the third airlock I stop dead in sorrow, staring at Hoyt lying half in and half out of the open inner hatch to Number Four pod. Hawk's pod. Now I know why it hung. Hoyt, suited up for action, lies in halves, his torso wedged against the bulkhead, his legs—I peer through the hatch—missing, but blood clings like liquid jewels to every surface. Hawk's pod arm has vanished along with Number Four stabilizer and the outer hatch. Someone blew the bolts anchoring the arm, venting this whole section.

Good thing I didn't take my helmet off.

Hoyt's open brown eyes stare at me through his faceplate, not bewildered or surprised, but accusing. "Don't look at me," I whisper. "I'm sorry, Danny. Dammit, I'm sorry!"

I hardly know why I'm apologizing. I have lost so many friends I can't remember them all. But I really liked Hoyt; he was so steady, so good to talk to about things that didn't involve guns and space and out-of-control politics. We only talked about how we ended up here just once, when he was a little drunk and missing home.

"Evil is just good run amok," he told me, with that earnest, owlly stare you get after too many honest-to-God beers, not the non-alcoholic swill that passes for entertainment in One World zones. "M'dad told me that, Sarge, and 'strue. All those good intentions..." He faded about then, but I never forgot a truth pulled from the booze, pondered through many hours in many pods since, watched by the white eyes of space.

Whose good intentions are sabotaging my team and the only place we have to stand until a PatForce cruiser can get here?

I sidle through the inner hatch and survey the damage. The missing stabilizer accounts for the vibration; the others are trying to compensate. The outer hatch quivers in my sight, framing only stars. The arm is gone but it doesn't mean Hawk is, too. She hates spacewalks but she's tough; she'll do whatever she has to if her orders are to take this place out. Come to think of it, that gung-ho streak of hers has always grated on my nerves, so at odds with her china-doll face.

I check the setting on my sidearm and click it up a couple of notches.

Scenarios tick relentlessly through the fog of exhaustion whiting out my brain. *Was it suicide, homesick farmboy?* We've been on duty forever. We were down to counting the minutes until our rotation Earthside when the word came down last week that *Southern Hope* was damaged in a firefight with our relief aboard. Now we simply wait, watching unreachable home spin below us and wondering if our boots will ever touch solid ground again.

Wary of the hatch standing open so innocently, I examine the inner panel in mounting rage. Someone has wired every function into the door controls. Hoyt must have tried to close the outer hatch and triggered a lethal trap. I picture him diving for safety, and feel sick.

"Sarge?"

The whisper in my helmet startles me half out of my skin. I flatten to the bulkhead, my heart stuttering in shock. Little Jordan Keller is going to die of heart failure before the bad guys get her, at this rate.

"Say again, over."

"It's Miyoshi. What's going on? Over." The soft Japanese sibilance is so quiet I can barely hear it, but relief washes over me in a flood. I have been, I realize, nursing a secret dread that maybe Hawk's pod took out Miyoshi's on its way to nowhere, or that whoever killed Hoyt has shattered my rock.

"Miyoshi, Keller. Come inside. Now. Over."

"Roger, out."

No questions, no doubts. I know without seeing it that he is already popping his hatch open. Hikaru Miyoshi, have I told you lately that I love you?

I push off toward the next section, hurrying to reach his hatch before anyone else can. He's had my back for so long; I've got his. Real simple.

"Sarge, Miyoshi. I have a prob—"

His voice cuts off. I am at the section seal; for a second I debate the wisdom of opening it, but Miyoshi has been with me since before the *Freedom* went up. I trust him. I *trust* him! I cycle through into still another empty corridor, twenty meters of gray walls and black floor. I launch myself from the airlock and make like a bullet to the arm access halfway down on the left. It's closed but the lights are blinking red above it. The outer hatch is open. Somebody is screwing around out there.

I reach to close it, my gloved fingers clumsy on the control pad. "Miyoshi, Keller. Where are you?"

"On the arm. I—Sarge!"

"What?" I scream, but no voice comes back. Instead, a massive hum groans through the whole outpost: power sucking into the conduits feeding the guns as the generator spins up. Someone is firing, but who?

"All stations, report!" I am screaming, but it is lost in the sudden *whang! Clang! BAM!* as junk impacts the outer hull. The hull breach alarm starts to shriek. Instantly, I kick off from the bulkhead in a desperate grab for an emergency handhold, in terror of explosive decompression in this section. I have done the surprise spacewalk, thanks, and once was enough.

"Which one of you crazy bastards fired at the outpost?" I scream into my helmet mic, but only silence comes back. Dammit, what is causing these intermittent outages?

The section does not decompress. The clanging and thumping stop. I cling to the handhold, unable to pry my hand loose for a whole minute. *Miyoshi's out there!* I tell myself, and it is that which finally unclamps my fingers.

The light over the access is still red. I don't care. If someone is in the well it can't be for a good reason. I key in the code to close the outer hatch and wait for the lights to turn green. For ten endless seconds I think the outer hatch is jammed and the lights will never change, but then the red goes out and I pull myself out of the line of fire, keying the inner hatch open with my free hand.

I expect the white gleam of someone's suit; what I get is a blank silver face with a spooky blue glow behind it. "Gren! What are you doing here?" Gren should be in a pod halfway around the station, watching for Worlie cruisers.

Then it jolts home. Hoyt, dead. Hawk, missing. Miyoshi in trouble. The pod guns can be test fired from the well....

"What did you do?" I scream. My sidearm is already in my hand; I point it at Gren's horror of a face, but before I can blow that bag of spare parts to atoms Gren throws itself backward out the hatch. I am so mad I almost go after it but some fragment of sense kicks in. I end up clinging to the access yelling every obscenity I know, venting ten years' worth of coiled-up scared all at once. But then something huge and white jumps up right in my face and I throw myself backward, spinning out of control. If I connect with something I'm going to rip hell out of my suit, and more visions of things I don't want to remember flash through my head.

I manage to grab a handhold. Movement outside jerks every reflex I own; I hit the emergency override that disregards objects in the opening and snatch myself downward out of the path of any aimed shot from outside. The hatch slams shut, but not before I catch a glimpse of something pale floating outside.

"Eat vacuum!" I scream, even though Gren will never notice; it spends half its time floating around the outpost doing exterior maintenance. But my nerves badly need venting and I have deprived myself of the more satisfactory method of shooting that android piece of junk full of holes.

From the corridor I code-lock the access to my command code. Gren will have to propel himself around to the next one, but I am already shooting myself toward the section seal. I have interior lines and a full head of anger. I make it through the seal and see the hatch still closed, and feel my lips stretching in the hellacious grin I thought had been lost forever with the *Freedom*.

"Miyoshi! Hawk!" I yell into my helmet mic. To hell with radio procedure. "Are you out there?"

Nothing. Cursing Gren's hashing of the comm circuits, I lock down the access and take stock of my position. Section 6. At the end of the corridor near the seal is the inner door into the operations center. I eye it, then the access, then the seals. The single viewport on the station is down there too, wedged between the section divider and the pod housing, shedding eerie Earthlight onto the operations hatch. I start to shove off toward it, intent on seeing what can be seen of the pods and Gren. But the hull breach alarm is still whooping; if I don't get it locked down none of this will matter. I slap the ops hatch open, eyeing the four-meter tunnel between the outer hex and the inner core. It is intact; the green tape remains of Ski's forlorn Christmas tree flutter on the wall in the air displaced by the hatch closing. I float past it, remembering how we laughed at him and then refused to take down the only festive thing in the whole damned place afterward. I remember us singing Christmas carols as I open the inner door.

A long, incredulous wail of rage rips from my throat. Ops looks like it's taken a direct hit from a cruiser, but this damage was done from the inside. A pulse gun up close on critical stations. The panels are in pieces. It will take days to get them back online. If we live long enough.

God *damn* it! I just want to go home! I want to feel dirt under my feet, gravity cradling my body, the delicious, dizzy certainty that when I fall there will be something to catch me. Even after the rescue ship plucked Miyoshi and me and the seven other *Freedom* survivors out of the void they didn't take us Earthside. Too far, then. Now we just have to wait our turn. But our turn to go home never seems to come. It's been ten years since I touched Earth; I am losing it, that visceral memory of having a place to go to that doesn't move, doesn't disintegrate in white fire. I am forgetting the feel of solid ground underfoot and the scent of living things in my nostrils and the touch of sunlight filtered through atmosphere. I am slowly being stripped of the place I fight for. God, God, *God*, I don't want to die in space, floating endlessly in a dead outpost, as weightless as a politician's promise.

I pry my clenched fists open and force myself to look at the mess. "Figure it out," I whisper into the silence. "Take care of your people."

One of the boards still works, flashing red on Sections 2 and 3. Their pressure reads zero, but the section seals are holding. I silence the alarm and take a quick look at the other boards. For a miracle the pod controls are working, but someone has shut them down. I start to restore power, and hesitate. Will that just give somebody a better shot at the rest? Hawk's pod is gone. From the sounds of it, someone fired at Miyoshi's. I try to remember whose pods overlook his.

"All stations, this is Alpha. Report, over."

Nothing. I mutter a few well-chosen words and try to think. I am so tired! Days and weeks and years of this endless watch, running on adrenaline, watching the world tear itself apart over ideas, has turned my brain to vacuum. I close my eyes, wishing for a time machine to take myself to some century that never heard of space flight, longing for green hills and heaviness in my bones and my old room at home and—

My eyes snap open. My room had been full of antique crap left by generations of my ancestors, including a box full of parts my dad once dared me to make into something useful. The result is now sort of a family heirloom, Jordan's radio, which wasn't really a radio, but could actually pull in nostalgia broadcasts. I know how to get comms up.

I start scrounging for parts, jerking open bins to find spares still snugged neatly into their straps. Our saboteur makes mistakes. Encouraging. I abandon neatness and start jamming stuff together. I work facing the hex access, turning now and again to look at the hatch into the living quarters that take up the other half of the core, convenient access in emergencies, just another problem right now. Time ticks like a bomb in my head, counting down to some ending I know will be bad.

The silence creeps up my nerves. I want—I need—to talk to my squad, to reassure them, to find out what is happening outside. Who fired? At what? My gut tells me somebody took a potshot at Miyoshi. Likely his pod is gone, or the arm, and probably him, too. Tiny voices of grief wail in the back of my mind but my hands work like automatons, divorced from the reality of dead friends. Hate crawls to the fore and stays there, fixating on a blank silver face and a squat android body.

I am trying to get the last two crystals to align when a thought brings me up short. If Gren is the traitor, someone made him so.

That makes two traitors aboard.

"Shit," I whisper, and work faster.

The thing I produce is a ridiculous bit of jury-rigging, but it works, slaved to a jack in my suit. "All stations, report," I say into my mic, and instantly I get Ari's voice back.

"Sarge! Somebody blew shit out of Miyoshi's pod!"

"Who?"

"My pod's frozen. I could only see Miyoshi's pod go up, not who fired."

Figures. "Ski? Keller. What have you got?"

Silence. "Ski! Report."

Nothing. My skin starts to crawl.

"Nguyen."

"Here."

"Miyoshi."

Static. I take that as a hopeful sign. "Hawk."

Silence.

"Gren."

I expect silence; the answer shocks me. "Alpha, Gren. Please open the airlocks. I must speak with you. Over."

"In your dreams," I mutter. "Do bags of spare parts dream, Gren?"

"Sergeant, I must come inside. I have—"

I slam the switch on my helmet comm. I have no desire to trade verbal shots with Gren. I know what it's done. Listening to excuses is a waste of time.

I find myself staring at the transmitter, grinding my teeth in helpless rage. Who—is—doing—this? Despair washes over me, so bad it gives me the shakes. For an instant I hate all of them: Nguyen, Ari, Hawk, Ski—Which of them sold out? Which of them is talking to a Worlie cruiser right now on an encrypted channel, about to thumb a ride while we all go to hell? I shut my eyes tight against a vision of this outpost flaming like the *Freedom*, a lightshow for eyes on Earth to wonder who has lost this time. Voices echo in my head: screams of dying friends, underscored by Miyoshi's voice yelling "Sergeant Keller!" It echoes through my mind like the distant fading thunder of a summer storm and rolls away into the depths of my head, leaving me dizzy and disoriented and caught in devastating déjà vu. For a moment I am not floating in the safe and enclosed control room of an outpost orbiting Earth, but in gut-wrenching infinity, dropping forever and ever through nothing, with not even the hope of a gravity well to catch my falling corpse. I cannot rid my mind of the sensation of falling, even knowing there is neither up nor down and nowhere to go, nothing to collide with. It hasn't been this bad in years; I start to flail in panic, and my glove impacts something hard.

It snaps me back to the control room. I open my eyes, gut-shocked and panting. I'm so tired I'm losing it, and I just can't. Not now.

Get serious, a voice tells me, my old sergeant from my recruit days. He's been dead seven years but I can still hear him yelling at us to get serious, get it together, get our minds into our helmets and keep from becoming PatForce statistics.

I bite the inside of my cheek, the only thing that reliably gets my attention, and shove myself over to the access. I'll take my chances outside.

Ahead is the observation window, the outpost's only graceful feature. It was made for practical reasons rather than aesthetics, but the view of Earth is magnificent. Usually. Today the blue and white and green has a fly, a giant white one bumping forlornly against the tough transparency. I float in the corridor, face-to-face with it, my fists clenched so hard I'm surprised my nails are not ripping holes in the tough fabric. I look at the name tag, dreading to read Miyoshi, but it is Hawk. Terima Hawkins, what is left of her, for she has been crushed by something huge, probably the retractor arm jack-knifing into the pod. She trails a small wake of beaded blood droplets.

"Sorry," I whisper for the second time today, because I doubted her. Because I failed her.

Miyoshi.

Grief twists through me again. I know there is no chance that he is alive. Not with Hawk out there as proof that somebody is gunning for us all. It's a waiting game. The squad can't remain outside forever. I must figure out how to get them in here before Gren picks them off one by one.

The hair starts to creep on my neck. Again. How is that I can*not* seem to remember the second traitor, the real traitor, the one pulling Gren's strings? With the vibration still rumbling through the deck plates, I have no way of knowing if someone were to crawl down a retractor arm and come stalking me as I am stalking Gren. Oh, cheery thought.

Can this day please be over?

Get serious.

Beyond Hawk's body I can see Ski's pod. If he's in there, he is keeping himself below the ports, his boots on the deck and his hand on the firing panel. Or he is not there, but out cavorting with Gren. For about the thousandth time I contemplate the folly of integrating machines into PatForce, as capricious as their programming, as fallible as—

Us.

Where are you, Ski?

I need to know.

I never actually saw him climb into the pod, did I? I just ran for my own when the alarm went off. I have never had cause to question Vronski's loyalty; I assumed he had followed orders like everyone else. Now I wonder.

The ops access is still open. I make my way back through the ruins to the inner door into the living section beyond the bulkhead bisecting the inner pod. The hatch slides open on the gym slash rec facility with its beat-up equipment and huge monitor that doubles for vid screen and briefing board. It seems haunted now. Hoyt's cable weights stand ready in their niches; I can almost see him, his boots locked to the floor, his corded arms straining against resistance set to maximum, pulling the weights from the wall in endless rhythm. Left, right, left, right, grin through the sweat when skinny Ari tells him to just drink the damned bone boosters. Hawk's collection of trashy vids peers from their transparent cabinet beside the monitor, a fistful of memories centered on her insatiable appetite for sex. And there is Miyoshi's banzai tree, his experiment in space that has occupied his spare time since the *Freedom* blew up with his last attempt. A gentle man, Miyoshi, a survivor who can gracefully begin again whenever life pulls the rug out from under him. I wish I had half his courage, for I look at these things and want to weep and throw things like a scared little girl instead of a master sergeant in Patriot Force. Maybe I have reached my quota of gruff and tough; maybe the courage has been leaking out since I first left Earth, quaking and puking in the strangeness of space and the white terror of ships firing at my transport. I have been living on dumb luck for seven years.

Something clangs softly. I spin around, zooming uncontrolled toward the ceiling. I correct and brace myself with one hand on the garishly-painted wall, gift of some psychotic designer who thought diagonal slashes of bright colors make great therapy for combat vets. My helmet receptors pick up the *whirr* and *hiss* of a door opening. After six months we can all identify every door in the place.

That one is mine.

Rage stabs red fingers through my brain. I am tired of screwing around with silence and echoes and missing squad members. I am tired of chasing emptiness. I am just—plain—*tired*!

My pulse gun is in my hand. I don't remember drawing it, or has it always been there? I can't remember. I make for the door and turn left toward the miniscule quarters that contain the sum total of my worldly possessions: three books and two spare uniforms. Unlike Miyoshi, I see no point in re-placing what was lost with the Freedom. My life is about patrols and standing watch and controlling my unbearable longing for the planet turning in lazy beauty below us, as distant as a daydream.

The door to my quarters stands open. "Who's there?" I yell, because even through the helmet my voice will carry in the outpost's atmosphere. "Come out of there!"

"Sarge? Don't be mad, 'kay?"

Disillusion falls like lead onto my shoulders. "Now why would I be mad, Ski? Just because you killed Hawk and Hoyt and Miyoshi?"

"No, no, no, no!" His voice rips the silence, shocked and aggrieved and thick with the accent of his native Poland. "I came to *help* you! Sarge, you have to listen! Here, I'm coming out!"

Good, I think, and fire at the first gleam of white in the dimness beyond the open door.

"SARGE!"

Damn, I missed. I flatten myself to the ceiling, the oldest trick of all but the best I have in this confined corridor. For a mad moment I find myself wishing for a popgun instead of the piddling pulse gun, something that will burn and rip air and flesh and reinforced titanium, but then sense returns and I find I am not eager to spend the next few days huddled in the rec room conserving air while PatForce detaches a cruiser to come patch up their holed outpost. I wait, my brain cool, clearer than it has been in days, or is it weeks? I cannot remember; I can barely remember this morning. For some reason I decided we needed to be in the pods, and thus Hawk and Miyoshi died. What was it? Oh, yes. Malfunctions. Alarms.

Except it wasn't malfunctions, was it? Sabotage, pure and simple. Who was the last one in there? Hoyt. But he's dead, so he hadn't done it. Gren, then. But somebody had to program it, and here's Ski. But Ski put the transmitters back on line, and why do that if you're going to let the Worlies come in and blow the whole place to hell on some predetermined schedule?

Oh, God, I'm tired.

"Sarge?"

His voice is a trickle in my ear. "Still here," I say pleasantly. "I've got all day."

"I saw the control room, Sarge."

"I'll bet you did."

"You think *I* did that?" Again the outrage sounds genuine. I never knew our stolid refugee from the heart of One World territory was such a good actor.

"Who else? I sure didn't."

A long pause whispers in my ear. White noise, static, ghosts from a dead life—I don't know what I hear, but suddenly a real sound breaks through, not from my quarters, but the outer hex, echoing down the spoke connecting our quarters to the outer ring.

Betrayal shocks up my nerves; I am caught between two fires, for there is a gleam of silver in the tunnel. I shove off hard, trying to outrun the pulse fire I know must come, and I have just enough courage left to dive toward that gleam, not away. Even as my eyes focus on Gren's blank face, I see it reaching behind itself, pulling something forward, surely its sidearm. I fire but miss, a disgrace to my old sergeant, and then Gren's metallic voice wails in my ear.

"Sergeant Keller! Stand down!"

God damn the Army. Drilled-in reflexes kick in for one critical instant. I catch at the wall before I realize I am doing it, altering my angle—just enough. I can't reorient fast enough, and Gren is right there in the hatchway, a man-shaped horror with no face. But then I see a white-suited arm and shoulder behind it, and a screech of fury echoes in my helmet, for still another of my team has betrayed me and climbed down from the pods, another traitor stalking—

"Sarge!"

The second figure shoves Gren aside and dives recklessly through the hatch. It only just registers on me that it has no weapon in either hand; once again reflexes kick in and I manage not to fire. Then its helmeted head tilts up, and the face inside the transparent bubble is oh so dear, and the name tag on the chest reads *Miyoshi*.

"You're dead," I whisper, and then scream it. "You're dead!"

Grief pulls me into a ball. If he is not dead then he is in on it, and I have nothing left to cling to but three books and an empty cabin.

"Gren saved me!" His voice comes distant and strange through my helmet. "When the pod malfunctioned Gren managed to snatch me into the well. I'd have been shredded otherwise."

His hand closes, gently, on my upper arm. Wildly I try to pull away. "No! No! This is a trick! You and Ski—"

His faceplate touches mine, as intimate a gesture as you can make in a space suit. "Oh, Jordan-chan," he says, so quietly. "It was not us."

I hear sorrow in his voice. "Then who?" I choke. "Hoyt?"

He shakes his head. "Come. Please. Let us talk about this."

"Talk!" I try to pull away but can't break his grip. Ski looms up beside me, and I see that it's a conspiracy, and I try to beat at Miyoshi, but that's a pointless exercise in null gee. Ski's hand shoves me back when I rebound from my own flailing. Raging, I try to wrestle my sidearm into position but Ski grabs my wrist, his other hand braced on the upper rim of the hatch where Gren has planted itself like an iron maiden waiting to swallow its next victim.

Hot tears of rage stream down my face, blurring my sight. "How could you?" I scream at Miyoshi. "I trusted you! I trusted you!"

"And Hoyt trusted you." Gren's voice booms through the two meters of dead air between us. "We all trusted—we still trust you. But you must be stopped, Sergeant Keller."

Something moves beyond the hatch. I flinch, picturing Worlie raiders boring their pitiless way through the hull. It will happen again if I don't stop it, betrayal from within, *Freedom* burning, falling...I run into Ski's hand again, and the rage shrieks out.

"Yes, you'd like that, wouldn't you? Another hour and the whole outpost would be just flaming debris raining toward Earth!"

"I have no doubt that is true," Gren says. How can a machine voice sound so sad?

Behind it, I see that the corridor is now full of white-suited figures. They have all betrayed me, climbed down from their posts, given up the battle. The Worlies have won, and I am falling to eternity.

"Deserters," I hiss at them. Gren answers.

"No. *Northern Light* is an hour out. There is no danger."

"No danger!" I scream. "There's a traitor among us!"

Miyoshi's hand drifts up, as though he would stroke my hair as he used to do in the days before the world shrank to the stripes on my arm and the endless night inside my head.

"No," he says, so softly. "No traitors. Just casualties."

I strike his hand away—and freeze at sight of my own. Flashes of pulse fire and wreckage make it through the fog. My hand blowing hell out of ops on my casual way out toward my pod as the alarm begins to shriek.

Oh, God.

I hear a voice screaming and screaming inside my helmet, but even Miyoshi's arms around me cannot erase the sense of falling.

UNDER PRESSURE
Lee C. Hillman

MAJOR BRINA DENNOBAR CHECKED THE FLIGHT PLAN AND ITINERARY AGAIN. From her calculations, the most dangerous leg of the journey would be transferring the new Governor from his private transport to his diplomatic quarters on arrival at Loniro Prime. If anyone planned to attempt a power grab, it would likely come early, before she could whisk Governor Tarin Barala into the protection of his hand-picked staff, who would then remain with him constantly until he could be presented to the Viceroy for official investiture. Once he was confirmed, Brina could add Galactic protection forces to Tarin's own officers for the duration of their return to Maiara.

She was fairly certain there *would* be an assassination attempt.

The threats had begun even before Tarin's mother, Governor Rissa, had died. Three days after the galactic news agencies had scooped the story of her illness, one of Brina's agents intercepted an encrypted signal feed to the Kenir sector. Within twenty hours they had scrubbed it clean and translated it: Wait and Watch.

Brina couldn't pinpoint the traced signal, but she had three obvious leads. There was Prince Warnam, head of the Gorashan Dynasty. His family had had its eye on Maiara's mineral-rich asteroids for generations, hoping to convince the Viceroy to name one of their scions to the Governorship. The other strong possibility was Lango Imholt, whose merchant ships would have a much easier time accessing central space if Maiara's defense grid were under their direct control. Imholt was notorious for his willingness to go around galactic diplomacy when it suited his purposes. But the Gorashan family was not known for playing fair, either. Brina sent out feelers for more information and instructed her teams to broaden the spectrum to intercept further communiqués. Sadly, they received more to go on over the next two weeks, but nothing conclusive.

The third option was one Tarin had dismissed out of hand, but it remained on Brina's list. His own cousin, Sald Barol, was ineligible to inherit by ordinary means, but if Tarin were killed before he could be invested, the interplanetary council could be persuaded to throw their support to him through the course of the election that would follow. Brina couldn't understand why Tarin insisted his cousin was incapable of that type of subterfuge.

"Major, we're beginning our initial approach into Loniro's space station," the comm officer announced.

"Acknowledged. If they offer escort, take it," Brina told him. She couldn't afford to insult the Viceroy by refusing, although she'd have rather had plenty of free space all around Tarin's ship until they made dock on the surface. She'd have asked them to clear the whole port, if she'd had a prayer of making it happen.

Knowing Tarin would want to pop onto the bridge, Brina tucked the itinerary readout into her tunic pocket and went to head him off. She moved swiftly through the gangways, her leg twinging the way it always did when she started moving again after a long sit. The synthetic cartilage tended to shrink at rest, but like real tendons and muscles, it stretched itself with use. By the time she reached the bridge, her gait had smoothed back to a steady, graceful lope.

Not that she was complaining. A cybersynth leg was a good deal better than no leg and mandatory retirement on disability. The galactic pension plan was good, but it wasn't meant to support retiring at the age of thirty-five.

The bridge doors slid open at her approach.

"...been a pleasure, captain," Tarin was saying. He turned. "Thank you all," he continued, and saw her. "Ah, Brina, good. I was just telling the captain it's been a smooth journey."

"So far," she agreed.

"Superstition doesn't become you," Tarin told her serenely.

He was so young, she thought. He hadn't had time to grow cautious. "I'm not superstitious, Governor, I'm careful. My job is to make sure you make it all the way to your investiture, not just to the Viceroy's central planet."

"Of course," Tarin agreed, "and you'll do that job admirably, I'm sure."

"Well, part of that job is waiting to celebrate until you're back on Maiara, all official-like."

Tarin chuckled. "I have perfect confidence. My mother thought very highly of you, you know." He looked around the bridge, smiling openly.

"I'm happy to hear that, Governor," Brina replied, "But as you know, we have reason to be concerned. If you'll accompany me back to your quarters?" She indicated the gantry to the bridge. "We can leave the captain and his crew to their business."

Tarin's bright smile faded a bit. "Oh. Yes, of course." He allowed her to escort him into the corridor. Brina kept him at her elbow as they walked.

"Have you acquired any more leads in the search for my assassins?" Tarin asked when they were alone. All traces of the conviviality he had shown on the bridge were suppressed now by a serious, sharp-minded attitude. As she watched him, Brina was reminded acutely of Tarin's mother. He had the same ability to gather information, assess it, and surprise the people around him with the results of his analysis.

"I thought you didn't think there was any real threat," Brina reminded him.

He smiled. "I never said there was no threat, only that I had complete confidence in your ability to neutralize it."

"My abilities are limited, Governor, by your willingness to comply with my instructions for your safety."

Tarin sighed at the reprimand in her voice. "I didn't take anyone with me to the bridge," he apologized.

"And you didn't tell me you were leaving your quarters," Brina agreed. "I agreed that on this ship, you could forego a constant guard on your cabin door, but that doesn't mean you can go anywhere you please without noti-fying us. And once we're planetside, I want someone with you every minute."

"Yes, but what if I have an assignation or a secret meeting?" Tarin asked. The glint in his eye matched the mischievous smile. Brina wanted to knock them both off his face. She resisted.

"No secret meetings. As for assignations, you can have them, but only if a guard comes with you."

Tarin tried again to make her laugh. "And if I suffer performance anxiety?"

Brina stared at him, deadpan, until he sobered. "Governor, this is not about your privacy. It is about your protection. I will not let you endanger yourself or keep me from keeping you safe. I've told you before that neither

I nor anyone on my team cares what you do—or with whom. But I'd like you to get into the habit now of making sure someone from security is with you at all times."

Tarin nodded solemnly. "Don't worry, major. If anyone has a stake in my staying alive, it's me. So. Tell me what you came to tell me."

Brina pulled the itinerary out of her tunic pocket. "I'd like to review the timetable with you one more—"

Her commlink pinged. "Major, we've intercepted another communication, this one from Maiara to Loniro Prime."

She looked up at her protectee as she replied. "Thanks, Colo. Have you decrypted it yet?"

"Working on it now. Andu thinks it'll take him maybe an hour?"

"We'll be in dock by then, transferring the governor to his atmospheric transport. Tell Andu to send it to my personal reader as soon as he's got a lock on it."

"Acknowledged," Colo told her.

"I'll be with the governor for the next ten minutes. Come up to his quarters to stay with him while we prepare to transfer."

"Yes, major, on my way." Colo cut the link.

Tarin pressed the security reader on his door and bowed to Brina so she could enter before him. Brina made a quick sweep of the cabin and then waved him inside.

"So, do you think it's Warnam or Imholt?" Tarin asked, as if they had not been interrupted. "Trying to kill me, I mean."

"I know what you meant. I wish you'd take it a little more seriously."

"My dear major, I see no reason to worry when you are doing it so effectively for us both." He lounged on the bunk. "Now, my guess would be Imholt. As much as Warnam would like my territory, he at least is possessed of a sense of nobility. Imholt has no such scruples."

"But Warnam has contacts in the refinery in Kenir," Brina pointed out.

"Ah, but that makes him rather the obvious choice, doesn't he?" Tarin grinned. "If I were Longo, I'd send a message to Warnam's contacts, as well."

"Why do that if it would tip us off?"

"For the simple reason that it will make it look like Warnam's people are involved," Tarin replied.

Brina frowned. "I'm not in the business of intergalactic espionage, but it doesn't really matter, we don't have enough yet. There's still the possibility that Sald is—"

"My cousin is not interested in Governorship," Tarin said flatly.

"I wish I could agree, Governor. But let's hope this newest set of instructions gets us the heads-up we need to keep you safe. Now. The itinerary?"

Tarin sighed. He recited in a bored monotone: "At ten-hundred, we'll be given clearance to transfer to my atmospheric transport. The trip from spaceport to the Viceroy's palace will take one hour; allowing for docking clearance, that's eleven-fifteen. At eleven-twenty, you and three of your operatives will accompany me through the palace to my private quarters. I am to remain there until nineteen-thirty, when we will be received by the Viceroy. He'll accept my credentials, invest me formally, and then we'll pose for the intergalactic news network. The event will conclude with a state dinner and investiture ball. You would like me in bed—alone, I presume—by twenty-two-hundred so that we can board our ship back to spaceport at oh-six-hundred the next morning."

"You left out—"

"Yes, of course. While we await the reception, there will undoubtedly be an endless presentation of gifts, any one of which may be booby-trapped. I assure you, you'll be given complete access to check all baggage, even mine, as well as all parcels and food items brought into the quarters before I touch, taste, or ingest anything."

"This isn't a ridiculous request, Governor," Brina insisted, teeth grating.

"I've told you, I agree. But you've been over this with me at least a dozen times." For the first time, Tarin sounded as young as his seventeen years. "I said before, I have complete confidence in you. What I don't have confidence in is whether I'll remember my oath, so I'd like to spend a little time working on it before we're overrun with reporters, digitographers, well-wishers, and gift-givers."

Brina fought the urge to groan. She reminded herself again that the pressure she felt to keep Tarin safe was probably nothing compared to the stress Tarin felt, to be so young and in such a public position. Then again, there could be no question that Rissa had raised him to be prepared.

"I'll be outside," she said, "waiting for Colo."

"What do you mean, there's a more urgent problem?" Brina demanded. She had barely made it into the lift before her comlink pinged. The bridge's unwelcome news did nothing to improve her sour mood over the incipient governor's glib attitude.

"Captain Rikl requests you join him and he'll explain," came the reply.

Brina sighed. "On my way," she told the ensign. She pushed the button for the bridge deck; the lift's pneumatic pistons complained at the schizophrenic request.

"Major," Rikl greeted her. "There's an issue with the governor's transport."

"What sort of issue?"

"It's out of service," he said. "Gravitational system failure. I've already asked for a full report on the malfunction, but in the meantime, I don't like the options they've offered."

"Which are?"

"Shared transport, or we can accept the offer of Princess Rylara's personal ship."

"The Viceroy's daughter?" Brina frowned. "What's the catch?"

"The Princess will be on board."

"You're kidding," Brina scoffed. "He'll never go for it."

"Then it's the public transport."

"No way," Brina objected. "I haven't vetted anyone who might be on that ship."

The captain nodded. "So?"

Brina stared at the display showing the spaceport dock from the angles of the ship's external cameras. Her job was getting harder by the second. "Fine. I'll break it to the governor."

"Why weren't we informed of the mechanical errors earlier?" Tarin asked when Brina told him the bad news.

"Because we weren't," Brina answered. "Because it's likely that the mechanical problems are a set-up to get you off that transport and onto one we can't control."

"That's a bit obvious, isn't it?" Tarin scoffed.

"Obvious, but effective. You're not getting on that transport."

"Which leaves us with two equally unpleasant choices. Either we travel without any ability to control who else is on board, or...." He grimaced.

"You could probably dodge having to review the Princess's paintings for the hour or so it'll take to get to the palace," Brina pointed out. She wondered if she should have appeared a little less amused by his discomfort.

"Undoubtedly, and insult the Viceroy in the process."

"Won't it insult him just as badly to refuse the offer?"

"No; I can make it sound like probity," Tarin said convincingly. "Besides, if someone wanted me unable to take my own transport, wouldn't they bet on us taking the next best?"

"I would," Brina agreed.

"Well, then: Public transport. Charming. How many seats are available for purchase?"

There were three passengers on the transport outside of the Governor's party—three too many, in Brina's opinion.

Two guards flanked Tarin to either side, Brina on point, Colo bringing up the rear. The rest of his essential staff, including his valet and personal secretary, would come on the Princess's transport, which was Tarin's diplomatic way of saving face while avoiding her enthusiastic but dreadful artistic endeavors. Some of Brina's people were with them in the hope the assassin would reveal himself onboard.

Brina clutched the profile chips for the three passengers and the four crewmembers. She'd reviewed them before allowing Tarin to set foot onboard, but there was always a chance she'd missed something. As they walked into the compartment, she felt an odd hitch in her cybersynth knee; a moment later, it righted itself.

"You okay?" Marse asked her. She was guarding Tarin's right, so she doubtless saw the sticky twinge in Brina's gait.

"Fine," Brina assured her. "Just want to get this over with."

"I hear that," Marse agreed.

"How behind schedule are we?" Tarin asked when they took their seats.

"About forty-five minutes, Governor," Brina said. "Luckily we had a few hours of downtime built in."

"So my beauty sleep will suffer, you're telling me," Tarin said with a wink.

The docking arms retracted with a lurch. Brina's leg twitched and relaxed as before.

"Muscle cramp?" One of the passengers commented genially. "Probably the anti-grav. My arthritis gets me every time," he continued, indicating his hip.

Brina smiled tightly. "We're on duty, sir," she said to cut off further conversation.

The ship pulled away from dock, thrusting into low orbit and closing quickly on the atmosphere. The captain (Captain Harig according to his dossier) announced that the cabin crew would be in shortly to guide the passengers through the heavy-G procedures for traveling through blackout. Their stewards assisted with the restraints. Brina tensed when Tarin fastened his restraints, but the stewards passed by without making a move toward him.

They fell toward the planet surface.

Brina read through the files again, still finding nothing out of the ordinary. But something didn't feel right, and she couldn't shake it.

"This is your captain again. We'll be entering blackout in just about ninety seconds, so relax, breathe normally, and when we're through I'll turn on the safety signal so you can move freely again. Oh, and Major, if you can access the downlink pad on your seat, there's a message for you."

Brina stretched her arm to key in her security clearance code. The message downlinked, but before she could read it, they entered blackout.

Around Brina, the passengers leaned back and closed their eyes. She resisted the urge to close hers, even though she knew no one could move around during blackout. Outside the portholes, bright orange flashes showed the burn and their rate of speed. She fought to breathe as the g-force pressed down on her chest. It was nearly impossible to move her head, but she let it fall back and then forced it to the side to check on Tarin. He had closed his eyes, but seemed to be breathing calmly. The muscles on his neck were corded with the effort.

Three minutes passed. The pressure lifted and Brina heard the collective intake of air as everyone in the compartment breathed in relief.

The downlink completed itself. Brina read the message. It was the decryption Andu had not finished before they were required to move onto the surface transport. "Arranged. No royal escort. Equipment in locker. Button on device."

Brina looked up, expecting the safety lights to illuminate or Captain Harig to announce their entry into atmospheric flight. Although neither came right away, Brina reached for her restraints to unfasten the harness. "Device" probably meant "bomb." She had to get to the captain right away, forward the message to her team on the Princess's ship. The killer was on one of the crews.

She had just opened the clasp when the gravity went out altogether. She lifted out of her seat and floated toward the bulkhead.

"Major!" Marse cried in alarm, unfastening her own restraints.

"Keep the governor covered," Brina said. She held up her hands to keep from bouncing into the ceiling, reversing her flow back toward her seat after pressing the emergency call signal to the cockpit.

The hatch at the back of the compartment slid open; a steward answering the call, Brina hoped.

"The grav's out in here," she started to say, but before she could voice more than "The grav," she heard the pop and sizzle of a blaster. Marse slumped over Tarin. Drops of blood flooded upward from her chest.

Tarin lost no time drawing Marse's own blaster and firing back. Brina twisted to see the figure, wearing an EVA suit, bouncing toward them.

Brina kicked away toward the assailant, who ducked behind an empty row of seats for cover. The assassin touched a button on a small metal box, worn on a belt around his suit, and gravity returned.

Not just returned, magnified. Multiplied. Brina dropped to the floor with twice her normal weight. She felt a rib crack, but luckily she'd landed on her right side—the cybersynth side, so no other bones were shattered or crushed under its mass. That didn't change the feeling of being crushed right against the deck, or the labor of her heart to keep beating. The assassin turned up the dial another notch. Not a bomb, then. That was good news.

But the hired gun wasn't affected by the device at all. In his suit, he raised his blaster again.

Brina struggled to lift her leg, her arms, anything to stop the attack, protect the governor. Her body refused to cooperate, except for her right knee, which jerked as if there'd been no change to the cabin pressure. She gasped for breath and at the same time shifted her hips as hard as she could. Freed of the weight of her body, the synth leg shot upward in a powerful kick.

Her boot landed squarely on the assailant's torso. With the added strength of the cybernetic leg, he fell backward despite the grav suit. Brina swept her leg in a wide arc, screaming with the pain of her ribs, but it caught his legs and sent him over the rest of the way. She became aware of the captain making an announcement about the emergency, but no one else had made it through the hatch with another EVA suit. She drew in another labored breath and slid down the deck toward the assassin. He was sitting up, aiming. She shot another roundhouse kick to knock the blaster from his gloved hands. On the back-swing, she sliced down toward the box on his belt.

Then three things happened in quick succession: the box smashed open; the assassin cried out in pain; and gravity levels returned to normal.

Ten seconds later, it was over.

Colo had struggled out of his restraints and captured both the blaster and the man wielding it. The remaining guards had Tarin out of his seat and down on the deck behind the last row of seats. Brina had collapsed, but could breathe again, at least.

"Is the governor all right?" she shouted.

"Perfectly well, major," the governor answered for himself.

"Check him for wounds," Brina insisted.

Her last image was one of the cabin crew leaning over her to check her own wounds. Then she passed out.

When next she woke, Colo was sitting next to her bed. "Hey, you're back," he said affectionately.

"How long—" Brina croaked.

"Few hours," Colo told her. "We're in the Palace, everything's fine."

"Assassin?"

"In custody. He was—"

"One of the stewards," Brina finished.

Colo pinched his eyebrows to peer at her. "How'd you know?"

"Andu decoded the message. Knew it was a crew member. Then I glimpsed his face through the visor. Recognized him from the file."

"Okay. He's made a full confession. Warnam was behind it after all."

Brina sighed. "How'd the governor take it?"

"He's not pleased. But he's officially Governor now and Warnam can't do a thing about it. When Captain Harig called in to report the disturbance, the Viceroy sidestepped protocol and invested Governor Tarin right away. He wouldn't leave, though, until you were feeling up to it."

"And Marse?" Brina asked.

Colo looked down. His frown and the sad shake of his head told her all she needed to know.

"Sorry. We should have—"

"Marse was doing her job. She knew the risks and she did what she was supposed to do." Still, Brina felt a catch in her throat. Marse had been a good agent. It was never easy to lose a comrade.

"Well, the governor wants her to get full honors, and no worries about the pension for her family," Colo said with more brightness than necessary, putting the brave face on it. "Did you see him take her blaster?"

"Yeah," Brina laughed weakly. "Wouldn't have thought he had it in him."

"Had what in him?" Tarin's voice came from the doorway. "Major," he said with relief, coming forward. "I'm so glad you're going to be all right. Thank you—and your staff, again."

"Doing our job, Governor," Brina said. But she found his joy at seeing her both genuine and infectious. He was a good kid—and more importantly, he had made it through his own ceremony alive. She'd get back on her feet and make sure he made it home the same way. "I'm glad you're going to be all right, too."

LIVE FIRE
Deborah Teramis Christian

To be synched with your weapons is to fly. It is to hurtle near light-speed down the barrel of an ion cannon, to thrum tight-stretched along the beam of a targeting array, your skin burning with the hail-bite of tachyons probing the deeps of space. *Quasar, quasar, burning bright, like a beacon in the night...*

I am the beacon in the night, when I am rigged at tac-ops. I am the far-cast energy frequencies of targeting sensors, and the predator's eye that follows their mark. I once was the Fire-Rigger, the finger on the trigger for the *Talisman*. My gun-hand was made of cybercircuits and plasteel, my digits were the five techs of my tactical weapons crew, their subsystems ganged to my control. Together we were the human interface to our ship's armament.

It was transcendent—but it was also mundane duty. Fire-rigger teams are required crew on every imperial patrol ship along the Hashmin Demilitarized Zone.

Yes, you heard right. Hashmin, that buffer zone between us and our long-shunned enemies, the Dalukin Empire. It is a place where our military presence may go from boring routine to brink-of-war hostilities in the blink of an eye.

They say the DMZ keeps the expansionist Dalukin at bay, but I'm pretty certain you've never heard news reports of the brinksmanship that is routine there. Dalukin slip through all the time, to test our security, and probe our borders at will. We are unable to detect their stealthed ships until they are well within deadly striking range. And these things will never be said publicly, lest it panic citizens and make our Navy look worthless.

But such a judgment would be very wrong. They may black out current news, but our triumphs are many, countering everything the Dalukin have tried over the years. Yes, you can sleep safely after all. The men and women who wear the golden starburst are watching over you in the night skies, though some may perish guarding you in your sleep.

My young career was nearly cut short by an incident on that border. It taught me the cost of vigilance, and the circumstance under which I might just throw my life away, risk vanishing into the cracks of space beyond reach of help or hope.

I've been there.

Part of me is there, still.

Before I ever joined the Navy, I was an officer in the Marines. I'd followed the footsteps of my older brother Vars, a decorated hero of the Amh campaign. Our Alshem-caste clan are the descendents of warrior monks, and the urge to prove ourselves in combat and service to a cause is deep-bred within us. Even for us women, and especially for this youngest sister of brothers in imperial service.

We are the Amisano, with roots on the high-g world of Casca, and like my brothers, I looked beyond our borders to make my name. The Marines taught me discipline and the hidden interplay of power and command, born caste and earned rank. I had it in me, I thought, to be a superior combat leader. I was just starting to realize that when a battery of tests cut me off from my platoon and marked me as something different.

The fateful question was asked: would I agree to rigger training? I had the reflexes and mental acuity, but more importantly, I had just that measure of active psi that would enhance, but not conflict with, wired nerves and cyberized brain functions.

It was a revelation to me. My eldest brother Oden was the psion in our family, so brilliant with his ability to manipulate the substrate of material and space—my measure of psi was feeble in contrast with his abundant talent. But this was a windfall, this question put to me by our division commander obliged to solicit enrollment in advanced naval systems training.

There was only one answer I could give. The nuances of Marine leadership would have to wait another day, another lifetime; ambition drove me to distinguish myself now. It required a transfer in service, a change from Marine cammo fatigues to the night-black jumpsuits and crisp, high-necked uniform tunics of the Navy. Suddenly I was obligated to unlearn my Marine arrogance and admit the utility of shipboard teamwork, of operations done in concert by many different systems and people.

With a stroke of a stylus, I became one of 'them': sent to the closest academy for indoctrination, then on to rigger training and the implant operations that cyberized my neural functions.

At the end of it I was not only something different, I was something more.

Colenis is the title given any master and commander of a vessel in the Sa'adani Navy. Colenis Bakadesh was on the flight deck of the *Talisman*, and I reported directly to her there, as expected aboard a destroyer-sized vessel. I came to attention and rendered a sharp salute, right fist to left shoulder.

"Simikan Amisano, reporting for duty," I recited the age-old formula, and held out my data pad with orders view-ready on the screen.

The Colenis gave me a dour look and a searching gaze before she took the pad. Her eyes lingered on the Alshem caste mark laserscribed on my brow, cataloging what that told about me. Calculating, no doubt, where I would fit into the complex stew of rank and caste relationships that is the subtext of any Sa'adani social grouping.

I scanned her surreptitiously for tell-tale marks as well. Nothing on face, ears, neck, no stylized clothing marks on her uniform—

There. As she took the data pad, I saw the gleam of a Gen Karfa caste mark on the back of her left hand. Nanite-graved colors permanently marked her skin with the sigil of her house and clan. So. High-born aristocracy she was, just a notch below outright noble blood, though since she commanded only a destroyer, she hailed no doubt from some minor house in the grander scheme of things. Fortunately, my Alshem caste placed me but one step below her own. It was a pleasant recognition for us both.

I breathed a bit easier, and her tone was less critical than her first assessing glance had been. "Your clearances are in order, I see. You're up to date on Ballista, yes?"

"Ballista" was the code name for the new weapons system we'd be testing. the latest in our battery of defenses against the Dalukin.

"Yes, Colenis," I replied. "Top of my class, and field victor in the combat sims."

"So I see." She waved the data pad. "I requested top of your class to fill this slot. Up-to-the-minute training is more important than past field experience for this cruise."

"I'm honored, ma'am."

A half smile tugged the corner of her lips. "I'm the I-Rigger," she said, referring to the integration interface function she served when the vessel was in combat mode. "We'll be getting to know each other very well, Fire-Rigger."

"I look forward to it, ma'am."

She swiped my data pad through her console reader, handed it back to me. "Go with Provisioner Chief Metrevar, here," she motioned to the non-com who'd guided me to the flight deck. "He'll get you squared away. Then report to the wardroom in an hour. We'll be underway in two."

"Yes, ma'am." I gave a parting salute, then followed the Prov Chief into the bowels of the ship.

Somewhere in a gunnery couch, my body breathed and adrenaline washed nerve bundles with chemicals of alertness. I barely noticed. I lived far beyond the reach of my fingers as they stroked console touch-panels. Those fingers were on autopilot, controlled by my hind-brain, that bit that remained in the couch. The rest of me...

Quasar-bright, I burned at the end of a tachyon targeting beam. Besakani ran the array. I felt him in our thought-network, a reflex twitching to my thought, *take aim.*

His feedback flowed like stream of consciousness. *Detection-Acquisition-Lock.*

My awareness rode a Ballista Spotter, a seek-and-destroy long-cruise missile. We stitched normal space like a needle, jumping in increments powered by a tiny on-board stutter-warp drive. In every cycle through n-space, we pulsed trace detectors strong enough to sense a Dalukin stealth screen. Jump, pulse, seek, repeat: we rapidly sampled a matrix of space that would take impossibly long for a ship to patrol, or probes to scan in the ordinary manner. Again we jumped, and again, until we found the thing that gave resistance.

The target decoy crunched like a nut between my teeth. Halting the stutter-jump cycle took only a thought; behind me gathered the strike pod, done playing leap-frog with the Spotter missile.

They were the fist that would drive home the killing blow: four Ballistas bearing the full ship-killing charges of traditional plasma torpedoes. I felt my gunners at the ready, coiled like myself in our couches, in our missiles. *Strike,* I ordered, and a final micro-jump to target ended with warheads exploding.

Only I remained, a lone observation point at a safe remove, the Spotter confirming the kill, Besakani my data-collecting shadow. While flash glare still washed over me, I felt my crew dropping back into the shipboard rigger system, one after another, detached from the sleek bodies they'd ridden to destruction and home again—

The error at Gun 1 sounded a high-pitched electronic scream in my left ear. It yanked my attention back to the ship. Now my hind-brain kicked the Spotter into homing mode while the rest of my senses flew to assess our systems. Out of startled human reflex I forced my physical eyes open, and saw what every fire-rigger dreads: red flashing lights on gunner status read-outs. I slammed my eyes back shut, plunging into our system to learn more.

Lead Crewman Eshra on Gun 1, my senior fire-rigger—gone. Off the boards, just like that. There was no disconnect record; only a spike in brain waves, and the abrupt dead air that meant one thing.

Eshra was dead.

Juro's brass balls! I cursed, and hit the emergency disengage sequence. I ignored the wave of nausea that rolled through my stomach, a physical reaction to the sensation of slamming back into my body, feeling weighty, meaty, once more.

Not pausing to equalize the neural chemicals that aid the rigger process, I dragged myself out of my couch like a dreamer running through molasses. By time I opened Eshra's hatch, my muscles were almost catching up to real-time. I bolted slow-motion to his side.

Too late. Blood from nose, ears, eyes glazed wide open, slightly protruding as if massive cerebral damage lurked behind those distended orbs. As it no doubt did.

What in the seven icy hells? I thought. This shouldn't...this never.... I was almost at a loss. Yes, they train us on rigger hazards, but if you fry because of a systems fault, it's a quick death. We learn that, and we put it out of our minds. It happens rarely, usually from catastrophic system failure in combat. But we'd taken no damage, and our systems were top-notch, meticulously tested for the Ballista project.

Executive Officer Etanen darkened the door, a haughty Delokar whose Aumori caste placed him several steps below me socially. You'd never know it to look at him. He had a proud, stiff-necked bearing, a permanent frown underscoring his hypercritical glare. I already knew to look sharp around him: his disdain for junior officers made him a rival for some Marine NCOs I recalled.

Now that glare was turned fully on me. During field tests he kept a general eye on operations while the Colenis integrated live-fire and direct ship control functions.

"What did you do?" he demanded. "You lost a man on an exercise. That's inexcusable."

I was so taken aback, I gaped like an ilu before I had the sense to respond. "We need to lock this gun unit down, sir. Tech Warrant Demel will need to test the systems, investigate—"

"Don't tell me my job, Simikan." He spit out my rank like it was a dirty word. "The Ballista Spotter's not home yet. Get your ass back on position and bring her in right now."

I looked down at poor Eshra, dead in his gunnery couch.

"And secure your crew. Every rigger on the ship felt that malfunction. Just tell them he's offline, until all stations are locked down. No distractions. This test isn't over yet."

It made a grim kind of sense. My fire-riggers had flown their missiles into oblivion, but they remained jacked in and had after-action procedures to follow, systems to stand down…

"Aye, sir." I headed back to my pod. Delokar Etanen locked Gun 1 as I hurried away.

I brooded over the tragedy as I jacked back into the system. Our fire circuits were all a-chatter. Queries streamed from my gunners and from Chief Engineer Linrastov at the lead power-rigger position, but the one I had to reply to immediately was from the Colenis herself. At i-rigger, she'd feel anything in synch or amiss in our systems.

Like me, she'd felt Eshra die.

I flipped the comm circuit with a mental nudge.

"Report," she snapped.

Words aren't necessary when you're jacked in. I streamed her an update transmitted in milliseconds. She was silent for a moment.

"I think—" she began.

It happened again. Another horrid, high-pitched screech in the cyber-connections, heralding failure and feedback where there should be none. And then the ship lurched beneath us.

We have grav plates. A warship under steady drive does not lurch.

A glance at the view screens showed why. An impossible void tormented our eyes with the black-light glare of warp space.

Colors like oil on water crawled across the screen before automatic compensators kicked in, dulling things to an almost tolerable hue. We'd slipped beyond n-space into that continuous realm that lies between dimensions. It was inhospitable to human life and mind, yet home to hazards living and natural. Warp is a place no vessel travels without precautions and preparations.

Training kicked in. "Gunners to point defenses." I sent the order with the speed of thought. Forget the missile test. Every crewman needed to stand in immediate readiness against the potential hazards of warp space.

Outside, the dark mind-twisting void swallowed us whole.

Rigged, you are fine-tuned to the systems you are a part of. Gunners breathe velocity and vector, weapons feedback, comms and sensor data. Anything else, an irrelevant distraction.

But I was the tactical operations officer, and it was necessary for me to have a background datastream tracking key ship systems. If there was anything amiss that affected gunnery, I would be alerted. Like now.

The pilots' go-rigger systems were lit up like a flare. Engineering failures were strobing hotpoints proclaiming shields weak and nearly offline. Our warp drive was functional but maneuvering engines unresponsive.

I heard the chatter of Engineering's second reporting to the Colenis: a cascading failure had ripped through Engineering while Chief Linrastov was interfaced with the warp drive. The man was dead. Systems he'd directed were locked down and uncontrollable at the moment by others.

On the tech channel, another emergency: core systems were in chaos, relays were damaged, some problem with sensors—

The XO's business-like voice cut through the chatter. "Damage control teams report to Engineering. This is not a drill. Tech, isolate functional systems and stand by. Tactical, maintain point def readiness. Stand by."

All right. Colenis and Delokar between them would sort this out on the bridge, and we had our own job to do. I looked over the cybershoulders of my crew, ensuring they were on point, weapons free and fire-ready. My target-rigger Besakani extended my vision and I swept the globe of other-space around us.

Sensor damage, indeed. My electronic vision was limited to something short of mid-range, and barely even that. I no longer tasted warp space's usual oily slickness, but something as muted as our filtered video portrayed.

Besakani, enhance.

That's as enhanced as she gets, Simikan.

I sighed. Our best defense here was early detection as long-ranged as we could see. The real peril of warp are the alien lifeforms that call that void home, like the "dust" fields of sego particulates, a hive mind that enveloped and corroded slow-moving intruders. There were other lifeforms as well, but the stellons were the worst: intelligent plasma gas clusters radiating like miniature stars, but prowling like hungry sharks after passing energy sources. They were the most aggressive, known to pursue ships until they fled—if possible—into n-space, or brought sufficient fire power to bear to make the price of lunch too high.

And that is what I saw, glittering like a headlight at the far edge of our functional sensor range.

It was a blue star, impossibly small and fast, closing from our port side. It sensed our resonant crystal drives, harmonics singing of radiant power. A banquet in a crunchy shell, we were to this thing. That people would die when it gutted our drive units was of no concern to it. We were merely a food item.

I began a targeting sweep. Ion cannons swiveled on gimbals to orient—

And froze in their tracks. Our gun units blinked offline one by one as power failed in Engineering, and our backup systems failed to come online.

"Gods dammit!" I shouted out loud. "TacOps to Bridge. Stellon bearing 268 Z-4-3, and weapons are offline!"

My outburst was a reflex driven by nerves. I'd never been in ship combat before. I realized my mistake as words left my mouth. Ignoring my gunners' frantic queries, I repeated my report through the cybersystem.

There was no response from the bridge.

I had to do something. A rigged system without response is so much useless hardware. I slammed a fist on my couch arm. *Stay ready,* I thought to my team, *for when our systems come back online. Fire at will when they do.*

Acknowledgments were still coming over my link as I severed connections and dropped out of the rigger net in a proper urgent disconnect. This time I was alert and adrenaline charged as I got out of my couch.

Out of the pod, up the short corridor of the tac-ops module, to the forward hatch. I palmed the lock. No response. Tried the manual override. No response.

I couldn't move forward in the ship.

I scowled at the comm panel as I addressed the ship's onboard AI. "Give me Colenis Bakadesh," I said.

No response.

I stifled the urge to scream, and turned back the way I came. Double-time now, I headed aft to Engineering. Damage control was there. Someone could tell me power status, get me a comm system that worked.

I ran past the first engineer before her condition registered on me. She was jacked into her console, slumped forward. Blood leaking from ears, from nose...

The hair rose on the back of my neck. Every sense screamed at me as my body shifted into battle alertness. I wished for my Marine platoon and some good hand weapons. What in the icy hells was going on here?

I paused just inside the drive unit hatch, beside a maintenance airlock, disaster before my eyes. A fire burned in the control systems, something with the actinic blaze of a plasma burn. Frantic figures struggled to attack the source, but it ate at internal systems like a demon thing.

A similar blue blaze caught my eye out the maintenance lock window. The stellon was near, and it sent a long finger of energy licking at the hull of our ship. The impact rocked the Talisman and ionized our hull. Static electricity crackled over surfaces everywhere.

Some part of my Marine brain read it before I knew it: where the next attack would come. What the consequence must be. I sprang into the maintenance lock and sealed the hatch not a moment too soon.

The next charge from the stellon blew one of our two drive units apart. The vacuum of warp space snuffed the flames even as explosive decompression sucked fire fighters, power-riggers, and debris from the ship and sent them pinwheeling into oblivion.

The maintenance hatch was just at the edge of the affected area. I felt the *Talisman*'s frame twist ominously around the reinforced box that was the airlock. Without thinking, my combat reflexes had taken over: I was halfway into an emergency maintenance vacc suit before I realized what I was doing. Out the view port I saw the deadly stellon come even closer. I was madly calculating how much time I had to get clear when a lance of light stabbed the plasmoid creature from the darkness of space.

Again, that spear of energy—and then multiple beams, coming from a single source. The stellon shuddered, twitched, began to move grudgingly away. The beams continued to blaze as I finished suiting up and pulled the helmet into place, flicked the polarizing visor down with one hand.

Filters engaged, and I gasped. The beams came from a Dalukin battleship off our port bow.

The Dalukin goaded the stellon away from our hull. The creature retreated reluctantly, but retreat it did. The hostile vessel followed it into the distance, herding it clear of the *Talisman* as she plowed on through warp space.

Our ship was crippled now, at half power with a single remaining drive, and who knew how many surviving crew. Our guns were useless and so was I, unrigged and out of touch with command. But the failures on the ship—they'd come before the attack, and no carefully vetted Sa'adani warship behaved in such a manner.

It could only be sabotage.

I had to reach the commander, tell her what I suspected, and report on the devastation in Engineering. My vacc suit comms were as dead as the rest of the ship channels. I already knew the hatchways forward were sealed. There was only one route left to me. Unhappily, I frowned at the exterior maintenance lock.

Common sense and primal reflex made every human resist contact with deep warp. It is inimical to human life. Everything about it grates the nerves raw and seeks to twist the mind. Never had I felt so ambivalent about my Marine training: as part of boarding operations, we learned to do hull maneuvers in warp as well as normal space. Not that we were likely to need the skill, but against an eventuality...

Like now.

Don't think about it, Amisano, I lectured myself. *Just do it.*

I had no time to wrestle with myself over this. The Dalukin ship had slid out of sight to our rear, lost in the refractive glare of the void, but when it was done with the stellon, I had no doubt it would be back. I gritted my teeth and worked the manual release for the lock. When air pressure bled to zero, I opened the hatch, and stepped outside.

Vacc suits of all designs have micro-grav plates built into the boots. They generate a localized grav field orienting toward the mass of the hull. I swung out of the hatch, found my footing as if I'd done this a hundred times. In fact, I very nearly had. I thanked my Name-Day deity for the endless repetitive training a Marine endures. Navy personnel know the inside of their ships intimately, but only engineering repair crews and Marines spend so much time on the outside of a hull that being there becomes second nature.

It was just as well, for even as I found my balance the full presence of warp space clawed through to the back of my skull and forced me to my knees. In the rush to get outside, I'd let the suit adjust automatically, instead of pre-setting it for warp screening. For an instant the blacklight glare of the void screwed my eyes shut; the energies of that space crawled over my skin, striking every nerve alive, threatening sensory overload.

Filter circuits kicked in nearly as quickly, and the mind-searing charge of other-space ceased, but not before a wave of nausea struck and I swallowed bile.

You will not *let yourself lose it inside this suit,* one part of me admonished sternly, a drill sergeant demanding control.

I faced the bow of the ship, blinked my eyes clear of moisture, and began to walk.

Searing blacklight careened from every surface, and made it easy to find my way aided by the screen visuals of my visor. The hull cladding beneath my booted feet glistened with an unnatural oily sheen, reflecting oranges and violets and hues we have no name for. My eyes were drawn to the hypnotic perversity of it and I wrenched them away, trying not to see the patterns and whorls that twisted the stomach like they twisted space.

Grimly, I set my navigation HUD to target the bow, and marched there in as straight a line as I could manage. Across plassteel plating I walked, clambered over the protrusions of gear housings, skirted the partially transparent blister of a gunnery pod and a lifeless form inside...

I pressed on. Look forward far enough to find secure footing, not long enough for the warp-sheen to beguile. Give your mind a focus on something real, something not warp. That was the way.

My goal became my mantra: *Find the Colenis and report.* It became a chant that saw me to the edge of the forward command unit. I spotted the maintenance lock where tech systems butted up against the flight deck beneath my feet and breathed a sigh of relief.

Also at my feet, the plasglass of the flight deck view bay stretched nearly to the airlock I'd found. The plas was hazed, an effect of its active warp filters. Looking in was like gazing through a semi-transparent window shade.

On the other side, two silhouettes fought.

I caught my breath. One figure grappled the other, bent back over flight controls—

I looked back over my shoulder, prompted by a psi-based instinct. Far to our rear, a glare of normal light splashed against the twisting void. Maneuvering thrusters.

The Dalukin were returning.

I flipped the cover of the airlock's manual override. Better to deal with conflict inside, than to stay on the exposed hull. My mind raced ahead. If the commander were still in charge, there would be no struggle on the bridge—

My fingers froze over the access pad. This was a code lock—dammit! Of course!—and I didn't know the access code.

No warship offered easy entry to any boarders on the hull. This lock was keyed to a punch-pad, a mechanical numeric plate designed for use in no-power emergencies. Punch the right sequence, the lever would free up, and I'd be in. The code would be known by any authorized personnel on the ship: Engineers and damage control teams. Marines, if the *Talisman* had shipped any. Command officers.

I was none of those. I was locked out.

The skin on my back crawled. *Stranded.*

I took a deep breath, calming my nerves, breathed out slowly. I called on a discipline from my martial arts practice, slipping into what I call 'slow time.' Where my mind should be racing, it felt considered. I mulled alternatives. I was sharp, gathering my energies while some higher part of my mind sought solutions...

There. So simple. I was in a maintenance suit. Stowed, they carry standard equipment used in ship repair: hull marker flares, line-of-sight comms transmitter...and somewhere here must be plasma cutters.

Check. Left cargo pocket.

My HUD told me three seconds had passed.

In moments I had the punch-pad out and its concealed lock-plate burned through. I pulled the lever and equalized pressure. I was in.

I entered a corner of the tech unit, shucking the vacc suit while I scanned the area. I recognized our warrant officer Demel, dead at his rigger jack of the same overload that had killed others. Something had surged through systems ship-wide, leaving death in its wake.

Still I had no proper hand weapons. I could hear the struggle on the bridge close to where I stood. I grabbed the cutter, and ran for the command deck.

Tech connected with the navigator's bay. I emerged in that corner of the flight deck. I hardly noticed the inert form of our nav officer. I thought he must have died like so many others on rigged positions—

then I caught sight of his throat, and the blood drenching the front of his chest.

It was a vibroblade wound. Slicing cartilage and flesh like butter, it had nearly taken his head from his shoulders. It would have been a silent attack from behind. The small hum of a v-knife would be lost in the background sounds of ventilation and system chatter.

My skin ran cold. I stepped out of the navigator's cubby and into the main flight deck, balanced on my toes, ready for anything—except what I found.

The XO and the commander fought on the flight deck. They staggered apart as I entered the bridge, eying each other for an opening.

Delokar Etanen's face was battered; a damaged knee hobbled him and handicapped the martial arts stance he was trying to assume. The Colenis bent to one side, favoring injured ribs; her hands were in a crane stance, ready to defend or attack. Red marks on her throat told me Etanen had nearly managed to choke her. A needle gun lay on the decking nearby. One of these two had tried to kill the other, and now they were both at it.

Etanen's eyes flicked to me, narrowed with hostility, then flicked back to his opponent. He moved to finish this before I came closer. Abruptly he dropped on one hand and thrust out his good leg, knocking the commander's feet out from under her.

His injured knee slowed him; before he could follow up, I was on him with the solid length of the plasma cutter. One blow behind the ear, and he was down.

Bakadesh regained her feet, the worse for wear. She took me in with a glance, took three strides and scooped up the needle gun. Then she turned, and coldly pumped three triplet rounds into Etanen's unprotected face.

They were explosive tipped. There was little left of the XO's skull when she was done.

It looked like murder, but her action had the harsh, obliterating quality of an honor killing, something Gen Karfa and Lau Sa'adani may do when they feel they must avenge an affront. I didn't know what to do. In our society at large, we follow the enlightened laws of the Imperium Codex, but the old ways still had their place in certain circumstances.

The Colenis' eyes still sparked with battle-anger as she turned to me.

"You're alive." It was a flat observation.

That was not how I expected to be greeted. I shifted uneasily. "I came to report. There's a Dalukin ship—"

She cut me off with a wave of her gun, which she left casually aimed in my direction. "Stow it, Simikan. I'm aware of our company."

"And the state of the ship—?" I began to ask. Too late I noticed the vibroblade sheathed at the waist of her flight suit.

It dawned on me. She already knew the state of the ship. She had put it in this condition herself.

I felt myself go white. "Why?" Pure disbelief drove the question, that and my brain, scrambling for solutions before the Dalukin were upon us.

Maybe she felt a need to confess before she wiped out the last witness to her treachery. She raised the back of her left hand to me. "Do you recognize this sigil?" Her caste mark was a linework disc of blue and gold framing a red bird of some sort. I shook my head. There was too much heraldry in the Empire for any casual observer to keep track of.

Her lip curled in scorn. "Then you'll know my House by its vulgar association. We're a sept of those called the Outside Lords, banished to the Coil Marches after the last Dalukin war."

Outside Lords: not traitors, exactly, but steadfast political opponents of the throne. They'd argued for cooperation with the Dalukin when that psionic race overran our borders centuries before.

"Outside Lords are the necessary opposition," I repeated what I'd learned in civics classes. "Do you want them to have a reputation as traitors, instead? What have you done with our ship?"

She regarded me without even the gleam of fanaticism in her eyes: just the reasoned stance of a misdirected patriot who has logicked her way to the wrong conclusions.

"The Dalukin are the most powerful race of psions known, yet we turned our backs on all they could teach us. Some of us think we can still benefit from closer association with them."

"By giving them our military tech?"

She shrugged. "Let's say we're removing obstacles to closer contact," she said. "The Lau Sa'adani bred for psionics in order to counter the Dalukin threat. We—" She cut herself off with a shake of her head. "There's more, but no time to get into it. Unless…"

She looked me over appraisingly. "You're smart, Amisano. Do you want to learn a new way to think about empire? Make real change happen?"

Do you want to forget your duty? She might as well have asked. *Forget your loyalties?*

"Embrace treason?" I retorted.

Her face hardened. A sound chimed from a console at the same moment, and she pointed upwards with a finger. "My friends are here," she said. "I'm afraid we have nothing more to discuss."

She angled her gun and fired.

I can't say I saw it coming, not with my physical eye. But psi-touched as I am, I sensed it. I darted to one side while her explosive-tipped needle charges tore up the padding of a flight couch behind me. I closed with her before she could take full aim with the handgun. She squeezed off another triplet burst while I got inside her reach and grabbed the wrist of her gun hand. Needles ripped through the starburst patch on my shoulder and detonated, taking a small surface chunk of my upper arm with it.

I cursed and swung at her with the plasma cutter. She deflected the blow with a neat forearm sweep, straight out of the Navy's Shai Den training manual. Her sudden cat-like twist in my grip was meant to free her wrist. I was wounded in that arm, and she was competent in this fighting form. It should have worked.

She didn't reckon on my physical strength. Casca is a high-g world, and I am deceptively strong. It would never be evident from seeing me sprawled in a rigger couch, or going about my ordinary business. She hadn't been paying attention to my shipboard workouts, I suppose. And didn't remember, in the moment, that a Marine is also taught their own unique style of martial arts.

I easily kept her wrist in my grip, and thumb-locked her as she twisted to get free. She looked surprised when she was unable to slip loose. I constricted her grip; a continuous stream of needles erupted from the gun, pocking the flight deck with deadly projectiles until the magazine stuttered empty. I was forcing her to her knees when, at some cost to her ribs, she drove a knee into my arm just above my elbow. My nerves went numb. She yanked free, then pulled her arm back, palm cocked for a killing blow to my face.

In that moment, the ship shuddered beneath us. It could only be a tractor beam, fighting our drive thrust to take us in tow. I saw Bakadesh's weight shift. It was all the distraction I needed.

I swung my arm up, leading with the butt of the plasma cutter. It flew up inside her guard. I could hear the crack as the tool connected with her skull.

She dropped like a rock.

I didn't care if she was dead or alive. I sprang to the flight console, scanned the information there. I wasn't a pilot, but I did know some basics from riding in the jump seat during dropship runs with my old platoon. There would be a proximity map—there. The Dalukin were tugging us within their warp effect bubble. When we synched within it, they would be able to board us. I couldn't let that happen.

I had to drop us out of other-space. We only had one drive maintaining warp. If I could shut that down, we'd be expelled from this perverse dimension like a watermelon seed shot from between two fingers. It was risky: it might throw us into the heart of a star, or cast us so far off the beaten path our star charts could not fix our position. Points in warp space do not map in a one-to-one analog to normal space.

And right then, risk didn't matter. The *Talisman* and her Ballista system would be out of reach of the Dalukin. That was all I cared about. Getting away.

The battleship pulled us closer. My mind raced. The only quick way to drop warp was to use the flight deck systems. I could operate them only in one circumstance: a disaster override. *Well,* I thought, *this qualifies.* In minutes, maybe ten, fifteen at most, the Dalukin would have possession of this ship and her advanced, secret weapons systems.

I checked Bakadesh's pulse. Weak but steady. She'd be out long enough for me to do what I needed to.

I climbed into her command couch, jacked into her systems, immediately met the standard warning. *Incompatible rigging,* the ship's AI flashed in my internal HUD. *Synch not possible.*

Synch this, I thought.

This is Tactical Operations Officer Simikan Amisano Marit, override code Esimir Den 3 7 Vandos 2. Confirm.

A heartbeat's pause. *No other command officers in system. Emergency access confirmed.*

My heart raced faster and I swallowed past a constriction in my throat.

Talisman, I addressed the AI by name, *you are controlling our warp effect bubble, correct?*

Yes. Maintaining warp, headings, and drive power at last authorized settings.

I need you to change them.

Arbitrary course changes are not authorized. The AI sounded almost scandalized. I drew a deep breath. Here we go...

I have emergency command of this ship, do I not?

Within certain parameters, yes.

I frowned. *What parameters?*

Emergency command is authorized only when appointed command officers are dead or incapacitated. This status obligates you to request emergency assistance, or navigate to closest location of friendly forces who may aid you in your distress.

I wanted to slam my hands on the control console. I nursed my wounded arm instead, and parsed AI logic with an effort.

Let me restate. Do you know our present location relative to n-space?

Negative.

I'd guessed as much. However Bakadesh had put us in warp, she hadn't stopped to map n-space referents first. *Is it possible for you to navigate us at this moment to the closest friendlies in n-space?*

Negative.

Good ship, good ship. Follow my logic just a little further... *Therefore, I need to take alternative action to contact friendly forces. Do you concur?*

Affirmative, the ship agreed.

Then cut our warp bubble and drop us into n-space immediately.

Hesitation. Our coordinates will be unknown.

Our coordinates are already unknown.

We have hull damage. Transition will be hazardous.

Transition is necessary.

Another ping from the console told me how necessary. I could see the Dalukin hull looming over us at the upper edge of the forward view bay. Warp fields were beginning to synch.

Talisman, you see the vessel trying for warp parity with us?

Yes.

You must recognize the Dalukin energy signatures. Your well-being and everyone on board will be endangered if we stay in this warp location a moment longer.

I could sense the AI thinking about that one. I felt like a minute passed. It was half a second by the clock.

You have a point, Talisman conceded. And the floor dropped out of the world.

To be synched with your weapons systems is to fly. To be cut off from them is to be isolated in mere humanity.

It is a state I endured for endless weeks. The Talisman was able to map our location: we were not lost, just far from traveled spaceways. The ship was damaged, the drive reduced to maneuvering thrust only. I set the rescue beacon to call for help, then waited for aid to arrive.

I buried the crew in space, all twenty-five, including memorials for those lost in the hull breach.

Bakadesh never came to on my watch. I stowed her unconscious body in the med bay's single stasis chamber and ordered the AI to seal that room lest I do something unthinkable there myself. What became of her after we were found, I was never told.

I never again experienced the live-wire existence of the rigged predator, the quasar-burn of energy weapons and targeting beams. Not directly. For now I command my own ship, a gunboat with a crew of three, where I am the pilot and the i-rigger all at once, orchestrating the dance for us all.

It is almost compensation for what I lost on board the *Talisman*.

VALKYRIES

Lisanne Norman

*V*ALKYRIES *THEY CALL US BUT IT FEELS TO ME WE'RE MORE LIKE* O*DIN'S RAVENS. Our part in the War is here on the planet Valhalla, near the front line, but everyone stuck on this damned ball of snow and per- mafrost calls it Hel, or Helheim. How'd it all start, you ask? Valhalla and its two moons are rich in resources that humanity badly needs, the Company says, so almost before the probe had finished sending its reports back to the Company ship, sitting in orbit nearby, the decision was made to land here and set up the mining operation. They'd been here for six months when the balloon went up and the real owners arrived.*

You think they were explorers like us, and just sore 'cos we beat them to it? Don't you go listening to the Company, gal, they knew from the get-go that the snow hid a permanent settlement and graves, many of which were obviously recent. Planet's a shrine for the aliens, place they come once a year to bury their dead.

Why? Damned if I know. They're aliens, aren't they? Who the hell knows why they do anything!

Who are you? Odin bless, lass, didn't they tell you? You're Sigrun, and when you get out of Medbay, you'll be in my unit. Now, you rest.

She forced her eyelids open as the voice in the dream faded. It had been years since she'd first heard those words, and months since Olrun, who'd said them, had died. The words were Olrun's way of introducing a new recruit to her unit to the reality of the War on Valhalla. But what had triggered the dream of her late mentor and friend, she'd no idea.

The alarm on her night table began to buzz loudly and she sat up,reaching to turn it off. As she did, the light in her small room, once Olrun's, automatically came on.

"Good morning, Captain Sigrun," said the warm neutral voice of the base AI. "Time to get up. There's a special briefing for your unit in forty-five minutes at 0800 hours. The weather outside is fine, with the temperature currently a bracing -50 degrees Fahrenheit, taking the wind chill into account."

"Uh... right. I'm awake, MIMIR." She threw back the covers and padded across the carpeted floor to her tiny bathroom, still not used to the perks of her month-old promotion. As she leaned into the shower cubicle to turn the water on, she wondered what the special briefing was about. Their work was so routine it almost became boring at times, but you couldn't afford to let your attention slip, not on Valhalla.

The mess was half empty this morning, she noticed, most of the units already out on their daily missions, the other half on either standby or R & R like they should be. She grabbed her meal from the server and headed to sit with her own women.

"What's with this special duty, captain?" demanded Hruna. "We're supposed to be on leave for the next three days!"

"You know as much as me," she said, sitting down. She noticed that they all had the double rations served up before a mission—two eggs, extra steak and pancakes, washed down with the good coffee or tea, not the usual brown, cardboard-tasting sludge they usually got.

"Must have been a push on at the front," said Mist, waving her fork in the air.

"We'd have heard about it before now," snorted Brynhild. "You can't miss the sound of those big guns, and besides, we'd all be battening down for lift-off to move this tub closer to the front."

"They don't move us until the advance has been consolidated, you know that. When they've held it for a week or two, then they'll move us," said Gudrun.

"It's gotta be a push, why else would they pull us off leave?" demanded Hruna.

Sigrun tuned them out, concentrating on her food. She was as curious as any of them, but she'd learned over the years that speculating got her nowhere: she'd find out soon enough at the briefing. It did strike her as odd, though. Why her unit? Was it perhaps because something had gone down in their patrol area?

"It's gotta be something at the 5th," she heard Gudrun say. "We don't know any other region well enough to go there."

Laughter and catcalls greeted that remark, drawing Sigrun out of her own thoughts.

"Gudrun wants to see her sweetheart in the 5th," laughed Eir.

"No I don't! I mean, I don't have a sweetheart in the 5th," protested Gudrun, turning on Eir. "You know I don't, it's against the rules to have relationships with the soldiers in our patrol area!"

"You better not," said Hruna. "Don't want to be doing a pick up of him one day."

"Keep it down, ladies," said Sigrun. "Other people trying to eat their breakfast, they don't need to listen to you lot."

She felt a nudge in her side and turned to look at Kara, her second in command.

"Captain, who's the suit over there with the brass?" she asked in a low voice. "He's not one of the visiting grunts."

Sigrun turned to look. He was young, maybe twenty-six at most, dark hair cut short, his complexion pale, but his ramrod-straight bearing and the expensive suit he wore yelled out Company man loud and clear. He was picking at his food, not joining in the general chat that seemed to be taking place among the officers at the table.

"Not a clue," she said. "Odds on the mission concerns him, though."

"Reckon he's as young as he looks? Or is he a Rejuv?"

"Possibly. He's way too stressed out for anyone older than, say forty, though."

A quiet but insistent buzzing began, calling them to muster. Sigrun grabbed the slice of buttered bread that was all that was left of her meal, and pushed her chair back.

"Muster, ladies. Now we'll all find out what's going on," she said.

They joined the general exodus heading out of the mess, each to their own briefing room. Theirs was on the starboard side of the old ship that was their mobile base. No longer capable of space flight, it served them well enough. It was home to the hundred odd Valkyries, their officers, and support staff. There was also the hospital section that could deal with two hundred people, though no one ever remembered more than about forty ever being in there, and the launch bays that acted as garages for the scout vehicles that the Valkyries used.

They settled down into their seats, waiting for the officer who would brief them to arrive. The speculative chatter and banter ranged back and forth, but at a low enough level that Sigrun ignored it.

As the base commander came in, though, everyone fell silent.

"Good morning, ladies," said Commander Vanadis as she walked across the small podium in front of the wall-mounted TAC screen. She stopped at the lectern set off to one side.

"Your mission today is a special one, that of locating a missing journalist. You may have heard of her, Kate Jordan. She was embedded with the 5th Battalion, until she decided to leave them and head off alone into No Man's Land."

"Why the hell did she do that?" Mist demanded.

"Seems she thought there was a story to be had about what we do out there," said Commander Vanadis drily.

"Nothing she could handle," snorted Hruna derisively.

"Can it, Hruna," snapped Sigrun, turning to glare at her.

Muttering under her breath, Hruna subsided reluctantly, and Sigrun retuned her attention to the commander.

The TAC screen came to life with a view of the current eastern war front.

"You'll be heading out to the Fenris Mountains where the 5th is currently based, some ten miles north west of the Bifrost landing site," said Vanadis, using a laser pointer to outline the area on the map. "The 5th made a push a few days ago, advancing the front line another two miles into enemy territory. It was then that our journalist went missing. Captain Sigrun, you'll land at the 5th's new base and glean what information you can from them before heading out into No Man's Land. Meanwhile, here's what little we have." She held out the manila folder she had in her left hand toward Sigrun.

"Does she have a tracker implant?" Sigrun asked as she got up to take it.

"No, but she was wearing one on her wrist. The 5th called us this morning as soon as they realized where she'd gone. Thankfully they knew better than to follow her."

Sigrun nodded, accepting the folder and returning to her seat.

"Your unit was chosen because you know that area, and you have the best retrieval record to date. There is one other matter, ladies. You'll have a passenger, an important Company one. Her brother."

Exclamations of disbelief and anger broke out, Sigrun's among them, until the commander raised her hand for silence.

"I know everything you're going to say, because I've already said it myself. Seems Mr. Jordan pulled enough strings that we've got no choice but to send him out with you. He's been told to stay inside the scouter at all times, and to obey your orders instantly, captain."

"He damn well better," muttered Hruna, almost under her breath. "Or I'll shoot him myself! If the aliens catch sight of him, then it's goodnight for all of us!"

"Hruna!" Sigrun hissed, again turning to stare the woman down.

"You'll do any pickups you see as usual, but just load them up and bring them back here for processing. Your main job is to find that journalist. Mr. Jordan will be waiting for you in your ready room. Dismissed, ladies."

As she followed her troop out into the corridor leading to their ready room and the hanger area where their scouter was parked, Sigrun listened in to the general grumbling, gauging the mood of her women. Like her, they were angry and worried in equal measure. In the War, they held a special status as both women, and non-combatants, and were allowed free access to No Man's Land.

The first women taken prisoner by the aliens had been in a convoy, taking supplies to the front line. They'd been prepared for everything but what had actually happened—they had been handed back unharmed after an agreement had been made between the two sides that women would never be involved in combat, nor with combat supplies, and that only the women would be allowed into combat areas unharmed to pick up the injured and dead. It seemed the alien Ymir held women-kind in deep reverence, and would not harm them in any way. Humanity had had to agree to it, and to date had never broken the agreement. For their part, only the alien females, much larger than the males, went into the same area to collect their injured and dead. The aliens were apparently big on symbology, and thus the Valkyries had been born. Tales of amicable meetings in No Man's Land between the females of both species that had passed into urban legends.

Like her troop, Sigrun ignored the man standing between two MPs just inside the ready room, and headed for where her armor was stored in its cubicle. Tyra, her adjutant, was already waiting for her.

"Morning, captain," Tyra said, taking the folder from her and placing it to one side. "I've checked your kit out already, just to be sure, since you're missing your down time this week. Everything's in the green. And I had my gals check out your troop's suits too."

"Thanks, Tyra," she said, turning round and backing into the small space before slipping her feet into the leg and foot sections.

"I put a couple of extra battery packs for your stunners in your left side ammo pack," she said quietly, waiting for Sigrun to lean back against the back piece of her suit before swinging the front chest and groin piece round on its mounting gimbals. "Same for Kara. Figure with that young man along, you may need them."

She looked up into the older woman's face and smiled, lifting her arms up and out of the way so the side latches could be sealed. "Good thinking, they may just come in handy."

"What they're thinking back at HQ, allowing him out in your ship, I'll never know," she grumbled. "We've never broken that treaty in over five years, till now. And all because of some journalist that should know better than to put everyone's lives at risk just for the sake of a story!"

"Doubtless, they'll have something to say to her when they get her back to HQ, assuming she's still alive, of course."

"A night outside on Valhalla probably finished her off, and good riddance, I say!"

"Now, Tyra, that's no way to talk about her," Sigrun admonished mildly as she lowered her arms and waited while her adjutant fitted the left arm and shoulder sections in place. "If she's embedded with the 5th, she'll have a power suit on too. She should be able to survive long enough, so long as her air and the heating system last. It's still summer out there, with no sundown for another couple of months yet."

Tyra sniffed loudly, moving round to her right to put on the other arm piece. "Well, let's hope she got the fright she deserves, wandering off alone like that!"

"I hope she didn't meet up with any of the Ymir," said Sigrun. "Not that they could understand each other. At least she won't be wearing silver-and-white armor, so there's no chance of her being mistaken for one of us."

Tyra grunted as she handed Sigrun her gloves. "Like that would ever happen! Well, at least they dressed him in furs, not in armor. He'll freeze in minutes if he leaves the ship."

"True, Now stop being so pessimistic, Tyra! Smiles as we leave, please. Never tempt the norns," she said, pulling on her gloves and sealing them in place.

"Aye, captain," said the woman, stepping back to give Sigrun room to move.

Her arm seemed to weigh a ton as she lifted it up to open the access panel and start the power-up sequence. She toggled the switch and instantly she felt the suit interior firm up and cling to her body. Heating came on, low level for now, but its tell-tale flashed green on her panel.

"Comm-set," she said, holding out her hand for it without looking up from the panel.

Tyra slapped it into her gloved palm. "Comm-set," she confirmed.

She clipped it over the back of her ear, then fixed the throat mic into its slot at the inner neck of her suit.

"Valkyrie One, checking in," she said.

"Affirmative, Valkyrie One, hearing you loud and clear," said control.

"Sound off, Valkyries," she said, checking suit air pressure, meds, and gravity adjustment to make sure everything was green.

"Kara checking in."

"Eir here. Good to go, captain."

"Gudrun here."

"Mist. All good."

"Hruna. Green and mean, captain," she said with a laugh.

"Brynhild ready to go."

"Gudrun checking in."

"All present and correct, control," Sigrun said, reaching out to pick up her helmet. She sucked in a breath as she did. Even after so many years, she still felt a thrill when she picked it up.

The silver helmet alone set the Valkyries' armor apart from any other. Designed like a helm from the early medieval period, it had small, laid-back silver feather-etched wings set on either side. The wing shape was echoed in black on the back of their white armor. She picked up her folder in her free hand.

"Captain Sigrun, can I have a word?"

The male voice broke into her reverie, dispelling her almost mystical mood.

Blinking, she looked up at him.

"You don't approach the Valkyries," snapped Tyra, pushing him aside. "They come to you, if they want to speak to you!"

"Now just a minute..." he began, staggering back slightly.

"It's all right, Tyra," she said, reaching out to touch her adjutant's arm reassuringly. "He doesn't know our ways."

"He shouldn't even be here!" the older woman muttered as Sigrun tucked her helm under her right arm.

"What is it, Mr. Jordan?" she asked.

"I just want to be sure we're on the same page," he said. "You're taking me to the 5th, where I'll presumably pick up the real search party, not to mention some protective armor. I can't possibly go outside dressed like this."

Sigrun's polite expression faded. "I'm afraid you've got it wrong, Mr. Jordan. We are, as you put it, the real search party. And your lack of armor is intentional. You will be remaining in the scouter at all times."

"What? Now look here, young lady, I made it quite clear that I intended to be outside with the search party!"

"We're in a war zone, Mr. Jordan, only three miles from the frontline. The rules of engagement count for more out here than the Company."

Jordan's face darkened in anger. "You forget you're an employee of Krafla Mining like everyone else on Valhalla! I'm going to take this up with your commander!"

"By all means, do that. But we're loading up now, and taking off within ten minutes, whether or not you're on board. If we delay any longer, we might not find your sister alive. Civilian armor isn't constructed like our military issue. They have to be recharged every twenty-four hours."

"Then I'll take it up with the commander of the 5th! He, at least, should be aware of where his loyalties lie!"

Sigrun shrugged and signaled to the MPs to take charge of him before she turned away to follow her troop out of the ready room to the launch bay. Jordan would get even shorter shrift from Ryan of the 5th, but he wouldn't be as nice about it as she'd been.

Kara was waiting for her at the door and fell into step beside her as she walked down the center of the echoing cavern that was the launch bay.

"I can see he's going to be a bundle of laughs," she said quietly. "And to think I thought he looked cute!"

Sigrun laughed. "Cute? Him? He's nothing but a Company suit on legs. I want you to keep a close eye on him, Kara. Make sure he stays in the ship once we're out in No Man's Land."

"Why can't we just leave him with the 5th?"

"He pulled strings with the Company, we have to take him with us. Just keep an eye on him, please."

"Will do. What other Intel did they give you?"

"Don't know, I haven't the time to look at it yet. I'll go through it while Mist preps for takeoff. Get our passenger stowed in the guest quarters, I want him as far away from us and sick bay as possible."

"And the fact you can remotely lock that cabin has nothing to do with it, huh?" Kara's eyebrow disappeared under her light brown bangs.

"There is that," she agreed as they veered off toward where the *Sleipnir* was berthed against the starboard hull.

Sleipnir was designed to support Sigrun and her troop of seven for up to two weeks in the field in Valhalla's harsh perma-winter conditions. It was roomy, with a little more than the regulation standard space per person. Cabins were double occupancy with their own tiny bathroom. Sigrun, as captain, and her second in command, had their own cabins. There was one at the rear, complete with its own small lounge area, reserved for the occasional time, like this, that they carried a passenger to and from the frontline and their base. There was a sick bay, a combined galley and mess, and a common area that included a briefing table and TAC screen. The small deck below, accessed via a floor iris and ladder, had their morgue where the storage and recharging cubicles for their armor were, and in the main cargo area, an all-terrain surface vehicle. To the left of the morgue was a small room with two cryo units, and in the main cargo area, a rack of eight more.

Sigrun settled herself at her console on the bridge and finally opened up the folder. Around her, Eir was settling in at her sensors and nav. station, pulling up the latest weather reports, while Brynhild stowed her helm in the locker for her gunnery station. Though non-combatants, it made sense to be armed and have the stations manned since friendly fire situations did happen. *Sleipnir,* and her sister scouters, fully capable of interplanetary flight, had been relocated to Valhalla by the Company when it became necessary to implement the Valkyrie units.

The file told her that Kate Jordan was a highly popular news journalist and host, whose style of journalism had her seeking out the hard facts in controversial stories. She believed in getting to the heart of a matter by going there herself and speaking to those involved, thus her two-month stint being embedded with the 5th to find out more about the War, and the aliens dubbed the Ymir by Krafla Mining Corp. The attached photo was obviously a press one, showing a well-manicured woman in her mid-thirties, shoulder length fair hair dressed in neat waves, with perfect make up. Intelligent brown eyes stared up at her from the glossy image.

"She looks nice enough," said Kara, resting her hand on her couch chair as she passed by her to reach her own communications console.

"She does," said Sigrun. "But I'll wager she's as much a handful as he is. I doubt either of them understands the words National Security, or even just No."

"That's good sometimes, when it exposes crimes and sleaze."

"But not when she's breathing down our necks," Sigrun said, closing the file and leaning sideways to place it in her locker, under her helm. "What we do here isn't wrong, it's vital to our war effort."

Kara nodded. "The MPs delivered Jordan to his room. I checked he was settled and locked him in."

"Thanks," she said, sitting up, and toggling the ship's comm as Kara went to her post. "Hruna and Gudrun to the bridge, please."

"Yes, captain?" said Hruna, saluting her when she arrived.

"I want the iris down to the lower deck security keyed, please. Usual key. I want to be sure our passenger can't get down there. I also want you armed at all times, and keeping a watchful eye on our passenger along with Kara. Gudrun, if we need to use the sick bay, call for Hruna to guard the door outside. Again, I'm taking no chances that anything can go wrong. See to it now, ladies."

"Aye, ma'am," said Hruna and Gudrun, saluting before leaving.

"You're that worried?" asked Kara quietly, turning round to glance at her.

"Yeah, I am."

"Ship prepped for takeoff, ma'am," said Mist. "Coordinates for the 5th entered. Transit time fifteen minutes. Ready when you are."

"Acknowledged. Sound the warning and wait for Hruna and Gudrun to check in. Kara, tell Jordan to get to his acceleration couch and fasten in." Sigrun began her pre-flight routine.

"Aye, captain."

The two-tone warning sounded throughout the ship, alerting the crew that take-off was imminent.

Mist let it run for thirty seconds then switched it off. Moments later, Hruna and Gudrun reported in as ready.

"Valhalla Base, *Sleipnir 1* requesting permission to take off," said Kara.

"Valhalla Base to *Slepnir 1*. Permission granted. Clear skies and safe journey to you. Base out."

"Thank you, Base," said Kara.

Sigrun eased *Sleipnir* out of her bay and began to taxi toward the actinic force field that covered the entrance. She stopped at the mark on the runway and began the power-up sequence for takeoff.

"Takeoff in ten, nine..." began Kara as the engines rose in pitch, sounding like the howling of banshees.

Sigrun could almost feel the ship straining against her control, as if it was a living entity, then as the pitch reached the right note, she released the breaks. *Sleipnir* seemed to leap forward and, in an instant, had left the base and was climbing into the cold, blue, cloudless skies of Valhalla. There was a slight thrust of gees pushing her into the padded acceleration seat, but it was familiar, and she welcomed it. Flying made her feel alive like nothing else could.

Reports from Kara and Mist came in, and Sigrun heard them with half an ear, not detecting anything that sounded like a warning. Her boards were clean and green as she leveled out at cruising height.

"Jordan's complaining in back, captain," said Kara's quiet voice. "What shall I tell him?"

"That we'll be there in fifteen minutes," she said.

HQ at the 5th was the usual muddle of prefab huts hidden under nets camouflaged to look like dappled snow. Sigrun brought the scouter down to hover above the hastily laid large red cross symbol, then slowly lowered it till it was resting on the ground.

"Power down to standby mode, Mist, but keep her running. We won't be long here," she said, shutting down her board. "Kara, you're with me."

Flicking a switch she called for Hruna to meet her at the airlock with their visitor, then pulled her helmet out of the locker and lowered it over her head, sealing it with a quick twist. She felt the instant rush of cool air around her face before she called up the monitors on her HUD. "Switch to 5th's frequency, ladies," she said over her suit comm.

As she emerged from the airlock, an armored marine ran over to the bottom of their ramp. He slid to a halt in the snow, sketching a salute to the side of his full-face helmet.

"Captain Sigrun, ma'am. Commander Ryan welcomes you to the 5th Battalion. Please accompany me to his office."

"And you are?" she asked as she began to walk down the ramp.

"Lieutenant Dalton, ma'am," he said. "Commander Ryan's office is over there." He waved in the general direction of one of the larger white buildings.

"We have a passenger," said Sigrun, drawing level with him as she saw his head turning and eyes widening as Jordan came down behind her, dressed in his furs. "He's the brother of your missing journalist."

"Uh, no one told us about him," said Dalton as he led the way over to the building.

"He's to come with us, don't worry," she said, amused as the few soldiers that she passed outside stopped to stare at her and her two team members.

"It's not often that the Valkyries come to the base, ma'am," Dalton said. "We're honored to have you visit, even if the reason is a missing civilian"

"The pleasure's ours, lieutenant," she murmured as the young man opened the airlock entrance for them.

They filed in, waiting while Dalton closed the 'lock behind them and began to cycle it to the habitat norm. Moments later, the inner iris opened to let them through.

"You can take your helmets off, ma'am, we keep the temperature at the regulation 70 degrees in all the habitats on base," he said, reaching up to unfasten his own helmet.

"Thank you," said Sigrun, doing the same.

Dalton waited while the three women took off their helmets, and Jordan slipped back the fur hood and his goggles, then unwound the scarf from across his face.

"Please, if you'll head this way, ladies," he said, gesturing down the corridor with a pleasant smile.

Sigrun grinned back at him, nodding her thanks and headed down past the other doors to the one at the end. Dalton slipped in front of her with a murmured apology, knocked, then opened the door.

"Captain Sigrun of *Slepnir 1*, Commander Ryan," he said, saluting the commander sitting at the desk.

"Captain, welcome to Fenris Base," said Ryan, immediately getting to his feet and coming round to greet them. He held his hand out to her, and she took it in her gloved one. "It's an honor to have you visit us. I just wish it could be in happier circumstances."

"Not your fault, Commander. There's no accounting for stupidity," she said, shaking his hand.

"Now just a dammed minute," said Jordan, pushing to the front and trying to elbow her out of the way. "It's not stupidity to follow up a hot lead on the truth of what actually happens out here on Valhalla!"

Ryan glanced from the angry civilian back to Sigrun, a questioning look on his pleasant features.

Sigrun found herself mentally giving the commander the once-over and liking what she saw—good looking for a man in his early forties, blue, friendly eyes, smile creases at the side of his mouth.

"He's her brother," she said, pulling her thoughts back to more mundane matters. "Krafla Mining sent him out here. He's to accompany us on the search mission."

"You have my sympathy," he murmured *sotto voce*, making Sigrun smile.

"I demand that a professional search team be sent out for my sister, and I also demand to know why it hasn't been done already!"

Ryan turned to look at Jordan. "Your sister left the base in the dead of night, without telling anyone where she was going, Mr. Jordan. She did this because I refused to take her out into No Man's Land. I have a war to fight here, I don't have time to go chasing after women who should know better than to act like spoiled children."

"Why did you refuse to take her? She's a major news host for the Interplanetary News Service! Her program commands respect everywhere that..."

"Mr. Jordan, stop right there," said Ryan, his voice taking on a hard edge. "I don't give a tinker's damn who your sister is. All I know is that she expected me and my men to drop everything to take her on some wild goose chase into No Man's Land when I told her I could not do that without breaking a five-year treaty we've had with the Ymir!"

"What does that matter," snarled Jordan. "They're only aliens, dammit! They don't matter when put against the story she was uncovering! You should have taken her then she wouldn't have needed to head out on her own!"

"I don't propose to even discuss that topic with you, Mr. Jordan. Sadly you are only too representative of corporate society today—no sense of values and morals. If you had, we wouldn't be at war in the first place! You seem to care more about Ms. Jordan's story than her, and you're obviously no one of importance in the Company, or you'd be well aware of our Valkyries and what they do here."

Jordan sucked in a breath and very obviously forced himself to calm down. "That's not true," he said more moderately. "I care deeply about my sister, but you should be sending out a professional group of soldiers to find her, not a bunch of girls done up in fancy dress!"

Hearing Dalton's gasp of horror, and seeing the look on Ryan's face, Sigrun was hard pressed not to smile. It wasn't even vaguely amusing, but for some reason, it did amuse her.

"Have you any idea what you're talking about?" Ryan asked quietly. "These ladies perform a vital service for us at the front line. They are the only ones allowed by the Ymir into No Man's Land to retrieve the injured and the dead! No men are allowed there, ever, not even their men! Not since they first found women among our soldiers. That's what the pact with them is about."

"As for professional," chipped in Dalton, "they are the professionals."

"Thank you, Dalton," said Ryan. "I happen to know Captain Sigrun has been doing this for years. How long is it now, captain?" he asked, looking back at her.

"About five years," she said, meeting his gaze. "I was... recruited about six months into the war," she finished, trying to control the faint feeling of disorientation that had swept over her. Why had she no memories that went beyond waking up on Valhalla with Olrun beside her?

Ryan's hand reached out to touch her elbow, ready to steady her should she need it. "There you have it, Jordan. Captain Sigrun and several of her team were soldiers like us before their recruitment into the Valkyrie units. Either they take you, or no one does and your sister stays out there. Dalton, take Jordan and Captain Sigrun's ladies to the Officer's Mess and offer them some refreshments. I have a few words I need to say to the captain in private."

"If you would..." Dalton looked hopefully at Kara, waiting for her name.

"Lieutenant Kara," she said, grasping Jordan by the arm and pulling him with her.

When the door shut behind them, Ryan gestured to a chair in front of his desk. "Please, have a seat, captain."

"Thanks," she said, sitting down.

He poured her a glass of water, passing it to her, then sat down on the edge of his desk.

"Kate Jordan got wind of what happens out in No Man's Land and was trying to investigate it further," he said bluntly. "I don't know how she got word of it, but as far as our Intel goes, only she has any suspicions. We obviously censored everything she sent out from the base, but nothing out of the ordinary was mentioned. I doubt her brother actually knows anything either."

"Perhaps it was just a hunch, then," said Sigrun, sipping the water.

"Perhaps, but let your people at the base know so they can deal with her if you get her back alive."

She nodded. "Will do. Was there anything else, Commander?"

"Ryan," he corrected her with a smile. "I'm sorry you got your leave cancelled. I actually requested your team be sent because I knew you had the expertise to handle this situation. Now I know about Jordan going with you, I'm glad I did. Perhaps I can make it up to you sometime, by taking you off the base for a decent meal?"

She hesitated, well aware of the regulations.

"The regs only apply to the front-line soldiers," he said, reading her mind. "It's to prevent you Valkyries having to pick up someone you're involved with. My rank means I have to stay in the base while they take the risks." He pulled a face, then grinned, the smile lighting up his eyes. "But right now, it does have its fringe benefits."

"In that case, I'd like that," she said, smiling back at him. "We don't often get to leave the base and go up to the mother ship."

"Then that's a date," he said. "There was one other thing."

"What?"

"I have a badly injured lad in the Medbay here. I'm afraid he won't last until the evac ship comes later today. Can you possibly put him in one of your cryo units and take him with you?"

Sigrun shook her head, regretfully. "I'm sorry, Ryan, but you know I can't. We only transport the dead."

"I know, but I had to ask. He's a good lad, took his injuries while saving one of my company commanders. Hate to see him die."

"If you think he'll die, then you know what to do."

"I always felt that procedure was rather hit and miss, not something to do if there was a chance of life being prolonged."

"I'm sorry, it's the best I can offer. Our medic sisters will get here as fast as they can if you have reported your young soldier's condition."

Ryan nodded, then reached back on his desk to retrieve a piece of paper. "Here's the frequency for Ms. Jordan's locator, and the one for the two-person scouting SnoCat that she took. We gave her a wrist unit when she arrived here. Hopefully she's still wearing it under her armor."

"What kind of armor is she in? And when exactly did she go missing?" Sigrun leaned forward to place the glass on his desk, but Ryan took it from her.

"Standard civilian armor, with a twenty-four-hour charge and air supply that lasts about the same. She'd been out that day for about eight hours when the unit she was with returned to base. Twilight is dangerous at this time of year. It confuses the senses easily, makes you disoriented. Her suit had had the air replaced, but had only been on charge for maybe another eight hours instead of the twelve those suits need." He glanced at his watch. "It's about 0900 now, I'd say she probably went AWOL about 0200, so she's been out there some seven hours."

"So she's probably got only another three or four hours left, given it wasn't fully charged," said Sigrun thoughtfully. "She may have air, but the cold will kill her long before the air runs out. What about the SnoCat? Does it have good enough heating for her to use it once the suit runs out? Or any chance she'd be savvy enough to take a spare battery pack for her suit?"

"The 'Cat uses the same battery packs as the suits, but in multiples. Theoretically, she could use them in her suit. The SnoCat isn't really built for use without a suit on, though it does have enough basic heating to allow you to take your helmet and gloves off when inside. It's a moot point if it would provide a better shelter than a snow dug-out in an emergency, though, given how an igloo actually keeps heat in."

"I'd better get moving, then," she said, getting up. "Thank you for your hospitality."

"Your next leave is two weeks after this, right?" he asked as he also got to his feet.

She nodded.

"Then I'll see you two weeks from today."

"I'll look forward to that," she said as he escorted her to the door.

No Man's Land for the 5th covered an area roughly ten miles long by two miles wide. It was the contested zone, and right now they were flying high over the fighting, transmitting their own special signal that alerted both sides to their neutral presence. Both the Ymir and the Humans were dug deep into snow bunkers and trenches, vehicles hidden under camouflage, neither side gaining an inch on the other. Mortars pounded away, bombarding either side but every now and then the flare of an energy canon lit up the sky as one side or the other thought they had an important target in their range finders.

'What a waste of lives on both sides," muttered Kara.

"I know, and I agree," she said. "Any sign of either of those signals yet?"

"None, and it's getting late. If she was in a SnoCat, she could be anywhere, even outside No Man's Land."

"Then we widen our search," said Sigrun.

"Light's going, soon it'll be twilight and the fighting will stop," said Mist. "Maybe if we can fly lower down we'll pick up something."

"Maybe, but widen the search for now, please. Eir, take a break, Kara can handle your board. I'm taking one now," she said, getting to her feet and stretching. "Back in ten, ladies."

She walked down to her cabin, going into the bathroom to wet her face and freshen up some. It had been a long day, and was promising to be an even longer night. There was still a small chance of finding the journalist alive, but that was shrinking with every minute that passed.

Coming out of the bathroom, her bed looked so inviting that she lay down, promising herself she was only closing her eyes for five minutes, armor and all.

She woke to Kara shaking her arm. "Sigrun! Wake up. We're picking up a signal from the SnoCat!"

"What?" she asked, sitting up and rubbing her eyes. "How long have I been asleep?"

"Only a couple of hours. I left you because you obviously needed it and nothing was happening."

Swinging her legs off the bed, she got up and followed Kara back to the bridge. "Where's the signal coming from?"

"Down in the lee of the Fenris Mountains," said Mist. "On the Ymir side," she added quietly.

Sigrun groaned. "It would just have to be there, wouldn't it? Bloody woman is more trouble than she's worth!"

"It's fully twilight now, and the fighting's stopped. Want me to take her down?" asked Kara, slipping back into her seat.

"Any comm chatter?"

"Some, from both sides."

"Can you make it out? Are the Ymir aware of her?"

"Not as yet, but this area did see heavy fighting earlier today."

"Take us down, carefully."

"Always, captain," chuckled Kara, beginning to bank the scouter and head back to the source of the signal.

"This is as close as I can get to the signal, captain," said Mist as *Sleipnir* settled gently down into the loose snow.

"Keep her powered up, Kara. Once we've recovered Ms. Jordan, there will be other bodies to check," she said, closing down her board and grabbing up her gloves.

"Aye, captain."

"Brynhild, Hruna, and Gudrun, meet me in the cargo bay," she said over the ship's comm. "Where's that mobile tracker?" she asked, rifling about in her locker.

"Here, captain," said Mist. "I set the frequencies in it already for you. Just switch it on and it's good to go."

"Take care out there, captain," said Kara as Sigrun grabbed her helmet for the second time that day.

"Always," she said, reaching up to put it on and seal it.

The other two women met her at the end of the cargo bay access corridor. The rear ramp was already open and they were carrying folding spades. Gudrun handed her one.

"There's a wind sprung up, got ourselves a blizzard building out there," said Hruna.

"Just what we need," muttered Sigrun as she walked down the ramp, her boots ringing on the metal plating.

Outside, loose snow was already beginning to swirl in the gathering wind. So far it was only at just above ground level, but before long, it would be swirling everywhere as the windstorm built.

Switching on the tracker, she walked a good ten feet out from the rear of the ship then began heading off to the south, following the tiny blip on the screen. "This way," she said.

The terrain was heavy going even with their powered armor. The land had been churned up by the movements of heavy vehicles, and from ordnance landing in it. Loose snow, blown about by the gathering windstorm, lay about six inches deep. They slogged along for several hundred feet before Sigrun finally stopped.

"It should be here somewhere," she said, unfastening the high-powered flashlight that hung from a clip at her waist.

The beam pierced through the haze of snow and the blue twilight, throwing everything in its path into stark contrast. Snow was churned about more than usual, and she could see the outlines of what could be a SnoCat.

"Let's get digging," she said, kneeling down at the edge of the amorphous shape.

Finally someone's spade hit metal and they heard the clang through their suit speakers.

"Pay dirt at last," said Hruna. "Bloody woman should be sentenced to six months digging up corpses here for this stunt!"

Sigrun ignored the comment as she began to scrape at the snow by where they'd heard the clang. Gradually the shape of the SnoCat was revealed, and inside it, they could see a hunched-up form.

"Well, she's there at least," said Gudrun, pulling out her scanner. "Not detecting any life signs, though."

"After all this time, it's what we expected," said Sigrun as they worked away at freeing the door into the 'Cat.

It was frozen shut when they finally had it completely exposed.

"Stand clear," said Hruna, pulling out her pistol and turning the setting to a low energy one instead of stun. She aimed at the seal between the door and bodywork and began firing, moving slowly along the seam as she did.

Snow hissed and spat, the metal heated up, sending puffs of burning sealing material into the air outside, and fogging up the inside.

"Good job she's wearing a helmet," said Gudrun. "If she wasn't dead already, she would be now."

"Stop bitching me about it. You want her out, don't you?" said Hruna good-naturedly.

"You're doing a grand job," said Sigrun soothingly. "The fumes won't matter to her one way or another."

Hruna stopped and took hold of the handle and pulled, hard. The door came flying off in her hand, sending her toppling onto her butt in the snow. Cursing, she got up and threw the door away.

"Let's get her out," said Gudrun, kneeling down and squirming her way into the cab to grab hold of the journalist.

"Captain," came Kara's urgent voice on the suit comm. "It's Jordan, he got out and I think he's headed your way."

"How the hell did he get out?" demanded Sigrun.

"He hacked the locks," she said. "It never occurred to me a Company man like him would be able to do that."

"Never mind. Stay with the ship, we'll be on the lookout for him."

"There's more Captain," said Kara.

Just then Sigrun noticed a shadow looming over her from behind—a shadow that wasn't human.

"Oh crap," she said. "I think I know what you're going to tell me."

"There are Ymir in your area. I'm picking up comm chatter from them about our landing. They know it's us, but they're curious about what's brought us down at this time of night."

"Yeah, they just found us, Kara," she said, slowly turning round. "Sigrun out."

The Ymir was tall like all their species, about seven feet tall, Sigrun calculated as she looked up the bright blue armor to the helmet the female wore. Slowly, she switched off the flashlight—not necessary because the group of Ymir had brought their own—and held her hands out in the universal greeting of unarmed friendship.

Beside her, Hruna, all marine and all paranoid, flicked her pistol back to stun and holstered it, then held out her hands.

Gudrun, still hauling the dead journalist out of the SnoCat, sat back on her heels and just looked up at them.

"Greetings," said Sigrun, then repeated it in her basic Ymir.

The lead female reached out toward her, touching the small ornamental wings on the side of her helmet.

"Valkyries," she said, her voice deep and sonorous.

"Valkyries," agreed Sigrun. Slowly she turned and pointed to Gudrun. "We collect the dead."

"Why woman dead?" came the slow, measured question. "Not fighting?"

"No, no," Sigrun reassured her hurriedly. "Journalist, writer of words with the soldiers. Not fighter. She left base at night to... explore," she improvised.

"Why?" asked a second Ymir.

"To write words of what the war is like for those on home world."

A torrent of fast speech between the women greeted this revelation. After a few minutes, the one in the lead silenced them and turned back to Sigrun.

"Understand. She die of cold?"

"Yes," said Sigrun, feeling relief flooding through her. "Yes, she did. Suit battery ran out."

"We take, you come," she said, gesturing one of the others forward. "Bakkra, I am."

"Sigrun," she said, moving aside as the other woman came forward and knelt down to pick up the body of the journalist.

"Bodies of yours find, load in ship for you," said Bakkra. "You want?"

"Please," she said. "I tell my people."

"Good. Now follow."

Hastily Sigrun gestured to Hruna and Gudrun to follow while she tersely relayed to Kara what was happening.

"What about Jordan?"

"I hope the fool falls down a bloody crevasse," she said. "I can't worry about him when we're having a contact with the Ymir like this. Do you realize how rare this is? And they are offering to help Ms. Jordan."

"I understand, captain. Want us to go look for him? He has a tracker on."

"No, stay there and help the Ymir. Load the ones we can Awaken or harvest into the cryo units as usual. Send his frequency to my tracker and I'll try to find him."

"Aye, captain."

The Ymir base was nearby. In fact, they'd only gone a few yards when out of the gloom and incipient blizzard, a fur-clad figure emerged and flung itself on the Ymir holding the body of the dead woman.

"What the hell are you doing with her? Put her down you alien bastards!"

The Ymir stopped dead in its tracks and looked down at the person beating his hands against her armored flanks.

"Man," she said clearly, her tone conveying a disgust that crossed any species' barrier.

"Crap," said Gudrun. "Crap, crap, crap."

Jordan turned away from the Ymir and flung himself on Sigrun. "And you! You're allowing them to take her! She's my fiancé! We planned to get married next month, and you let her die!"

The sheer impact of his body hitting hers toppled Sigrun over on her back into the snow as Jordan began to pound his fists on her helmet visor. She felt a tug at her side, then he was gone. There was a scream from Gudrun, followed by a shot.

Rolling to one side, she pushed herself to her feet, terrified at what she'd find. It was Hruna that lay dead, her head a ruin of blood and bone and bits of helmet. Across from her, Jordan was held suspended in the grip of one of the Ymir.

"Not soldier," Sigrun said weakly. "Company sent him. Told us brother of dead woman, not fiancé—husband-to-be."

"He break treaty," hissed the woman holding Jordan as he began to swear and struggle in her grasp. "Ours now."

Sigrun knew the treaty by heart, they all did, and by its rules, any male who strayed into No Man's Land belonged to whichever side caught him. She nodded, feeling sick to her stomach, not just at the loss of Hruna, one of her most trusted troops, but also at having to give Jordan over to the Ymir alive.

"Yours," she said.

"Good," Bakkra said. "Now we treat dead one."

"You're giving me to them?" yelled Jordan. "What the hell kind of woman are you? You can't hand me over to the aliens like this!"

"Oh, yes I can," snarled Sigrun, anger evaporating any pity she might have felt for him. "You broke the treaty despite being warned to stay in the ship! You murdered one of my women! The treaty is more important than you or me! It allows us to Awaken the dead soldiers so they can live again, to harvest the organs of those who are only brain dead so their injured comrades can be saved! Had you stayed where you were, you might have gotten your girlfriend back, but not now. Now she'll take Hruna's place in my troop, and no one will fault me for leaving you with the Ymir!"

Hello there. Take it easy. You've had an accident, but you're all right now. Who are you? Your name is Olrun, and you're a Valkyrie like me. When you get out of Medbay, you'll be in my unit. Our part in the War is here on the planet Valhalla, near the front line...

ENDINGS
Judi Fleming

STARED AT THE BLANK STATUS PANEL ON MY SERVO-SUIT'S CRACKED FACEPLATE AND asked myself if I'd ever been so exhausted that I couldn't take another step before in my life. I don't mean when you give up because you felt worn out or your muscles burned. I mean when you really couldn't move another muscle. Not even when your life depended on it. I was at that point and it was frightening.

I struggled to keep this thought going, pushing the adrenalin through my system, hoping that there were enough undamaged solar cells on the armored exterior of the space suit to recharge when the sun came up in six hours while I fought with my overwhelming fatigue. The soft starlight reflected off my face plate, but didn't fog up. Good news there. It meant life support was still on line, so the three-hundred-pound battle suit surrounded me in coffin-like comfort.

The alien commander and I had blasted each other at the exact same moment. Our guns had only enough charge to knock out the computers and weld the power plants, which ran our heavy-duty suits into unusable lumps. This left us lying on our sides staring at each other, barely five meters apart and both unable to move. Hoping that the backup solar power panels still worked.

We'd fought the better part of a day and a half. We'd grounded both of our ships through precise strikes, hoping to capture each other alive. The planet had low gravity and sharp rocks, so I'd ordered my surviving troops into the cumbersome gear after we'd crashed. I'd carefully set up the perimeter and strategy, but despaired as we lost one woman for every alien we took out.

There was no hope of rescue for me now. My soldiers lay dead around me. Who knew how long the main battle above this planet would go on. Who knew who would win and arrive unannounced.

I wanted them to swoop in and save the day. To heal my wounds and fix my broken arm. Was I bleeding? I wasn't sure, but I sure wanted to stand up because these suits were never meant to be horizontal.

But right now it was down to just the two of us and I knew this alien I faced had to be at the edge of physical endurance as well. If I closed my eyes for more than the space of a blink, I would pass out. So I stared at the figure before me. Anything to keep my edge.

The Gullagh appeared to be female like me. I felt mild surprise at the realization. Her green, leaf-patterned skin was beautiful this close up. I had spent my five years in space battles and had never been this close to one before.

Videos didn't do justice to the lovely twists of fine tentacles around her face that mimicked hair. Her wide golden eyes examined me with the same curiosity. I'm sure she cataloged my short brown hair and brown eyes against the other variety of humans she had seen and killed in her lifetime.

The battle between our two species had lasted decades. Seventy-five percent of the human male population had died defending the solar systems we'd inhabited. Now the bulk of the soldiers who fought on were women. And perhaps it was the same for her too. Both ready to fight to the death to save our species.

I struggled to focus, unwilling to give into the exhaustion that ate at my mind, whispering for me to sleep. I desperately wanted to let go, but knew it would be my last rest if I did. What had the original battle been about?

Was it something about an ill-mannered response to a question that had started all this? History said it had been bad translators between our two races. Was it the accusation of our lack of compassion as we colonized other planets? The fuzzy recollections eluded me, my mind tumbled into confusion.

Focus. Focus. I reminded myself over and over. My new mantra as I inspected her and our surroundings. I could see that she had several human technology solar cells tacked onto her suit. How clever of the Gullagh to take advantage of our technology so that she too would be "up and running" when dawn broke over our prone figures. Moving toward me to finish the job if my own weren't able to beat her technology. We had a whole night to find out which suit's self-repair programs were better. Could the nano-techs working to solder microscopic circuits in my suit beat out whatever repaired hers? Was the cold I felt an infinitesimal leak or tissue dying from blood loss?

My fatigued mind slipped sideways. Did I care anymore? The thought shocked me like a small jolt of electricity. How could I not care? These beautiful beings had killed billions, cleaning us off of planets like fleas off a dog. I stared at her again, willing hatred to well up inside of me like the academy training videos had.

But I had been a slightly unwilling soldier. Even now my face burned in shame at the thought. Yet I'd always been dedicated to the cause and took my commission with pride and followed every order. I have always believed the human race well worth saving, so I had fought, always secretly hoping this war would end in my lifetime.

That tiny, niggling bit of disgust and doubt over all those I had killed never quite stayed buried in my subconscious like I told it to though. Now I was dying, trapped in this blasted suit, unable to find any comfort.

Tears rolled down my cheek and I blinked my eyes shut a little too long. The world spun, turned black, and I slipped into the oblivion of sleep.

I was suffocating in my dreams. My mind latched onto the urgency of waking and I surged through the layers of exhaustion that had clamped onto me like leeches. My muscles quivered with pain. The agony of my body reprimanding me as all my actions that had been beyond its ability came into sharp focus. Swollen and battle-damaged tissue pressed into the heavy suit surrounding me. Thirst gnawed at my throat like an animal.

I forced my unwilling eyes open. The grit of dried sweat and tears compounded my discomfort as my muscles screamed in disobedience when my arm tried to automatically reach up to clear them despite the suit. The suit was too heavy to move without the computerized servos.

I drew a calming breath and relaxed, focusing my attention on the slice of black sky and stars within my field of vision. No point in doing anything but rest and let my nanos work. The tiny cracks in the visor connected the stars like a necklace of diamonds. In my peripheral vision, I could see that she gazed at them too, then looked back at me.

I jerked when she spoke. The confusion of exhaustion tangled with the realization that parts of our suits worked. She had external speakers and I now had translators. Was she really pinned down by its weight or did she have plans for me? I focused on her words.

"Beautiful, aren't they?"

"Yes," I croaked in response. My throat dry and unwilling to do more. The sound of my own external speakers sparked a small hope in my breast.

"I'm Commander Jualla." The translators made her voice sound like liquid music.

"Commander Guinevere." Human language was clearly not as melodic as the Gullagh's. I turned my head to face her square on, wishing I could adjust my body for better blood flow in my limbs. I didn't want to think about how many parts I could no longer feel.

"I'm sorry about your ship and your people." The words were out of my mouth before my brain could censor them. I closed my eyes as if I could take the words back with that action. How could I be sorry for killing those who had killed so many? My crew. My friends.

More tears spilled between my lashes and a sob ripped through my chest, up and out of my mouth. I wept and it wracked my body, involuntary and painful. Snot ran down my upper lip mixing with the tears that flowed down my face. I squirmed in my suit, seeking release from my prison, only awakening the fire of broken bones.

The grinding of metal on stone snapped my mind back into focus. My finely honed fighting instinct screamed for me to stand and face her. But I could not, locked in this metal cage. My gaze focused on her, seeing that she had only been able to shift her weight before the red status lights flicked on inside her visor.

Gulping, I calmed my breathing to restore my focus. I had not wept like that since I was a child and it embarrassed me at this age. How could I break down so easily? Then I realized that exhaustion is a wicked second foe on this battlefield. Anyone could be affected by it. I was okay. My focus was restored.

Jualla smiled at me. The Gullagh physiology was much like human. Cosmic odds should have been against that, but there it was.

"I am sorry for your losses as well." Her golden eyes deepened to a copper tint.

Military Intelligence had learned that color change was a manifestation of sincerity.

I smiled and thought about the odds stacked against both of us here fighting our female instinct to nurture rather than fight and found it even more outrageous. Women soldiers had to overcome our compassionate tendencies, the Psych Officers had told my class of female fighters. Save the human race. Defend your kind. Pull up that maternal instinct and twist it to help us survive.

"Why do you fight?" I asked her.

"Because you do."

I let my weary brain digest this and watched a pale glow start on the horizon behind her back. I so wanted to sink into a soft warm bed and sleep and not think of what might happen to me beyond that sunrise.

Did I want it all to end or just my own misery of fighting? Fighting myself and the Gullagh. Or was it just the exhaustion speaking again?

The soft roar of distant engines crept up behind me on the edges of my consciousness. Another shot of adrenalin spiked through my system. I could not turn and see who approached. Her eyes tracked the ship thundering down, the vibrations shook my suit, shooting daggers of pain through my injuries.

The status lights inside my visor flickered to life in the thin rays of the false dawn. She shifted up onto one arm, stretching inside her suit like a cat waking up from a nap.

Panic pinched my throat closed. The outline of the ship reflected on her visor was unmistakably Gullagh. My muscles seized and I lurched in my recharged technology, the suit's servos whining with the effort in the breaking dawn.

Jualla watched me with confident curiosity. Her cavalry had arrived and here I was with nowhere to go.

She waited to see my reaction. What would I choose to do? A quick lunge to pin her down and crush her, only to be hunted down by those on the ship? Or would I surrender and become the next prisoner of war, interrogated and told to sign the peace treaty like all those who had been captured before me? What kind of captive would I be?

I sat and let the pins and needles stab my arms and legs as feeling returned. She waited and watched. Her eyes bright copper now as the reflection of the ship's doors opened and the troops marched down the ramp.

The numbness in my mind grew. Deep down inside, I only wanted to sleep. To be home on my porch with a cool breeze blowing the trees and the scent of pine in the air. Was that so much to ask, so far from home on what could be my last day of life? I didn't think so. Yet there it was.

She talked on her comm to her newly arrived troops. Jualla's demeanor did not change. I had a few more minutes to choose the actions of the last few moments of my life and she respected that.

"Am I to be tortured?" I asked.

"No. Never," was her instant response.

"Will I be asked to sign that peace treaty like all the others?"

"Yes. It is your choice. You will speak for your race," she replied. She held out a hand. Was this an offer to help me up or to accept such a peace?

I gnashed my teeth in frustration. "I'm a battleship commander, not a Council member. I have no authority. My signature isn't worth a thing since I have no power. Don't you realize that what I do doesn't matter?" Fresh tears threatened to spill down my cheeks.

"Every person matters." Her logic was like a sledgehammer on my brain. Every message that they had sent to the Council for decades was simple. "Show us some compassion and we will do the same and show you peace."

My world, no, my belief system crashed down around me. Decades old puzzle pieces clicked into place. We humans had been given this message on every planet they obliterated us from.

The Gullagh had shown us the same mercy that we had shown to every native species we didn't like or find useful on those planets. We colonized whichever planet we liked and stripped others for their resources. No compassion. No peace for those that lived there before us.

They would stop if we would stop. Every person mattered. I mattered. I could stop the fighting. And they would stop fighting. There would be an ending. How splendidly simple.

M.O.V.E.

Jennifer Brozek

Senior Cadet Natara Kintares looked out the Space Station Command and Control window and saw her future. The view was filled with military vessels of all types coming and going from Space Station Killingsworth. Her future probably did not involve this particular space station but it was a possibility. As a graduating military cadet, these Military Observation Visit Experiences—or MOVEs—were designed to give the student a taste of what was to come. Natara could not be happier. Ever since she was a little girl, she wanted to join the Guard and to work in space.

"Cadet, look at this screen and tell me what you see."

"Yes, sir," she said, paused and then restated her response, "I mean, 'yes, Guardsman Harber.'"

The middle-aged man gave her a severe look softened by the twinkle in his eyes. "What's wrong with this situation?"

Natara studied the monitor. "You're gonna have a jam in Port Alpha-3. The two Explorer class ships are too big to be rubbing hulls in there."

"Good. How would you fix it?"

"Shift the *IIS Lifeline* to Port Charlie-2 and shift the two smaller scout vessels to Alpha-3."

"Good. Anything else?"

Natara thought about it and shook her head. "I don't think so."

"That plan will work fine but there's one more thing to do—give everyone an extra five minutes lag to allow the switch and trajectory calculations. It'll take a bit more time and some will grouse but the extra fifteen minutes isn't going kill anyone. Just because you shift things on the computer doesn't mean they shift automatically. The pilots of these ships are human with human foibles."

"Yes, Guardsman."

Harber was about to say something else but the sudden influx of ship signals detected on the edge of one of his screens made him pause. A moment later, he said, "You're dismissed, Cadet. Go to your quarters." He turned from her without waiting for an answer and hit a series of buttons on his console. As she left, knowing that a large fleet of ships was suddenly descending upon the space station, the first battle alarms sounded in the corridors.

Instead of returning to her quarters, Natara stood in one of the viewing rooms on the observation ring, watching the orderly dance of large military supply ships being shunted to one side while the space station all but vomited its short-range fighters to set up a protection grid between the advancing armada and the strategically placed military base. She sighed as the observation ring rotated away from the ports she had been watching and showed the next quarter of the station. She turned to hurry to the next observation room and almost ran into Soolee.

"I knew you'd be here. Are we gonna be all right?" her bunkmate, and the only other female cadet on this MOVE, asked.

Natara shrugged, ignoring the implied disregard of orders—admittedly, something she was known for, "I don't know. I think it's the Epiets. I got kicked out of CnC before I could get a good look at the ships' silhouettes. But I'm pretty sure it was them."

"Why are they attacking?"

Natara shook her head, "Don't know. Maybe because this is a strategic station on the border between their space and ours? Not sure. I do know if they take the station, there'll be trouble. It breaks the treaty the Council of Primes ratified." She paused, "You've got dirt on your face."

Soolee rubbed at her nose, smearing the dirt rather than cleaning it up. "That's what you get when you crawl around the hydroponics gardens. Dirty. My MOVE has been all about 'move this' and 'move that.'"

"Lucky you. Mine's been all observation. Look but don't touch. I should be up there right now. I should see what really goes on in CnC when there's an emergency." Natara looked out the observation window and frowned at what she saw there. Off in the distance, a lone scout-like ship was headed toward the space station. It was coming in from the opposite direction of the fighting. She stared at it, trying to identify its race and type. Her frown became a scowl when nothing came to mind.

"What? What's wrong?"

"That ship. Do you know it?" She pointed at the rapidly growing speck.

Soolee looked out the viewport and stared at the incoming vessel. She shook her head. "Not my area of expertise."

"I don't know it."

"So?"

"You don't understand. I don't recognize that silhouette. There are 402 space-faring races in the Kember Empire. From those, there are 3,689 different types of military space-worthy ships, averaging nine different types of ships per race. I just passed my identification class. I'm the third cadet in the last ten graduating classes to get the silhouette test perfectly correct. I identified all 3,689 ship types based on the silhouette alone... and I don't know that ship."

Soolee whistled. "Impressive... but also bad. Maybe it's a civvy ship?"

"No. Can't be. Shouldn't be. Civilian traffic is restricted in this part of the sector due to the... ah... contested nature of the border. Besides, it's too small to have come in on its own. There's got to be a mother ship somewhere within range." She looked out the viewport again but the rotating deck had moved them out of view of the unknown vessel. "C'mon."

Natara and Soolee hurried down the empty corridor. Everyone was either at their battle stations or in their quarters staying out of the way. They ducked into the next observation room that was rotating into line-of-sight of the unknown ship. It was much closer now. Natara pressed against the viewport, trying to get a better view as the ship came in toward the station.

"It's got to be all right, right?" Soolee asked. "They wouldn't let the ship this near if it wasn't."

"Probably. But I want to know what it is."

The two cadets watched as the small ship, the size of a one- or two-man scout vessel, dived down away from the docking port ring and flew parallel to the station's body. "Oh, that's not right. Ships aren't supposed to..."

"What's it doing?" Soolee pressed herself against the viewport. "Why's it doing that?"

"I don't know," Natara admitted.

"Why isn't anyone doing anything about it?"

"I don't know," Natara said again. "There should be tug drones out now, trying to move the ship back to the space lanes. It's an automatic thing but... nothing's happening. It's like they can't see it."

"We can see it."

"We're using our eyes and not machines. It's got to be a new stealth technology." Natara watched the small ship land itself on the space station like an insect landing on an animal too big to notice it. "This is bad."

"Real bad," Soolee agreed. "That's the hydroponics ring."

Natara turned to her classmate. "Are you sure?"

"Yeah. I'm sure."

"We need to report this."

"Please, I really need to talk to Guardsman Harber," Natara tried to keep her voice level and professional as she faced the guardsman in the doorway to CnC. Behind him, hunched over their consoles and talking in quiet, tense voices, were the Command- and-Control personnel and Guardsman Harber.

"Cadets, you're supposed to be in your quarters," Guardsman Oberman said with little patience. He eyed them up and down with irritation. "You need to be elsewhere. We don't have time for inconsequentials."

"But this is important." Soolee insisted, disregarding Oberman's fearsome glare, as she remained at attention before him.

Inside Natara cringed. She knew this old Guardsman could only see a couple of young girls, much less mere cadets, and not the trained Guardsmen they were becoming. She wished Soolee had not said anything at all. He wanted and needed details.

His eyes narrowed. "What is so important that two cadets need to interrupt someone in the middle of an attack?"

"There's an unknown ship. It landed on the station but not—"

Oberman interrupted Natara, "There are thousands of ship types out there. I'm not surprised you don't know one. The Guardsmen in CnC have a handle on things. They know what's coming and going."

"But—"

"But nothing, Cadet. I've read your MOVE file, Kintares. I admire your enthusiasm but this is neither the time nor the place for it. I've also read about your tendency to bend the rules. That doesn't fly on a real space station and we *will* discuss this on our shift tomorrow. Count on it." He raised a finger to forestall another protest. "One more word from either of you and

I'll have you both thrown into brig for disobeying a superior officer. Return to your quarters. That's a direct order." He turned his back on them and shut the door to the control center in their faces.

"Damn. What'd you do to him? Piss in his morning drink?" Soolee asked.

"You idiot," Natara muttered to the closed door and blew out a gusty sigh, "I've only had one shift with him but I get the impression he really doesn't think females should be in the military, much less in CnC."

"What are we gonna do?"

"Not talk to the Cadre, that's for sure." Natara wondered what else was in her MOVE file. Then her scowl turned into a smile devoid of joy. "We're going to deal with this ourselves. Are there any back ways into the hydroponics ring? The section that the ship landed on?"

"Oh, yeah. Lots. I've been spending most of my time doing maintenance in them. You wouldn't believe how dirty hydroponics can get."

Natara looked at Soolee's smudged face and half-smiled. "Yeah I can. Let's go."

Within minutes, the two of them made their way to the hydroponics ring, avoiding as many of the station personnel as possible. The one time they did run into someone, they bluffed the Guardsman into ignoring them by pretending to be on an errand.

"Guardsman Rillion will have our heads if we don't get this to hydroponics maintenance yesterday. Come on!" Soolee said and pulled Natara's arm. The Guardsman barely looked at the cadets as they quickened their pace, passing him in the hallway.

Natara let Soolee pull her along until they reached a door marked: Maintenance 26-D. Soolee waved her ID bracelet next to the security pad and they were rewarded with the opening of the door. Once inside, the two of them breathed a sigh of relief. "Ok. We're good now," Soolee said. "All we have to do is slip into the maintenance tunnel that leads into the garden."

"What do you maintain in the tunnels?"

"The water lines, nutrition to the plants. That sort of thing. Why?"

"Just wondering how dirty it'll be."

Soolee rolled her eyes, "Not very. They run a tight station here. At least, Rillion does on the hydroponics ring. 'An ill-maintained garden makes for an ill space station.' I'll go first. I know where to pop out so it won't be right next to where the ship landed.

"Good. Then, I'll take the lead."

True to her word, the maintenance tunnel was small but relatively clean. There were no leaky pipes and no puddles of dank water. Still, it was not a comfortable place to be. Too short to stand, you had to crouch or crawl to move. It was slow going. The lighting was sparse and motion-sensitive so it felt like they were crawling in circles within a bubble of light.

Still, Natara was impressed. Coming from an acquisitions base with water as the main export, she knew just how tough it was to keep containers and pipes completely watertight. Even so, crawling on hands and knees wasn't the cleanest thing around and that's what these tunnels required. Natara vowed not to tease Soolee about the dirt smudges again.

Natara could have shouted for joy when they paused and Soolee took a small tool from her belt to unlock the maintenance panel. She did not like the dark, cramped space and mentally urged Soolee to move faster. But her companion worked in slow, silent motions to free them from the maintenance tunnel. Once unlocked, Soolee pushed the panel out and slid it to the side, taking care to be as quiet as she could. Then she and Natara crawled out of the maintenance tunnel. Once out, they hunkered down and listened before Soolee replaced the panel. They could hear movement; soft, under the hum of the machinery around them.

Soolee brought them to the far side of the hydroponics garden where the hanging plants, filled with ripening fruits and vegetables, hid them from view. The walls and ceiling sprouted with both plants and water spigots while the grated floor, littered with specialized hydroponics tools, revealed softly humming fans that kept the air moist and the room clear of plant debris.

Natara crawled forward, parting the plants in front of her, and then stopped. She motioned Soolee to her. When the other girl came forward, she saw what stopped Natara. It was an Epiet. She could tell by his basic humanoid appearance, grayish skin, and the iridescent scales on his head and neck. He had two vials of liquid and was pouring the smaller one into the larger one, changing the liquid's color from clear to murky green.

"What's he doing?" Natara asked, keeping her voice low. "What's that thing he's standing over?"

"It's one of the water sample valves. It feeds into the water supply for this garden."

The answer made Natara feel cold and then angry, "We need weapons."

Soolee pointed at two gardening tools on the floor nearby. One was a metal-handled net and the other was a pair of long-handled clippers. "Those do?"

Natara nodded as Soolee crawled behind the hanging plants to get to the tools. She handed the cutters to Natara who dropped into Guardsman hand language and signed, "You go high. I go low."

Soolee nodded and stood up. Natara maintained her crouch and scuttled forward, through the plants into the open, staying low. The Epiet was fully involved in whatever he was doing to the water supply and did not see the two cadets creep up behind him. With a signaling yell, Natara dove low at the Epiet's knees, swinging the clippers so that the metal head of the tool hit behind the Epiet's right knee. At the same time, Soolee brought the net down over top of the intruder's head and yanked backward, putting the Epiet off-balance.

As the Epiet went down with a hiss of surprise and pain, he dropped both of the vials he was holding into the open water valve. On the ground, tangled in the net that Soolee held down on his head and neck, his hand went to his sidearm but Natara used the clippers to break his wrist with a single sharp blow. Soolee gave the Epiet two hard kicks to the head and the alien lay still. Natara took the sidearm from the Epiet's unmoving body and stepped back.

Both girls were panting with excitement and suppressed terror at what they had just done. Natara nodded, "Good. Good." She looked at the weapon and then pointed it at the Epiet's leg. The energy pulse struck the Epiet but the alien did not move. Both cadets jumped at the sound the weapon made.

"Seeder's Balls, Nat! Why'd you do that?"

"I needed to know if the weapon was bio-locked to the species. Besides that, the weapon fire should bring security."

Soolee crouched down over the Epiet. She placed her palm on the alien's chest. "No heartbeat. But that doesn't mean he's dead. He may have dropped into stasis."

She nodded, "You should restrain him."

"Yeah," Soolee agreed and rummaged around for tie down cords. "Why didn't an alarm go off when that thing cut its way in?" she asked, cords in hand, working to restrain the unresisting Epiet.

Natara looked at the opening in the space station wall, "There's no pressure change. The ship must be sealed to the station. With no pressure change, there's no hull breech to detect." She walked to the opening and looked inside the Epiet's ship.

It was compact and highly sophisticated. There were three chambers that she could see. Probably a fourth one she could not. Natara recognized many of the Epiet language symbols but did not know enough of the language to understand the symbols on the doors.

Soolee came up behind her. "He dropped the vials. I have to know what they were. Get an untainted sample. We need to know what he did to the water supply."

Natara nodded. "I've got to see what stealth programs are running. Security should've been here by now. Whatever technology it's running, it has a larger radius than the ship." She looked over her shoulder at the unmoving body of the Epiet. "He secure?"

"Yeah. Five minutes. Five minutes to do what we can do and if we haven't figured something out, we hand it over to security. Any longer is too dangerous for the station."

"Agreed." Natara stepped into the Epiet vessel and put her hand on the pad next to the door nearest her. It opened with a soft hiss. "Control. Excellent. Check the other rooms."

She stepped into the control room of the small scout ship and marveled at its engineering. Every inch of space was used for controls, screens, and devices she had no hope of understanding in the five minutes they had given themselves. But she knew military intelligence would be all over a ship like this. There were blinking symbols, lights, and buttons everywhere. It was a lot to take in. As she stared at the pilot's center, she heard a noise and turned around, whipping the Epiet gun up into a firing stance.

"Natara?" Soolee's voice sounded strange. "I found something. Could you come here?"

Natara frowned. The five minutes was not up. She stepped to the doorway of the control room, keeping the Epiet weapon at her hip. "What is it?"

"I... I found the samples. You need to see them."

"All right." She stepped forward, cautiously looking into the doorway that Soolee stepped through. The tall redhead stood at an angle to the door, not looking at it. She was looking at something else in the room.

For one instant, Natara was sure someone else was in the room with Soolee. In the next, she was positive she was being paranoid. Her next step told her that her gut instinct had been correct.

Another smaller Epiet was in the corner of the room with a weapon pointed at Soolee while looking at the door. The Epiet opened its mouth to speak but Natara did not hesitate. She opened fire on the alien. The first shot missed, hitting the cabinet next to the Epiet's shoulder. The second shot hit her in the chest. The Epiet got off one shot that grazed Natara's left arm. Natara yelped in pain and fired again. She struck the Epiet in the chest again. This time, the Epiet dropped its weapon and slumped to the floor. As its last living act, the Epiet reached over and twisted something on its belt. The light in the small ship blinked from the standard white to an ominous yellow.

Natara dropped the pistol and reached for her wounded arm, only to be stopped by Soolee grabbing her wrist. "Don't. It'll hurt worse if you touch it."

"It hurts now."

"Yeah. Well, it'll stop hurting permanently if we don't figure out what she just set off."

"She?"

"Yeah. She. Small, more purple in the scales. My area of expertise."

Natara nodded and turned for the control room. Inside it, the main console displayed what clearly was a countdown. Everything was bathed in yellow light. "It's a self-destruct."

"Ya think?"

"Yeah." She put her hands down on the glowing hand prints next to the display that had not been there before. Nothing happened. Her heart sped up. "Ideas?"

"Hit the big yellow button there?"

"You do it. My hands are full."

Soolee reached over and hit the yellow button in-between Natara's hands. Again, nothing happened except the countdown continued to get smaller.

Natara raced over ideas in her head. "I've got one last idea and then we run for it." She turned from the glowing console and ran into the other room. Grabbing the dead Epiet by the arm she yanked the dead body toward her and dragged it through the ship back into the control room. As soon as Soolee saw what Natara was doing, she hurried to help. Between the two of them, they each managed to get the Epiet's hands pressed to the glowing handprints. Natara slapped the large yellow button in the middle and prayed that it was the right thing to do.

It was. The countdown disappeared and the light in the Epiet vessel returned to normal.

Natara collapsed into the nearest seat and then jerked herself back into a standing position with her hands in the air as space station security personnel shouted for them to freeze and to identify themselves.

Soolee responded first, "Soolee Moore, Cadet, Senior Class, 992-236-510-288."

"Natara Kintares, Cadet, Senior Class, 611-444-972-313," Natara added on the heels of Soolee's answer.

The faceless security personnel in their combat helmets did not relax their guard as they pulled the cadets from the Epiet vessel. The girls saw that security was covering the male Epiet who was still down or unconscious while the female Epiet was dragged from the vessel and dropped to the floor next to her companion. They all stood there, cadets with their hands raised, covered by two security men while a third reported the situation.

"Your sponsors, Guardsmen Harber and Rillion are on their way, cadets. I hope you have a good explanation for what happened here," the security officer said as he got off the com-unit.

"We do, sir. It's one for the books," Natara said.

"I'll bet. At ease."

Soolee and Natara dropped into a semi-formal parade rest stance. They glanced at each other and smiled. Disobeyed orders or not, they saved Space Station Killingsworth from a sabotage attack and that was something that could never been taken away. If the two of them could just get through the next day with their skins intact, they would be all right and they would both have one hell of story about their MOVEs to tell their peers back home.

Brenda Cooper
CRACKING THE SKY

Brenda Cooper has published fiction in *Analog, Asimov's, Nature, Daybreak, Strange Horizons,* and in multiple other magazines and anthologies. She is the author of the Endeavor award winner for 2008: *The Silver Ship and the Sea*, and of the sequels, *Reading the Wind* and *Wings of Creation*. She co-authored *Building Harlequin's Moon* with Larry Niven. Watch for *Mayan December*, coming soon from Prime Books. By day, Brenda is the City of Kirkland's CIO, and at night and in early morning hours, she's a futurist and writer. See her website at www.brenda-cooper.com.

Nancy Jane Moore
GAMBIT

Nancy Jane Moore writes everything from flash fiction to novels. Her novella, *Changeling*, is available as an ebook from Book View Café and in print from Aqueduct Press. Her collection, *Conscientious Inconsistencies*, is published by PS Publishing. She is a founding members of Book View Café, where she published a series of 51 flash fictions in the first year of operation. Her fiction has appeared in magazines ranging from the *National Law Journal* to *Lady Churchill's Rosebud Wristlet*, various online venues, numerous print anthologies, and several ebook anthologies.

Maria V. Snyder
GODZILLA WARFARE

Maria V. Snyder switched careers from meteorologist to fantasy novelist when she began writing the NYT best-selling *Study* Series about a young woman who becomes a poison taster. Maria dreamed of chasing tornados and even earned a BS degree in Meteorology from Penn State University. Unfortunately, she lacked the necessary forecasting skills. Writing, however, lets Maria control the weather, which she gleefully does in her *Glass*

Series. Maria's published science fiction novels include *Inside Out*, and its sequel, *Outside In*, both are about the dystopian and fully-contained world of Inside. Readers are invited to read more of Maria's short stories on her website at www.MariaVSnyder.com.

Danielle Ackley-McPhail

GHOSTS ON THE BATTLEFIELD

Award-winning author, editor, and publisher Danielle Ackley-McPhail has worked both sides of the publishing industry for longer than she cares to admit. She has published eight novels, ten short story collections, three writers guides, and two cookbooks. She also edits many anthologies, and has contributed to numerous other collections, including all of the *Defending the Future* anthologies.

Ann Wilkes

IMMUNITY PROJECT

Most of Ann Wilkes' fiction found in anthologies and magazines leans toward tragic, funny or both. Her first published novel, *Awesome Lavratt*, is a tongue-in-cheek space opera filled with mind control, passion and adventure. She is also founder and editor of Science Fiction and Other ODDysseys, a blog with book and other media reviews, author interviews and commentary on writing and science fiction. She lives in California's wine country with her husband, Patrick. When she's not writing, she's dancing like a Greek at her favorite Taverna or listening to the blues. Visit her at www.annwilkes.com.

Laurie Gailunas

IN THE MIDDLE OF NOWHERE

Laurie spent her earlier years living in Mexico and traveling in Spain. She likes to think she's settled down, but isn't fooling anyone. She's lived with her husband in the same house in Ann Arbor, Michigan for many years, but uses it as a base from which to travel. Laurie is a two-time Finalist in Writers of the Future and author of non-fiction articles in professional nursing journals. She's worked as a nurse, church administrator, spiritual counselor, office manager, and, toughest of them all, wife and mother of three. You can find her online at http://laurie-gail.livejournal.com.

S. A. Bolich
FALLING TO ETERNITY

S. A. Bolich was a former Regular Army military intelligence officer who, as a young communications exploitation platoon leader, spent significant amounts of time running around Germany in a jeep at the height of the Cold War, when American forces trained in expectation that "Ivan" (the Russians) might someday come bursting through the Fulda Gap. She remembered clearly the looks on the faces of her young men and women the first time they saw the minefields on the East German border and the border guards in their towers ready to machine gun their own people rather than let them cross into West Germany. She met people who braved—and survived—that crossing. Her stories were colored by that experience of seeing up close what oppression looks like.

She passed away on October 4, 2016, in Spokane, Washington after a long and courageous battle with cancer.

Lee C. Hillman
UNDER PRESSURE

Lee C. Hillman has a diverse background, from theatre performance to conference and event planning, project management, podcasting, project management, and even a little editing now and then. While she looks for work, she has been working on a CD of her songs, learning the guitar and harp, and a few other projects. She is also active in the Organization for Transformative Works and online in several fandoms. She currently lives in the Boston area.

Deborah Teramis Christian

LIVE FIRE

Deborah Teramis Christian wrote her first book when she was 9. Her path to professional writing has been circuitous and shoehorned in between such eclectica as the Army, NASA's Jet Propulsion Laboratory, rpg design, librarianship, sociology research, and consulting in business automation. She has authored three books published by Tor Books, the first of which was the science fiction novel *Mainline*. The Sa'adani Empire setting of *Mainline* is the same backdrop used in the short story *Live Fire* in this anthology. Teramis does not generally write short works of fiction, and *Live Fire* is the first work of hers ever to appear in an anthology.

A long-time resident of San Francisco, Teramis is presently doing an extended writing retreat on a farm so she can better complete works in progress and undertake some new creative endeavors. She is currently finishing the novel *Splintegrate*, a science fiction tale that takes place in the same setting as *Mainline*, a few years after that story's events. Interested readers can learn more about the status of *Splintegrate* and Teramis' other projects at her website, http://www.deborahteramischristian.com.

Lisanne Norman

VALKYRIES

Lisanne Norman is the author of the *Sholan Alliance* novel series, from DAW Books. Her battlefield days—28 years as a skirmisher with the Scottish Reenactment Society—are over now, and she has moved again, hopefully for the last time, to America, where she lives in California with her son and daughter in law. She continues to write down her dreams of magic, and warriors, and alien worlds, her writing obviously enriched by the many varied experiences she has had and the skills she has learned along the way. These skills have brought her many readers who write to her, among them serving members of the American Military.

Judi Fleming
ENDINGS

Judi Fleming works as a training specialist and instructional designer for the federal government in her day job and thus much of her writing is of the non-exciting technical sort. She is a graduate of Seton Hill University Writing Popular Fiction Master's Program.

Jennifer Brozek
M.O.V.E.

Jennifer Brozek is a freelance author for many RPG companies including Margaret Weis Productions, Savage Mojo, Rogue Games, and Catalyst Game Labs. Winner of the 2010 Origins Award for Best Roleplaying Game Supplement, her contributions to RPG sourcebooks include *Dragonlance*, *Colonial Gothic*, *Shadowrun*, *Serenity*, *Savage Worlds*, and *White Wolf SAS*. Winner of the 2009 Australian Shadows Award for edited publication, Jennifer has edited several anthologies with more on the way. Author of *In a Gilded Light* and *The Little Finance Book That Could*, she has more than 25 published short stories, is the creator and editor of the webzine, *The Edge of Propinquity*, and is an assistant editor for the Apex Book Company. She also writes the monthly gaming column *Dice & Deadlines*. Jennifer is a member of Broad Universe, SFWA, and HWA. Read more about her at www.jennifer-brozek.com

Mike McPhail
SERIES EDITOR

Author, Editor, and Designer Mike McPhail, a member of the Military Writers Society of America, is the co-founder of eSpec Books and the founder of McP Digital Graphics. He is the creator of the science fiction universe, the Alliance Archives (All'Arc), and its related Martial Role-Playing Game (MRPG) system.

Collections by DTF Authors

Vox Astra: The Black Box by James Chambers
Vox Astra: When Clouds Die by James Chambers
Written in Light by Jeff Young
A Legacy of Stars by Danielle Ackley-McPhail
The Die is Cast edited by Greg Schauer
Dawns a New Day by Danielle Ackley-McPhail

https://especbooks.square.site

Novels Based on DTF Stories

Daire's Devils by Danielle Ackley-McPhail

Shattered Dreams by Bud Sparhawk

Devil Dancers by Robert E. Waters

Issue In Doubt by David Sherman

In All Directions by David Sherman

To Hell and Regroup by David Sherman,
with Keith R.A. DeCandido

Finally, There's Something We Can All Agree On.

It's something we've all said many times. And it does seem to be one of the few things that Americans unanimously agree on. But it takes more than agreeing with each other. It takes the USO. For more than 60 years, the USO has been the bridge back home for the men and women of our armed forces around the world. The USO receives no government funding and relies entirely on the generosity of the American people. We all want to support our troops. This is how it's done.

Help support our troops.
888-USO-5566/www.uso.org